The Finding of Martha Lost

The Finding of Martha Lost

Caroline Wallace

BLACK SWAN

TRANSWORLD PUBLISHERS
61–63 Uxbridge Road, London W5 5SA
www.penguin.co.uk

Transworld is part of the Penguin Random House group of companies
whose addresses can be found at global.penguinrandomhouse.com

Penguin
Random House
UK

First published in Great Britain in 2016 by Doubleday
an imprint of Transworld Publishers
Black Swan edition published 2017

A CIP catalogue record for this book
is available from the British Library.

ISBN
9781784160821

Typeset in Giovanni Book by Falcon Oast Graphic Art Ltd.
Printed and bound by Clays Ltd, Bungay, Suffolk.

Penguin Random House is committed to a sustainable
future for our business, our readers and our planet. This book
is made from Forest Stewardship Council® certified paper.

MIX
Paper from
responsible sources
FSC® C018179

1 3 5 7 9 10 8 6 4 2

LG, to remind you (that I'm always thinking about you).

'I believe in everything until it's disproved. So I believe in fairies, the myths, dragons. It all exists, even if it's in your mind. Who's to say that dreams and nightmares aren't as real as the here and now?'

John Lennon

Liverpool Lime Street Station, May 1976

~~Once upon a time . . .~~

This part of my fairy tale begins in May, in 1976. It's perhaps Part Five in the story of my life. And, before anyone thinks to ask, I've no idea what happened in Part One.

Right now I'm spinning my way across the station's main concourse, shouting 'Bonjour' at everyone I know. As I spin, my black polka-dot dress fans out, and it swishes with each turn. I squeal as dizziness overwhelms me, and I giggle into a heap on the concrete floor below the departures board.

'Bonjour, Jenny Jones,' I shout.

She's sitting in her kiosk – it's across the concourse, close to the exit. A man's buying a packet of ciggies and box of matches. He's bending over and counting out his pennies on the stack of newspapers in front of the kiosk. Jenny Jones is watching him, but she's got one hand in a bag of Frazzles and the other's turning the pages of a magazine. She looks over at me and waves, her hand still in the bag of Frazzles.

'You on your morning spin?' Jenny Jones shouts, and I nod. 'Did you step outside, queen?' she asks.

I shake my head. 'Liver bird,' I say, pointing at myself.

Jenny Jones shakes her head, and I start to spread the skirt of my polka-dot dress out into its full circle. Folk scoot around me – some smile, others swear. But I close my eyes and lift my arms up towards the station's iron rafters. I pull in the biggest sniff of grime and soot and cigarettes. There's a hint of diesel and vinegar and vomit; there's a sprinkle of leather luggage and oil in there too. That sweet and sharp smell of train station tingles my nostrils before I lower my arms and let my breath out slowly.

'Thank you for letting me live here,' I whisper.

'Lime Street wouldn't be the same without you, queen,' Jenny Jones shouts, and I open my eyes. I look at Jenny Jones, and she's smiling as she shakes her head again. I smile too.

'Bonjour, Stanley,' I shout over to Stanley the cleaner – he's brushing the entrance to Platform 6, just next to the public telephone box.

He holds up his wrist, points to his watch. 'You seen the time?' he shouts, and I turn and look up towards the big clock that's next to Mother's window.

'Goodness,' I say, attempting to stand up and feeling dizzy. 'I'm late!' I add, yet I still decide to spin my way across the concourse, avoiding the bench, to the lost property office.

I love spinning. It's not the most efficient way of getting around but, after months and months of trying, I think I might have perfected the most brilliant way to spin. It's all thanks to a ballet technique I read about in a lost book, and it's all to do with keeping your eyes fixed on one spot. I've learned that it's best when that spot isn't a person, because people tend to move, and that makes the spin go wonky. I can spin for ages now, and I hardly ever vomit on my dress. I did want to write a letter to Margot Fonteyn, to ask if she'd ever vomited on her tutu, but Elisabeth thought it best I didn't.

I'm laughing then whistling, and folk are having to stop as I attempt to pirouette in a straight line from below the departures board to where I work.

The postman stands in the open doorway. He's tall, he's

skinny, his moustache's an upside-down u-shape and looks like a hairy horseshoe around his mouth. Folk call him Drac, on account of his front teeth sticking out weird. He's been delivering letters for as long as I've been here, and right now he's fanning his face with the lost property office's mail.

'Bonjour, Drac,' I whisper, leaning against the door, my breath coming out in pants. I bend and take off my black heels, then I hurry behind the counter.

'Turn around,' I say to Drac, and he does. I bend down behind the counter, pulling my dress over my head and replacing it with one of Mother's black smocks. It almost reaches my ankles and looks a bit like a huge polyester sack. I push the polka-dot dress and the shoes into the secret compartment under the counter.

'Sorry, Drac,' I whisper, popping my head back above the counter and seeing him turn to me.

'Morning, Martha Lost,' Drac says. 'Is *she* about?'

I point up to the ceiling, and Drac nods.

'If I had a pound for every time I've been soaked by her chucking that Jesus fluid at me,' Drac whispers. He jerks his head at the ceiling. He's still not moved from the open doorway.

'You'd be a rich man, Drac,' I whisper, putting my hand over my lips and trying to stop a giggle from escaping.

'Last week she chased me all the way down Platform 3 with a pan of her Jesus fluid,' Drac whispers. 'For a larger lady, she sure can run. Sloshed it all over the station concourse, she did.'

I giggle through my fingers, even though he's told me the same story every morning this week.

I sit down on my stool behind the counter. I look down to my ledger sheet and whistle. I like Drac, but hopefully he'll go in a second. He's not very good at knowing when to leave. Elisabeth's said I need to be harder, not make him feel quite

11

so welcome, or he'll stay in the doorway whispering in his hissy, lispy voice for hours. I quite like the way he whispers though. Sometimes I close my eyes and imagine he's a snake.

'One for you today,' Drac whispers. 'First time I've managed to get one to you without *her* getting to it first.'

'For me?' I ask, looking up.

He nods; he's smiling.

'I've never had a letter before,' I say.

'I stashed it safe,' Drac whispers, unzipping his jacket and pulling out a little brown parcel. 'Didn't want Mother swiping it.' He nods towards the ceiling and gives me a long wink. He moves into the lost property office, puts the letters on the counter and then holds out the little brown parcel.

I don't move.

'It's for you,' he whispers. 'You're the only Martha Lost I know.'

He smiles; I nod. I take the parcel and put it on the counter in front of me. I run my fingers over my name on the parcel.

'Liverpool postmark,' Drac whispers, and I look up at him. His fingers dance around his moustache. 'Best open it.'

My hands shake. I'm careful as I try to open the brown paper without ripping it. One side of the parcel loosens, then the other side. I peep and a tiny squeal escapes.

'A book,' I whisper. 'The sender must know how much I love reading.'

'Knew it was!' Drac says, forgetting to whisper.

I pull out the book. I turn it over and flick open the pages. There's words written on the inside cover – an inscription just for me.

Loud stomping footsteps sound on the floor above the lost property office. I jump in my seat. Drac and I look up to the ceiling. One hand shoots up to cover the bruise on my cheek. The footsteps stop. I wait. Drac stays as still as a statue, with his eyes focused on a point high above our heads. Nothing. I let out my breath in a loud sigh.

'Best leave you to it then,' Drac whispers.

I nod, but I don't look at him. I'm reading the words written on the inside cover. Four words: 'MARTHA, YOUR MOTHER LIES'. They're written inside the book. On the outside, the title of the book is stamped in gold letters, *The History of the Night Ferry – London to Paris.*

I notice one page that has a folded corner. Page ten. I read it. I read the words over and over. At first I'm feeling a bit lost as to why someone thought that page was so very important, and that's why I read the page again and again. If I'm honest, it's not the most interesting page I've ever read. But then I realize, and then I read it once more just to make sure. It's not what's on the page that's supposed to interest me; it's what's not on the page.

The Night Ferry wasn't a train that turned into a boat when it went on the Mersey. It was an international sleeper train between London Victoria and Paris Gare du Nord. The Night Ferry never travelled to Liverpool.

And that's that – there's absolutely no way I can concentrate on my work.

Elisabeth pops in at nine a.m. She's my best friend. She owns the coffee bar next door, and she's that beautiful she could be a Hollywood star. I could watch her all day and never get bored. Sometimes she dances instead of walking. I think there might be music playing inside her head all the time. She's quite tall for a lady, and she's super slim, even though she eats cake for breakfast every day. She wears all the latest fashions, but she doesn't buy them. I don't think she's got loads of money; instead, she's clever and copies dresses she sees, draws out patterns and makes them all on a sewing machine. Nothing about her is like Mother.

But today I don't really talk to Elisabeth at nine a.m. And I don't eat my slice of lemon drizzle at ten a.m. I stop any thoughts that might cause smiles at eleven a.m. Instead, I let my face wear a frown, I keep looking at the inscription, and I think about how the nearly-beginning part of my fairy tale's full of lies. And after a few hours of thinking about that, I'm confused as to why someone would send me an item that would take away so much of Part Two but not think to offer a telephone number so that I could call them up and have a natter about it all.

I don't know who to believe, so I do what I always do when I'm not clever enough to make things better or when I've gone too long without smiling. I lock up as usual at one p.m., I go upstairs to the flat, I shout to Mother that I'm poorly, and I close my bedroom door behind me. I perch on a little stool at my dressing table, I stare into the mirror, and then I smile.

I read somewhere that most four-year-olds smile four hundred times a day, but then, by the time they become adults, they only smile twenty times a day. I'm not sure I want to be an adult.

I keep looking into my mirror. I think an hour or two flies by, and in that time I manage to smile seventy-three times, as well as perfecting what I'd consider to be a sophisticated look. It includes an eyebrow wiggle and a nostril flare. I like to try out new expressions in the privacy of my bedroom, before I bring them into public view.

Later, as I wait to fall asleep, I hold my book close to me. Mother doesn't pop into my room to check on me. Mother doesn't pop into my room to punish me. Mother isn't a popping-in kind of person, really.

I tossed and turned all night, but I've already been for my morning spin and right now I'm standing in the open office doorway, looking out on to the concourse of Lime Street

Station. I glance up at the departures board. There'll be a rush to Platform 6 and to Platform 1 any minute now. Trains to Warrington and Manchester are pulling in. I'm whistling, and people are fast-walking across the concourse. They can't run, because they're adults, and adults aren't supposed to run or spin in train stations. I like how their not-quite-running makes them wiggle. They're glancing up at the departures board, hurrying to find the platform they need. The lost property office is open, but at this time of day people are hurrying to work and not really needing me. I don't mind. I like to watch them.

The ticket booth is below the departures board. The queue there is longer than usual this morning. The lady at the back of the queue turns and smiles. Her hair's dark-brown like mine, and it bounces off her shoulders. Her neck's long, and her ankles are thin like mine. I wonder if we're related. I curtsey, she stares for a moment, and then she walks over to me.

'Why the long queue?' I ask.

'New girl,' she says, rolling her eyes. 'Can you sell me a ticket, queen?'

I shake my head. 'Sorry.'

She looks at the queue. 'Bugger,' she says, 'it might go down in a couple of minutes.' She turns back to me and steps into the lost property office.

'Do you work here?' she asks, her eyes scanning the metal shelves that line the right and left walls.

'Yes,' I say, 'I live in the flat upstairs with Mother.'

'No commute – you're lucky,' she says, and I nod.

'It's the best place in the world to live,' I say. 'You know those bronze liver birds on top of the Royal Liver Building?' I say. 'You know how they're chained down so they can't fly away? You know how it's said that if those two liver birds fly away, then Liverpool'll cease to exist?'

'Mmm . . .' she says, but I'm not convinced she's listening.

I think the lady might reckon my storytelling's rubbish. Of course she'll know about the liver birds, everyone in Liverpool knows about them, my question was just me trying to set the scene. Then I was going to tell the lady that I've never stepped outside of Lime Street Station, and then I was going to tell her about Mother getting a letter shortly after I came to live here and how that letter said I was the new liver bird of Lime Street Station. Then I was going to tell this lady how the letter told Mother that if I'm not touching the station at all times, then it'll collapse down into the underground tunnels, and then Liverpool Lime Street Station will cease to exist for ever.

Instead, I watch her scanning the lost property office. It's a perfect square and its lost items tell perfect stories. Metal shelves line all of the left wall, metal shelves line all of the right wall, the back wall has two doors in it. I love watching people's reactions to all the shelves and boxes.

'Is that cardboard box really full of false teeth?' she asks. All of the metal shelves have cardboard boxes on them, each labelled with what's inside. I nod.

'Is that a stuffed monkey?' She points to a stuffed monkey sitting on the counter.

'Yes, just logging him in,' I say, 'and there are seven straw donkeys on that shelf.' I point to the shelf that ends in the left-hand corner, next to the door that leads to Mother's flat upstairs. That door's always closed.

'So organized,' she says and laughs. 'Could do with you in our house, queen.'

I smile. 'Being organized is a must,' I say. 'But I'm thinking about making some changes today.'

'Don't think you can change much, not with that counter being there.' She points to the wooden counter that runs across the room, making the letter H with the metal shelves.

A small part of the counter bends upwards, allowing me to walk behind and sit on the stool.

'The counter and my stool are just right,' I say. 'I'm facing anyone who walks in and I've a perfect view of the bench that's in the middle of the concourse. That one.' I point out into the concourse and see the queue from the ticket booth snaking around the bench. The lady turns back to look at the queue, sighs and then turns back to face me. 'Mother prefers that stool, near the door to the flat, she says it stops people from asking questions.' I point at Mother's stool.

'Not a people person?' the lady asks, then she looks at her watch and lets out a tiny squeal. 'I'm so late,' she says, turning and stepping towards the concourse. 'Doesn't look like the queue's getting any shorter,' she says.

She's leaving. I panic. 'Are-you-my-birth-mother?' I ask her, the words coming out like they're one big word.

'Your birth-mother?' she asks, turning back and looking confused.

'Did you abandon me and leave me to sit on that shelf?' I point to the shelf on the right, the one near the glass front of the lost property office.

'I'm twenty-three. You're what, fifteen?' she asks.

'Sixteen,' I say.

She laughs and then she looks at her watch again. 'Got to go, nice talking to you . . .'

'Martha Lost,' I say.

'Nice talking to you, Martha Lost.'

I stand up from my stool, lean over the counter and watch her turn right out of the lost property office, past the coffee bar and towards the main exit.

'Come back soon,' I shout after the lady. She doesn't look back.

Lime Street Station's buzzing this morning. It's only eight

a.m., and there are already crowds of people waiting. I'm beginning to wonder why everyone's wanting to leave Liverpool today.

Stanley the cleaner's brushing around huddles of people near the queue for the ticket booth, but there isn't much space for brushing today. I don't think his name's really Stanley. Folk say he looks like Stan Laurel. I step out from behind the counter and back to the open doorway. I shout to him, and he brushes his way over.

'What's going on?' I ask, nodding my head towards the crowds.

'Rumour that the Liverpool lads are arriving in later today,' Stanley says. 'Loads of coppers outside already.'

That makes sense. The other day I'd read all about it in Elisabeth's newspaper, and then she'd had to explain it all a few times until I understood. The paper said that a couple of days ago Kevin Keegan scored an equalizing goal in the second leg of the UEFA Cup final. It was against Club Brugge.

'How do you say Brugge?' I used my French accent and said it 'Brug-gee'.

'I think the "gg" sounds like a "huh" and the "bru" is more "br",' Elisabeth said.

'But that makes no sense,' I said. 'Why spell a word with the wrong letters?'

'Br-huh,' Elisabeth said.

'I might as well call it Bugger,' I said.

Elisabeth laughed. 'That works,' she said.

'But why give a word letters and then tell people not to say them?' I said. 'At least with Bugger I'm using all the letters.'

'It's all foreign, doll,' Elisabeth said.

We asked Stanley, and he said we could say it any way we fancied. Elisabeth said that Kevin Keegan's goal led to Liverpool FC winning the final 4–3 on aggregate. Elisabeth explained what that meant, but mainly I focused on the word aggregate and how it made my mouth roll into different shapes when I said it aloud. Elisabeth said the city's been celebrating, that there's sheets hanging out of people's windows with 'KEEGAN for KING' written on them. She explained that meant King of Liverpool and that I was wrong to be excited about him becoming King of the World. She said that the city's been swarming with people wearing Liverpool FC colours and scarfs and paper hats with all the players' faces on them, and that some man down St John's Market was selling them on the cheap. I had to take her word for it. Because I never leave Lime Street Station, I've not really seen that much of the celebrating, apart from a few drunken supporters stumbling through here to find their way home.

Elisabeth has a thing for Kevin Keegan. She said that she's going to write him a letter and invite him round for one of her French Fancies. I can't wait to tell her that she might get herself a glimpse of him today.

'Thousands expected,' Stanley says. 'Second UEFA Cup win; bastards won in '73 too.'

'You a blue, Stanley?' I ask.

Stanley sighs, nods, then he walks off and carries on with his sweeping around people, which is OK when people are huddling but quite tricky when they're walking. I like that Stanley's a blue; most people I talk to are reds. I told Elisabeth once that I can't understand why folk round here can't support Everton AND Liverpool. Elisabeth just sighed and said something about me living on a different planet.

I walk through the gap in the counter and open the door to Mother's flat.

'Mother,' I shout up the stairs.

'What?' she shouts down the stairs.

'Liverpool FC won the UEFA Cup final. They beat Club Bugger 4–3 on aggregate. The final was a two-legged tie, with Bugger hosting the second leg,' I shout. 'Full squad's arriving here today, thousands of men expected. Best bring your pan of holy water down.'

Mother doesn't answer.

'Mother?' I shout.

'What the bloody hell's aggregate?' Mother shouts.

'They won – scored the most goals overall,' I shout.

'The Devil likes football,' Mother shouts, but I can hear her stomping around. She's probably filling the pan up from the holy water tap.

It's a good ten minutes before she comes downstairs.

'Brew up,' she says, plonking herself on her stool near the door to the flat. She pushes the pan of holy water under the stool.

Mother looks like a fat prune. She might once have been tall, but now she's all scrunched up, wrinkly and plump. Her hair's entirely white, cut into a bob with rubbish scissors, and her teeth are yellow. She sits with her legs wide open, her baggy bloomers reaching her knees. She's out of breath from walking downstairs, and she's wheezing like she smokes fifty ciggies a day, even though she only smokes ten a day, because Mother says the lost property office doesn't pay enough for more than that. She's got her leather belt in her right hand.

'Could really do with an armchair down here,' she says, then there's silence, and she watches me as I move over to put the kettle on.

'You wearing mascara?' she asks. She slashes the leather belt at my calves. She misses. 'Devil's rats wear mascara.'

I shake my head.

I make sure that I'm too far from her for her to reach me with her belt. And I ask her, 'Tell me again, how was I found?'

She answers, 'Oh, for bloody hell's sake, Martha Lost, my dear, do we have to do this again?'

I say, 'This'll be the last time, I promise.'

She sighs and tuts, then she says, 'Your story started on a gust of wind, Martha Lost, my dear.'

That's a lie.

I ask her, 'Can you be a little bit more precise?'

She answers, 'On a sleeper train from Paris Gare du Nord journeying the eleven hours to Liverpool Lime Street.'

That's a lie too.

I'm clutching the book, and I guess I hope that she'll just open up and tell me everything.

'Make yourself more comfortable,' Mother says, but I know that's so I'll be close enough for her to strike. I sit on the cold floor in the lost property office. I cross my legs and wait for her story.

'It's complicated,' she says.

That isn't a lie.

She says, 'The year was 1960. The passengers were seated for their *oeufs sur le plat* with ham. And as they nibbled on cereals and baskets of hot toast, croissants, brioches, and fresh fruit . . .' She pauses. 'As they breakfasted and the sleeping-car conductors made down the beds . . . something remarkable occurred.'

She's sticking to her story. I've heard this a million times before. She's using her Blundellsands voice. It's the same one she uses when she's on the phone to Management.

'It was then, as the passengers were breakfasting, in both comfort and in style,' she says, 'that a single suitcase fell from the overhead luggage rack.' Mother describes the suitcase. She says that it was old, battered, scratched and had two luggage labels on its lid.

'One, Adelphi Hotel, Liverpool, circular, black and orange,' she says. 'The other from the Scribe Hôtel, Paris, oval, black and green. The suitcase landed in the aisle with an almighty thud . . .'

She bangs the buckle of her belt on to the metal shelf. She startles me. She smiles.

'One lady, French, middle-aged, delicate, sipping only on orange juice, was said to have screamed,' Mother says. Her arms wave in the air, the belt waves in the air, she laughs at her acting expertise. Mother's a master performer. Today she's playing Lady Muck of Muck Hall.

'Another, British, middle-aged, common.' She says the word 'common' like she's from Blundellsands and owns a million pearl necklaces. Mother's enjoying herself. 'She was said to have shouted her disgust at whoever it was that had tried to murder her. But it was the Parisian lady who fainted into the aisle. It is she who was said to have caught the other passengers' attention; it is she who was said to have silenced their screams and muffled their shouts.'

'Mother,' I say, but her eyes flick to her belt, they tell me to hush.

'That was until all attention turned to the reason why she had fainted, to that tiny gurgle emerging from the old, the battered, the scratched suitcase, the one with those two luggage labels peeling from its lid. For sitting, smiling, gurgling, in that open suitcase, in the aisle of the dining car on that Night Ferry, an international sleeper train from Paris Gare du Nord to Liverpool Lime Street . . . was a baby girl.'

'Me?' I ask. I can't help but smile.

'You, Martha Lost, that baby girl was you.'

More lies.

'You were a truly beautiful baby girl, a right bobby dazzler. Yet we were never sure of your age. Some insisted that you must have been six months old; others said that you were almost one year old.'

'But, Mother—' I say.

Mother interrupts. 'I brought you here, to this lost property office,' she says. She spreads her arms out wide, as if welcoming me for the first ever time. I bend backwards to avoid the metal buckle. 'And here you waited for ninety days,' she says.

'But, Mother,' I try again.

'But nothing,' she says. 'I was the manager. I cared for you as best I could as we waited.'

'We waited?' I ask.

'For ninety days – every day I waited to see if someone would claim you – you waited on that shelf.' Mother leans forward slightly, she points to a set of metal shelves near to the office's glass front. 'No one wanted you and so I claimed you. I paid the pound fee. You were my gift from God.' Mother does a sign of the cross on her chest. I sigh.

'But how?' I ask her.

'How?' she replies.

I see her eyes switch. I see the fury beginning to bubble. I shuffle backwards.

'You talking wet?' she asks, her Blundellsands accent slipping away.

But I'm feeling brave.

'You see, Mother, someone sent me this little book.'

I lean forward and hand her the book. I've read it fifteen times. My hand shakes as it waits, outstretched. Mother doesn't speak. Her eyes are locked on the cover of the book, on its title in gold letters. She doesn't want to touch it. I'm waiting for the belt to strike, but she seems to have forgotten she's holding it.

'And there are words written on the inside cover.'

Mother looks at me. Her voice is sharp as she speaks. 'You're getting right on my tits today,' she says. 'And what do they say?'

'They say, "MARTHA, YOUR MOTHER LIES".'

Mother doesn't speak. I wait for her to batter me with her belt. But after a while, she unfreezes, shrugs and says,

'Sometimes you have to believe in stories, Martha Lost, my dear,' and then she adds, 'You proper think too much.'

'The book told me that the Night Ferry never travelled to Liverpool. And BOOKS DON'T LIE,' I shout.

That's when Mother tries to stand. She wobbles and uses the metal shelf to steady herself. Mother takes a few steps and then turns to the shelves in the lost property office. She reaches up. She's still gripping her belt in her right hand, and all the time she's huffing and puffing. Then she pulls down a battered brown suitcase from the very top shelf and shuffles her way back to me.

'Here,' she says, 'this is yours.' She holds out the suitcase. I put the book on her stool.

I've seen the suitcase up there before. It's been there as long as I can remember. I'd never figured it could be mine. Mother's always said that she burnt the suitcase I came in, just in case the Devil'd done a wee in it. I take the suitcase, battered and scratched, the one with those two luggage labels peeling from its lid.

'You were so beautiful, a right bobby dazzler,' Mother says again. 'I expected someone would claim you. I kept you there, on that shelf.' She points to the shelf again, a metal shelf, in view of everyone who wandered past the lost property office. 'I kept you there for ninety days and still not one enquiry. You were as good as gold back then.'

'But, Mother, I couldn't—'

'You're being as daft as Soft Mick,' Mother proclaims, a tremble in her voice. She's standing over me, and she's bursting with anger, or possibly she's bursting with something new that's making her shake. 'You dare to call me a liar? That's your story, evil child, there's no other that I can offer.'

'YOU ARE THE DEVIL!' I scream at Mother.

I watch her, and I see something flicker in her eyes. That word brings her back to herself. Talk about the Devil is language Mother understands. She looks at her stool. She chucks the small book at me. It misses and lands on the floor. She moves towards me and smacks her leather belt across my face. I've learned not to make a sound, and I've learned not to cry out in pain. Mother no longer cares that my bruises can be seen. The sound of the leather slap bounces off the walls of the lost property office.

And then Mother turns and waddles towards the stairs to her flat above the lost property office. I hear her stomp up the stairs, and I hear the door to the flat slam.

Reported in *Liverpool Daily Post*

SUITCASE WITH BEATLES MEMORABILIA FOUND AT A FLEA MARKET IN AUSTRALIA

A man in Australia is reported to have uncovered a suitcase jam-packed with irreplaceable Beatles memorabilia at a flea market this week.

The treasure trove of memorabilia, including unreleased recordings, is yet to be authenticated, but some experts believe the collection is the lost 'Mal Evans archive'. For the last few months, ever since Evans' death, fans have searched for this 'archive', a large collection of memorabilia from Evans' time with the group.

Mal Evans, the former Beatles roadie and friend, was shot by police in Los Angeles in January this year. Not only were his belongings lost during the police investigation, but the urn containing Evans' ashes was also mislaid in transit back to the UK.

Max Cole, 37, from Melbourne, Australia, is reported to have purchased the suitcase from a small flea market close to Melbourne for around $50, just under £20.

'I can't believe my good fortune,' Cole said. 'I spotted this scruffy old suitcase and when I opened it up I was shocked by its contents. I'm a writer, so, of course, I immediately knew that I had uncovered a story.'

Now Cole, a shop assistant by day and a paperback writer

by night, is said to be researching the life of Mal Evans before writing a book based on both Mal's life with The Beatles and the suitcase's contents. Unfortunately, Evans' ashes were not discovered as part of this find.

Nine a.m. and Elisabeth walks in. Elisabeth's carrying a newspaper. She looks over the counter and at me on the floor. I've not moved since Mother threw the book at me and stomped upstairs. A man came into the lost property office, walked to the counter, we stared at each other for about five minutes and then he walked back out the open front door. Apart from that, the crowds of people are staying out on the concourse. I've not spoken another word since I told Mother she was the Devil. I must admit that I spent some minutes worrying that I was starting to sound like Mother, but I've pushed that aside and I've been using the time to catch up on my whistling practice. I'm not feeling up to smiling practice just yet.

'Have you seen yesterday's *Post*?' Elisabeth says, uncurling the paper and pointing to a page. Her voice sounds excited.

I shake my head.

'Doll, look, someone found Mal Evans' suitcase,' Elisabeth says and then, 'Bloke who found it's writing a book about our Mal. He'd better include about our Mal being the fifth Beatle. He was the glue that stuck them together, would have done anything for those boys.' Elisabeth's talking quickly. She's talking to the newspaper rather than to me. 'He even used to buy their socks and undies! And I heard rumours that he might have helped write some of The Beatles' songs. But it didn't bring him fame and fortune. No, doll, he was the Cinderella of that story, without the happy ending, poor bloke. Only a matter of time before someone finds those missing ashes, then our Mal'll come back home. I bet his mother . . .' She stops talking, looks at me and puts her newspaper down on the counter. Her eyes look sad.

'It's hard being a liver bird,' I say, looking down at the concrete floor in front of me.

'Look, doll, the station won't—' Elisabeth starts to say, but I interrupt her. I've heard her arguments a million times before.

'All that responsibility on my shoulders – one step outside the station and all of this,' I say, holding my arms out wide, 'will sink into the ground. Sometimes I wish I could spin away from it all.'

'I've been getting next door ready,' Elisabeth says, which is her way of letting me know that she's heard some of the shouting between me and Mother. 'I'm making extra cake for the crowds. Want to help?'

I nod, I look up at her and I smile. I do want to help.

'Have you had your hair done?' I ask. Elisabeth nods.

'It suits you.'

Her hair's a yellow bob, with the straightest fringe ever. Some days I wonder how old she might be. Mother said it's impolite to ask a person's age. Sometimes I have to press my hand to my mouth to stop all the questions Mother says I'm not allowed to ask from escaping.

'Thanks, doll,' Elisabeth says, then she flicks her hair with her right hand and smiles. 'How about you pick yourself up and come help?'

And because I'm confused, and because I miss smiling, and because I'm full to the top of my head with puzzles, I stand up. I know that when Mother finds out that the lost property office is closed and when she finds out that I'm next door listening to the Devil's music and eating the Devil's lemon drizzle cake, that she'll come down and stomp next door to collect me. But still I nod at Elisabeth as I pick up my book. I take the key and lock the lost property office, then I follow Elisabeth next door into her coffee bar.

I've never done anything quite this rebellious before. I've never openly gone against Mother's wishes and deserted my post during opening hours. Elisabeth knows the rules. She visits me in the lost property office during working hours, when Mother's not around and I'm not busy. I never visit Elisabeth in the coffee bar. Yet here I am, in the coffee bar ('the Devil's front room'), with Elisabeth ('that trollop next door'), having closed the lost property office ('provides you with bread and butter'). Elisabeth's making scones – fruit and cheese – cherry pie, apple pie and a couple of Victoria sponges ('the Devil's snacks'). Mother prefers to eat a meat and potato pie, with chips, for every meal (including breakfast). She says that it's God's favourite food and eating it makes her extra holy. She never cooks for me, but I don't really have much of an appetite and Elisabeth's super clever at sneaking food to me.

'We don't know if the lads are arriving today, but the crowds'll be hungry and they'll have their beer money to spend,' Elisabeth says.

I nod. I'm sitting on a tall stool next to the counter. I've got the copy of *The History of the Night Ferry – London to Paris* hidden under a napkin on the counter, next to the biggest bag of flour I've ever seen.

'Did the Devil tell you to paint your walls red?' I ask with a smile.

'You tell Mother that the tables are a pure white,' Elisabeth says, returning the smile.

Elisabeth's behind the counter. The espresso machine's steaming away, the glass display cabinets and the mesh domes on top are packed full of sugary goodies. Elisabeth's kneading a huge ball of dough. She's making fists, her hands and her forearms covered in flour.

'Look at the state of me,' she says.

I look at her. She's managed to get flour all over her face and into her new hairdo. I smile. I think she looks beautiful.

'You're making a right mess out here. Shouldn't you be doing it in the kitchen?' I say, looking along the counter. The mess is glorious. The counter's covered with cutters, measuring jugs, rolling pins, palette knives, scales, sieves and all the flour in Liverpool.

'Where's the fun in that?' Elisabeth asks. 'This way, you keep me company. Want to natter about it?' she asks, her eyes flicking to the napkin and then to my cheek. There must be a mark. I shake my head and smile. 'When you do, I'm here, doll,' she says.

'Can't believe I told Mother that I thought she was the Devil,' I say. 'Do you think I'm starting to sound like her?' I ask.

'No, doll, you're nothing like her,' Elisabeth says. 'And I don't think she's the Devil either. I mean, have you had a good look to see if she's got any horns or a tail?' Elisabeth's turned her back to me while she washes her hands, and I can hear that she's trying to stifle her giggles.

'It's not funny,' I say, but it is. I laugh, then I laugh some more.

While the cakes and scones rest and bake, I sit slurping tea and eating lemon drizzle cake with Elisabeth. People crowd in around the white tables and sink into the red chairs, happy to be taking a break, shopping bags lying at their feet. In between serving and baking, I chat with Elisabeth. Mainly she talks about Kevin Keegan's thighs. I don't tell Elisabeth about the book arriving. For the last ten years, Elisabeth's been picking me up when Mother's knocked me down. Elisabeth's taught me everything I know about grabbing the good in each day, but I've never told her about my being a foundling. Mother taught me to be ashamed. She said it was our secret, so I've tried my hardest not to think about Part One and Part Two of my life when Elisabeth's around.

Instead, Elisabeth tells me about a dress she's making, she tells me about the time John Lennon almost kissed her, and she tells me about her plans for the coffee bar. She has this ability to make everything exciting. I like that she doesn't try to nose into my head and that she doesn't frown when I don't want to share. And today, at this very moment, all I need and want is to be hearing Elisabeth's enthusiasm about the future and details of Kevin Keegan's body parts that I've never considered before.

But every now and every then I get a wave of guilt. It makes me shiver and check the doorway to the coffee bar. I'm waiting for Mother to barge in, rant and batter me with her leather belt.

'Penny for them?' Elisabeth asks.

I flick my eyes away from the doorway and look at her.

'I should be at work. Management might turn up today and sack Mother,' I say.

'If your gaffer turns up, he'll see how busy it is out there and think you've done the right thing,' Elisabeth says.

'What if my not working leads to Mother being homeless?' I ask, and then I say, 'She'd have to live in an enormous cardboard box outside, next to that Punch and Judy man, and I'd be stuck in Lime Street Station, trying to learn sign language from lost deaf people.'

'Sign language?' Elisabeth asks.

'To communicate with Mother through one of the windows,' I say.

'You've an old head on you, doll. Sometimes you speak and I swear you could be sixty years old,' Elisabeth says.

'Responsibilities—' I start to say.

'Responsibilities, my arse. That lazy madam should be doing the job she's paid to do and not making a sixteen-year-old kid do it for no wages,' Elisabeth says.

'I don't mind mucking in,' I say. 'I owe her—'

'Mucking in? You run the place, while she sits on her rear all day,' Elisabeth says.

'She'll hear you,' I whisper. 'You should apologize to her, just in case. Shout out that you're sorry.'

'Balls to her, I'm fireproof,' Elisabeth says, then she pauses before adding, 'I wish you'd stop with all your shoulds and coulds and ifs. All you seem to do round Mother is apologize for what you haven't done or how you haven't been what was expected of you. I tell you, she makes me bust a gut.'

'If I tried harder—' I start to say.

'You'd still get a pile of grief off Tilly Mint upstairs,' she says, rolling her eyes.

'But look at me,' I say. 'I'm here today, in the middle of opening hours, eating cake.' I stand up from the stool and curtsey. 'Meet the new and improved, rebellious me,' I say.

Elisabeth looks at me and smiles. I smile too.

'In that case,' Elisabeth says, 'pop "Save Your Kisses For Me" on the jukebox and let's have a whirl. It got loads of points in the Eurovision Song Contest, even beat the French, and I reckon it needs to be played proper loud in case Keegan's listening. Then, how's about I serve you up a cream scone with a slice of cherry pie on the side?'

'I've not brought my purse,' I say.

'I'll pop it on your slate, doll,' Elisabeth says and winks.

All day people come and go, in and out of the coffee bar. Some join in the dancing, because it's that kind of day in Liverpool today, others offer their own football chants over the jukebox. I've been learning new steps. Elisabeth says I've my own unique style. Sometimes I dance and I forget that others are watching. I dance for me, I dance and people point and laugh. I like that.

Elisabeth's spent the day rushing between behind the counter and dancing with me. I've been catching glimpses of her smiling all day, proper smiles that bounce right up to her eyes. I know that the music's been louder than usual. I know this because I turned it up (even when Elisabeth suggested that Mother might splinter with wrath at the volume), and I'm sure that Mother would have heard the chuckles and the laughter from the customers joining in too.

But today I don't care; today I'm new and improved. Today I want to start Part Six in the story of my life. I want Mother to know that her lies haven't worked and that I need to know the truth. But even when I think those words, I'm filled with a mix of nerves and dread. I know what Mother is capable of doing to me. I know that a battering will be waiting for me later. Yet still I've decided that I'm going to confront Mother again tonight. I need answers; I'm ready for answers.

By five p.m. it's pretty obvious that the Liverpool squad aren't going to arrive. I don't know who started that rumour, but it's led to thousands of football fans descending on Lime Street Station and loads of them are still out there on the concourse. I move to the doorway of the coffee bar and see Stanley out there, just chatting. He's not working, he's not even trying to sweep round people now that there's so many of them.

'Stanley,' I shout, and wave my arms at him. He walks over.

'All right, Martha Lost?' Stanley says, and then, 'Heard 'bout all them blokes turning up outside? Them urchin blokes?'

'Urchins?' I ask, picturing Oliver Twist with a Liverpool scarf.

'Reckon they're footie fans, but they're all skinheads here to batter and bevvy.' He points over at a man sitting on the bench opposite the lost property office. He isn't wearing a top and blood's streaming from his eye and his nose. The police seem to be both restraining and helping him.

'Don't look like the red bastards are coming,' Stanley says, smiling, then he waves and goes back to talk to his mates. I stand watching the men walking past the coffee bar. They're mainly wearing Liverpool colours with 'Scouse Power' and 'Liverpool FC' in bold letters. They're wearing scarfs, even though Elisabeth said it was a sunny day outside, and they're chanting. I smile. The songs and the atmosphere are all new to me. No one bothers with me, as men are hugging, chanting and swaying to songs that they all know. The football fans are here to welcome home their heroes, and even though it doesn't look like their heroes are about to turn up, it doesn't stop them from celebrating.

'Penny for them,' Elisabeth says. She's come to stand next to me, handing me a fresh brew and taking away my half-cup of cold tea.

'I like that they've had a good day,' I say, nodding towards the last group of hugging football fans.

'You look like you're full of thoughts, doll,' Elisabeth says.

'Just wishing I could get myself out and about in Liverpool. I want to know the city and the people,' I say. 'I've been thinking. Mother said that if I left the station it'd collapse, but what if I took the station with me?'

'You know Mother talks bollocks—' Elisabeth starts to say, but I interrupt her.

'I'm not willing to take that risk. Do you want Liverpool Lime Street Station to cease to exist?' I ask.

'No, of course not, but—' Elisabeth starts to say.

'I'm a liver bird, I have—' I say.

'Responsibilities, I know,' Elisabeth says.

'But I've been thinking hard about it and there might be a way,' I say, and Elisabeth laughs. I laugh too.

'Well, when you figure it out, I'll be your guide around Liverpool. I'll show you all the best bits,' Elisabeth says, and then, 'Shame Keegan didn't make an appearance.'

I laugh again. 'Best be getting back,' I say.

'You going to be OK?' Elisabeth asks, her eyes flicking to my cheek.

'Can't hide from Mother for ever,' I say. I smile, but I'm not feeling brave. It's all an act. I'm already shaking.

Today has been the best of days. I spin my way over to the counter, put down my cup, grab my book and make my way back through the doorway.

'Laters,' Elisabeth whispers, peeping out from the entrance to the coffee bar, as I unlock the door to the lost property office and step inside. I make my way through the office and up the stairs to the flat. I'm tiptoeing like a clumsy ballerina, still quivering. I'm thinking about how I'll get my apology out straight away, how I'll say the words really quickly and then how I'll tell Mother that I deserve answers, before she starts screaming and lashing out.

I creep into the parlour. Mother's heavy drapes have been pulled closed. The room's shrouded in a darkness that doesn't feel quite right. A huge wooden crucifix hangs in the corner – a focal point for anyone who enters the room. I wobble while attempting a curtsey at the crucifix, my knees quivering as I try to stand up straight.

My teeth start to chatter, and my arms feel heavy, I'm full of ice. I imagine Mother must have had one of her headaches, probably brought on by my being full of the Devil. I stand perfectly still and let my eyes adjust. I'm holding my breath, trying not to make a sound, but I reckon the chattering of my teeth is echoing around the room. I bite my lip to stop the noise – it stings. I'm waiting for Mother to pounce. I'm waiting for the barrage of words that are sure to hit me at any moment.

I'm waiting for her leather belt to make contact. I quake. My eyes have adjusted. I can see that Mother's asleep on the sofa. I can see Budgie perched on her head.

'Budgie,' I whisper, then do a new whistling thing I've been practising. That's sure to wake Mother and make him move, but it doesn't.

'John,' I whisper, thinking Mother might have finally convinced him that he isn't called Budgie. Mother never liked that I called him Budgie. She said a name wasn't a name unless it was in the Bible.

There's still no movement. I'm tempted to go to bed, to leave Budgie to poo on Mother's head, and maybe escape a battering tonight. I start thinking that I could always say what I want to say in the morning. I reason that Mother really needs her beauty sleep, that the number of unhappy lines on her face has increased recently, that lately her mouth is always turned down, and that waking her's likely to make her explode.

The drape flutters at the open window that looks down over Lime Street Station's platforms. A strip of orange light filters through a gap in the drapes – it brings an eerie glow to Mother's face and to Budgie's eyes. I shiver again. I step over to close the drape. I'm no longer tiptoeing, but I'm not spinning either. I pause as my hand grips the material. From this spot, I can see as far as my land stretches in front of me. A single curved roof covers the station, made of iron and glass. I've read that it dates from the 1880s. It stops me, the liver bird of Lime Street Station, from flying away. This view from Mother's parlour is my favourite. Liverpool Lime Street's huge clock is near to this window.

When I was younger, I once tried reaching out to touch the clock, but my arms were too short. So I sat on the windowsill, with my legs dangling over the station concourse, trying to lean that little bit closer to the clock, when Mother rushed to me, screaming. She pulled me back into her parlour and on to her carpet. She held me tight to her for at least a minute till my chest started to hurt and my face turned red. Then she pulled my hair back so that I was looking at her, and she slapped my face three times. Mother said that the Devil in me was trying to escape and make Lime Street Station cease to exist. Two days later, Mother had the windows replaced. Now they only open the tiniest of amounts.

Sometimes people look up at the clock and see me waving; sometimes they wave back. Sometimes people look up to the window and jump when they see me watching them. I like it when they jump. I jump too and fling my arms in the air. Elisabeth says that one day I might win an Oscar for best facial expressions and dramatic gestures.

As I reach up to close the open window, I see movement on one of the platforms. The platforms curve out, stone and metal. They bend to other worlds as they turn out of my sight. Far away down Platform 7 I can see a moving shadow. It's an empty platform, but there's a silhouetted figure of a man wearing a bowler hat. I'm feeling uneasy now; I'm feeling queasy. Everything feels off-balance. I blink and the silhouette disappears. I open the curtains to let some light from the station into the parlour, and I turn to look at Mother.

Budgie still isn't moving. Mother's eyes are closed. Her Bible has fallen to the floor near her feet, and her leather belt rests on her lap.

'Mother,' I whisper. She doesn't respond.

'Mother,' I say. She doesn't respond.

'Mother,' I shout. She doesn't respond.

I walk over to Mother. Her face is grey and her mouth is open slightly. She's not dribbling, which isn't like her, as she usually dribbles loads during naps.

'Mother,' I shout. She still doesn't move. I'm hoping for her to open her eyes, even though right after that she'll leap on me. I'm hoping that she'll open her eyes, even though right after that she'll be calling me all sorts of horrible names. I'm hoping for noise and pain and anything but this silence. I can barely breathe. Budgie lets out a tweet or two. I jump, and I wee a little in my knickers.

Budgie tweets again and again. Mother carries on not dribbling; Mother carries on being grey.

I can't control myself. My teeth are chattering, waves of cold rush through me and my whole body is rattling in a shake. I fall to my knees, but no sound escapes me. Tears are streaming from my eyes and snot is pouring from my nose. I crawl out of the flat, trailing a track of snot behind me, and I climb down the stairs on my backside. I crawl from the bottom step and into the lost property office. And that's where I curl into a foetal position on the cold floor behind the counter. My sobs are beyond my control; the sounds escaping from my mouth are no longer mine.

I'm lost again.

I don't belong to anyone any more.

'I am the Devil,' I whisper.

'No, doll, you're not,' Elisabeth says.

I hadn't even noticed her coming into the lost property office. I must have left the door open.

'Did she hit you?' Elisabeth asks.

I don't look at her. I stay curled on the floor and shake my head.

'Where is she?' Elisabeth asks.

'Upstairs,' I whisper.

'What did she do to you, doll?' Elisabeth asks.

'Nothing,' I whisper. 'She's not dribbling and her skin's gone grey,' I whisper.

'Two minutes, I'll be back,' Elisabeth says.

I see her feet as she walks to the door and on to the first step up into Mother's flat. I start counting to one hundred and twenty in my head, but by the time I get to twenty-four I'm already trying to work out which is worse – confirmation that Mother's dead, or Mother miraculously coming back to life and finding Elisabeth in her flat.

I haven't moved. My tears have stopped. Elisabeth's back, and she's sitting next to me on the cold floor in the lost property office. She knows better than to reach for me and pull me close to her, yet all I'm longing for is to feel safe and secure and loved. Neither of us are looking at each other; we're talking into open space.

'I'll make this all better. I promise,' Elisabeth says. She places a hand on my head and strokes my hair.

'Did Mother die for my sins?' I ask Elisabeth. 'Because my very being was the worst sin there could be.'

'Why would you think that, doll?' Elisabeth asks.

'Mother,' I say. 'But what if she's right?'

'She'd pinch the pennies off a dead woman's eyes, that one,' Elisabeth says.

She's talking like Mother's still here, but Mother's dead. She's upstairs. I'm going to have to tell someone official.

'How am I going to make arrangements and do the official responsibilities? I've never left Lime Street Station. I've never stepped out into Liverpool,' I say.

'She had a gob like the Mersey tunnel,' Elisabeth continues, to herself.

'Sometimes I'd walk right to the exit. It's like there was an invisible line that I really wanted to cross. I'd look out into Liverpool and wish I was someone else . . .' I say.

'But, you can—' Elisabeth says, finally listening.

'I wanted to explore, but my responsibility to the people of Liverpool stopped me stepping over that line. Mother said it was an honour, me being chosen to be the liver bird of Lime Street Station. She said her getting the letter was one of the best days of her life. And I get that it makes me special, but . . .'

'Did you ever see the letter?' Elisabeth says, and I shake my head.

'Now it's even worse. If I left now and something happened to you or to Stanley or to Jenny Jones, that'd make me a serial killer. I've already killed Mother,' I say.

'Doll, it's not your fault,' Elisabeth says.

'I'm to blame for the person Mother became,' I say. 'I turned her black hair white. Because of me, the skin on her face's drawn into an everlasting pout.' I pull my lips into a pout. I bite the inside of my cheeks to hold the scowl. It isn't my favourite expression, but I perfected it a few months ago. 'Even the black circles under her blue eyes from those count-less sleepless nights – I was to blame. I was never good enough. She regretted devoting her life to me . . . I broke her.'

'You're talking wet. That woman was broken a long time before you got here. I think you saved her,' Elisabeth says, but I'm not convinced.

'I'll always be grateful to her,' I say.

'For being your mum?' Elisabeth asks, but I shake my head – a definite no.

'Because of her I stopped asking questions. It was during Part Three, I was something like six, I think. I learned to stop talking to keep myself safe. I stayed out of her way, and I skulked in corners. It was before you arrived. I gave up, Mother had won, she had full control over everything I did. But that's when I fell in love with stories and inscriptions in books. I couldn't stop myself,' I say. 'I have Mother to thank for my last books and for teaching me how to read.'

'You and your books,' Elisabeth says, and I think I hear her smile.

I uncurl from the floor. I sit up and reach for the

screwdriver under the counter. At the very bottom of the counter there's a wooden panel. I unscrew the four screws and let the panel fall to the floor. Behind the panel is a gap – it's where I'd hide books from Mother, until it was safe for me to move them down to the basement. Behind the panel's where I hide my dressing-up clothes and shoes too. Today there are five books, three pairs of high heels and six fancy dresses hiding behind the panel.

'See this one.' I open up the book and point to the words written on the inside cover. 'Someone's written, "You're going to be a daddy" inside *Worzel Gummidge and Saucy Nancy*.' I close the book. I look at the thin paperback – a blue cover, a blue spine with curled edges.

'That's nice,' Elisabeth says. I know that she's confused.

'Don't you see?' I ask. 'Those words tell me a different story to the one inside the book. It turns the book into so much more . . . Those words weren't meant for my eyes; it's like I've overheard a secret.'

'But they lost the book. And they've never claimed it, so it can't be that important. They've probably not even realized that it's gone,' Elisabeth says.

I run and rub my finger over the cover of the book. I have this trick that I can do – sometimes I think it's a gift from the gods of the liver birds, maybe even a magical sorry for trapping me here with Mother. Because when I rub my finger over something that's lost, I can tell how that item came to be lost. I can't explain why it happens, and it only works with truly lost things. I rub my fingers over *Worzel Gummidge and Saucy Nancy* and the image of a man on a train, pulling the book out of his briefcase, jumps into my head. I can feel that the man is full of sadness. I watch him open the book. He sees the inscription. It's as if the book's on fire. He throws it to the floor and stamps on it. He never got to be a daddy, not then. It was a miscarriage – at around ten weeks their baby died. He didn't mean to leave the book on the floor; he was just reacting. The inscription was a reminder of what couldn't be. That's how the book ended up here, in the lost property office. I sigh. I lift my fingers from the book.

'The inscription's a flash into a moment. This book was lost because someone wanted to forget,' I say.

'You can't possibly know that, doll,' Elisabeth says. 'It's just a lost book. People lose things all the time.'

'It's a found book,' I say. 'The book was for a man, his name was Justin.'

'You and your imagination,' Elisabeth says, and I smile.

'Books are magical. I like that the reason behind the giving of a book is another story,' I say.

'I've never known anyone read as many books as you. You'll read anything,' Elisabeth says.

'If a book's been found, the least I can do is read it. Then it won't feel lost any longer,' I say. I especially like it when I come across words I don't know how to pronounce or I don't know what they mean – I make a note of them. Then, next time I spot Stanley the cleaner, I show him the words and he helps me. He's really clever with difficult words.

'I think I like books more than I like spinning,' I say.

'I've never met anyone quite like you,' Elisabeth says. She laughs, she takes *Worzel Gummidge and Saucy Nancy* from me, she stretches up and places it on the counter. 'You don't have to hide this any more,' Elisabeth says.

I pause. It's not just the books that I'm grateful for. I think about all those hours I spent helping in the lost property office, unpaid, learning to listen, learning how my gift worked, and I think about the weight of the responsibility of being the liver bird of Lime Street Station. Because of my gift, I'm really brilliant at reuniting lost items that want to be found and, because I can't leave the station, I make my own adventures every day.

'Thanks to Mother's neglect, I found the thing I was good at and the thing that makes me happiest,' I say.

'You're a little finder,' Elisabeth says. 'But that's down to you, not Mother.'

'There's more and more demand for my services in the lost property office,' I say.

'Why do you think that is, doll?' Elisabeth asks.

'People are always in a hurry,' I say, and Elisabeth nods. 'They only realize the worth of something after they lose it,' I say.

'There is the great lesson of "Beauty and the Beast", that a thing must be loved before it is lovable.'

G. K. Chesterton

And so my fairy tale continues. Part Six begins at the end of July, still in 1976 and still in a time when wishes mattered and magic existed.

But right now I'm behind the counter in the lost property office. I'm sorting out the latest deposits of lost property on to the correct metal shelves. I'm writing down the date they arrived and calculating when their ninety days will be up. I do this on a ledger sheet, a new one for each week. When the items arrive, they're placed on the shelves for the first ninety days. When a person comes in to collect their lost item, they pay a small fee (depending on the size and value of the item), and then they're reunited. Sometimes I forget to charge people the fee. I keep a tally of those amounts, and once a month I write a cheque from Mother's account to cover the missing totals. Mother never noticed when she was alive; it doesn't matter now she's gone.

After ninety days, the unclaimed lost objects are placed in cardboard boxes with similar items. Then, every few months, I select several of those lost items from the boxes – it's always the items without a story – place them into bin bags and take them down to the basement. There's a room down there that's full of black bin bags of lost items. Mother once told me that at some point, usually in the night, someone travels up by train from London, picks a couple of black bin bags from the basement and then takes them back down to London. I never even know they've been. I like to imagine that the mysterious someone originates from Loompaland and that they don't really travel by train, rather that they actually travel by tamed Vermicious Knids.

I told Mother that theory and she slapped me with her leather belt; I told Elisabeth and she offered me an extra slice of lemon drizzle cake.

Today, as I'm placing the lost items on to the metal shelves, my fingers can't help but brush over them. For the two months and three days after Mother's death, I wore gloves when I sorted the lost things, mainly because my head's been full of my own sorrow and I didn't want to fill it with stories of how others might have lost something they loved. If I'm completely honest, I don't know if I ever loved Mother. I might have loved her at some point, maybe. I've been focusing on how she claimed me when no one else wanted me and how she must have looked after me when I was tiny and couldn't walk or talk or fend for myself. But I don't even think that the grief I've been experiencing is about her death. It's more that Mother knew answers – answers that I'd hoped she'd one day decide to share with me. Is it wrong that I'd like to know my actual birthday? Is it wrong that I'd like to know my real name? Is it wrong that I'd like to know Part One of my fairy tale? I guess those answers died when Mother died.

But today I'm feeling brave, and maybe I'm finally starting to feel better. I'm not wearing gloves, and I'm allowing my fingers to dance along items. As I touch a lost wedding ring, running a single finger around its circle, I see man and a woman. I see them counting out coins in a desperate attempt to be able to afford this ring. They're smiling, they're in a café, sharing a coffee. Next, I see them in a shop, handing over a paper bag full of coins. The owner of the shop is called over—

'Martha?' Elisabeth says. She's walked into the office without me noticing. 'Daydreaming again?' she asks.

'Just wondering who this belonged to,' I say, holding up the gold band, then turning to place it on the metal shelf beside the kettle.

'No gloves, doll?' Elisabeth asks. I nod.

'Does my face make me look like an ugly Audrey Hepburn?' I ask.

'What? Where did you get that from? You really are a quilt,' Elisabeth says.

'A man said so the other day,' I say.

'What? I'll batter him—' Elisabeth starts.

'And I've been looking in my mirror and trying to figure out if it's a compliment or not,' I say.

'Was it that young Roman soldier that's been hanging around here?' Elisabeth asks.

'No. Anyway, he doesn't hang around; he just stares at me from that bench over there,' I say, pointing to the bench opposite the lost property office.

'And what did you conclude about Audrey Hepburn?' Elisabeth asks, her voice switching to calm. I must look confused. 'Was it a compliment?' Elisabeth asks, smiling now.

'I think so. Even an ugly Audrey must still be beautiful,' I say.

Elisabeth shrugs.

'Brought you some lunch,' she says, placing a plate of butties and a bag of ready salted crisps on the counter. 'Eat up. Got to keep your strength up,' she says.

'I'm still not quite myself, am I? Do you know that I haven't whistled for ages?' I say.

'Today might be the day, doll,' Elisabeth says, and I nod. 'And maybe it's time to stop wearing Mother's smocks for work,' Elisabeth says, and I shrug. Elisabeth's been bringing me different clothes to wear, but I've been paying my respects to Mother. 'Heatwave's in full fury and you're spinning around in massive black smocks,' she says.

'I'm not spinning as much these days,' I say. Spinning in Mother's smocks is far too difficult.

'Drac mentioned Dead Mother's funeral again.' I take a bite of my butty.

'Did you tell him to mind his own?' Elisabeth asks.

I shake my head and swallow. 'What kind of daughter doesn't even go to her mother's funeral?' I ask.

'The kind who's been kept like a slave for years. You can't just snap out of these things,' Elisabeth says.

'Drac says I should have paid my respects,' I say.

'Drac's an arse who needs to stop nebbing in other people's business,' Elisabeth says. 'It was a small turnout, but enough from the station paid their respects. Everyone knows what Mother was like. No one judges you.'

'Do you think my not going makes me like the Devil and the worst daughter in the world?' I ask. 'I wanted to go, but I just couldn't risk Lime Street Station ceasing to exist. Mother would have hated that.'

'You don't need to justify it,' Elisabeth says.

'If the funeral had been in Lime Street Station, I'd have been all right,' I say. 'It's just that my responsibilities—'

'Don't worry, doll. Mother wouldn't have wanted you to leave the station. We had that little service of our own upstairs.' She points up to the ceiling. 'Eat your butty, don't dwell in the past.' I nod.

'Not just for me. Budgie wanted to pay his respects too,' I say.

'Before he buggered off,' Elisabeth says, and I laugh.

Dead Mother's funeral was a church service and then a cremation. Elisabeth convinced those few from the station to go along and pay their respects by promising them a bit of a spread afterwards. Mother would have probably preferred a burial, but we didn't have the money for anything fancy, so Elisabeth organized a cremation and came back with Dead

Mother in a silver-coloured urn. We had a little service of our own, upstairs in the flat, with Dead Mother on the mantelpiece. I even sang Mother's favourite, 'Rejoice, The Lord Is King', and I only made up half the words. After that, we left Dead Mother on the mantelpiece, I closed up the lost property office and we went next door to Elisabeth's coffee bar to celebrate Mother's life with the few who'd been to the funeral. I took Budgie with me, had him perched on my finger, but when I stepped out on to the concourse he saw the iron rafters and flew up high. I stood watching him for ages. Elisabeth said that with Mother gone, Budgie could be free. She said that I could be free too.

Elisabeth reckoned that Mother would have enjoyed loud music and cake at her wake. Something about keeping the Devil distracted while Mother made her way to heaven. I wasn't sure that sounded like Mother, but in the end dancing to Elvis's voice and seeing Elisabeth gyrate to the beats left me feeling at peace. Of course, I wish Mother'd been nicer, but I've had time to think it through and talk about it to Elisabeth. I reckon Mother had her own rubbish 'once-upon-a-time' to deal with, and she did the best she could, trying to drag me up. But I don't want to be like Mother. I don't want to store up my bad once-upon-a-times until my face is etched with lines from heartache and bitterness. Life's too short to be unhappy.

'No more smocks from tomorrow,' I say, and Elisabeth smiles.

Elisabeth's kept her eye on me for the last two months and three days. She is brilliant. Sometimes I watch her as she's buzzing around her coffee bar and I can't help but call out her name. Then, when she looks, I stand up and do the most ridiculous of dances. It's one that I've made up myself, just for Elisabeth. It's the only way I know to thank her.

*

51

The next day and Elisabeth's drinking tea with me. She doesn't like the taste, so she asks for three heaped spoonfuls of white sugar. We stand at the open door of the lost property office, I whistle five notes of a tune and she tries to name that tune. So far she's got three out of seven right. It's nearly time for me to close up for the day. Jenny Jones from the kiosk is working with Elisabeth today, but it's quiet, so Elisabeth's keeping me company. We look out on to the busy concourse. We watch people weave and bob; we watch them leap into the gaps in the crowds. I like how they dance.

'That man came in again earlier,' I say.

'The Audrey Hepburn one? Was he handsome, doll?' Elisabeth asks. I laugh.

'He popped in on his way to catch a train to Preston from Platform 3. He said he'd had his eye on me for ages,' I say. I'm watching the departure board. I like how it winks as a train leaves and a new departure is shown. I like to wink back at it. Or rather I try to wink back. I've never been able to wink. I do a double eye closing and opening thing and contort my face in a way that resembles gurning.

'Creepy watching?' Elisabeth asks.

'Not sure. I think he might be old,' I say. 'This time he said he liked the look of my face and that I could be Audrey Hepburn's uglier sister. He said that my face wasn't quite like any other face he'd seen before.'

'And what did you say?' Elisabeth asks. She doesn't turn to look at me; we watch as life rushes past us.

'I said thank you, even though I wasn't sure it was a very good compliment,' I say. 'Then he asked me out for a walk in the park and I said I had to sort the false teeth.'

'Oh, you quilt,' Elisabeth says.

'He left without saying goodbye and his cheeks were red,' I say.

'I'd be made up if you said yes to at least one of the loads of men who court you,' Elisabeth says. I turn to look at her. She's smiling.

'Responsibilities,' I say, turning back and winking at the departures board.

'But, doll—' Elisabeth says.

'And now this,' I say. I take a letter out from the back pocket of my denim skirt and hand it to Elisabeth.

'Who's it from?' she asks.

'Management,' I say. 'I think they're going to chuck me out on the streets. They must not realize I can't ever leave Lime Street Station.'

She moves away from the doorway. She puts her cup on to the counter and then moves back to me to take the letter. I watch her pulling the sheet of paper from the envelope and watch her eyes as she scans along each of the lines of words. I see a frown gathering on her forehead.

Minutes pass.

'They can't throw you out!'

I shrug as I walk over to her.

'They're taking the Soft Mick! This is your home. This is where you work,' Elisabeth shouts.

'I never really worked here, not officially. I worked instead of Mother but was never on the payroll. I never really existed and now with Mother gone . . .' I say. 'Still, it could be worse, at least they recognize that I'm good at my job.' I point at the final paragraph in the letter. 'At least they're giving me the chance to carry on working here—'

'Of course they are! Well, you can understand their point of view. It's got to be all official like. They can't just have *anyone* working here – and you've got to pay your stamp,' Elisabeth says.

'I was paying it, just under Mother's name and not mine—'

'Doll,' Elisabeth interrupts, 'you're the best employee they've ever had. You're a right little finder.'

53

I'm still pointing at the letter. 'It says that all I have to do is present my birth certificate and National Insurance number. Then I get to keep my home and my employment. It says I've only got six weeks.'

'So,' Elisabeth says, handing back the letter and picking up her cup of sweet tea. She takes the tiniest of sips. 'That's easily fixed.'

'Not for me,' I say. And that's when my tears start.

'I don't understand,' Elisabeth says. 'Have you misplaced your documents? I can help you apply for copies.'

'I . . . don't . . . exist,' I tell her. I'm still sobbing. 'I don't know who I am.'

'You don't know—' Elisabeth starts to say.

'I was found on a train, but then I got a book that showed me I couldn't have been found on the train I was told I was found on,' I say. I'm talking quite quickly.

'Slow down,' Elisabeth says. 'Start at the beginning.'

And so I tell her about the book and the inscription. I tell her how I'm scared that, now Mother's gone, I'll never find out who I really am. Elisabeth nods and she smiles and she listens.

'And you've been carrying this upset with you for two months?' Elisabeth asks.

'Four days and two months,' I say.

'Oh, doll, we can fix this.'

'I don't even have a birthdate,' I say.

'You must do – everyone has a birthday,' Elisabeth says.

'I've never had one. Mother didn't believe in make-believe, and she said my being born wasn't worthy of celebration,' I say. I'm sobbing again. 'And I don't have a surname.'

'Of course you do, you'll have the same one as Mother,' Elisabeth says.

'I don't,' I say. 'Mother said she'd hate anyone to think she gave birth to someone like me. Mother said I didn't deserve her surname and that all foundlings didn't deserve surnames. She said the only surname I deserved was Lost.'

'Oh, doll! I thought Martha Lost was a nickname, what with you working here,' Elisabeth says.

'Mother said that's how people knew when someone was a foundling, because they had the surname Lost. She said it stopped the natter and told the world you were unwanted, but I've never met anyone else with that name.' I'm gushing and the words are rolling too quickly. 'Are birthday candles made from the Devil's earwax?' I ask.

'Oh, doll,' Elisabeth says.

'I just don't know what to believe any more,' I say. Snot's dripping from my nose. I wipe it on the sleeve of my blouse.

Elisabeth moves in to hug me, then I see her remembering that I don't like touching, and she pulls herself back. I hear her drawing in a deep breath. She reaches up her sleeve, pulls out a few squares of toilet paper, puts them on the counter and nods to them. 'Practical issues – let's see what we can fix. First off, wipe your snot . . . Everything's still OK with the bank account? You're still getting at the money?'

'I've never needed money. Mother paid for everything,' I say. I'm gulping in breaths to stop my sobbing.

'And since she left?' Elisabeth asks.

'I kept Mother's account open, and I've been faking her signature on cheques. There was also some cash that Mother kept in the rainy-day box. I dread to think what my slate must be with you.'

'Oh, doll, you'll get yourself in trouble. Not with me, with the bank. Let's wipe your slate clean, but it's best we look into opening you your own account.'

'But I don't exist,' I say. I'm crying again.

'But think about it,' Elisabeth says. 'Someone's sent you that book with them words written in it just for you.'

I nod.

'Well, that's great!'

I'm confused. And then she gushes, 'So someone must know who you are. And all we have to do is find that someone.'

'But I don't—' I start to say.

'You're the little finder. I can't think of another soul in the whole of Liverpool who's better prepared for the task.'

I nod and smile. I wipe my snot and tears on to the sleeve of my cardigan.

'Use the toilet paper,' Elisabeth says. 'Have you been in Mother's bedroom yet?'

'It's too soon,' I say. I pick the squares of toilet paper off the counter.

'Well, how about you start by writing a letter to someone official and seeing if they can help?'

'But I don't know any of my details,' I say.

'Doesn't matter – just write down everything you do know. I bet they can help,' Elisabeth says.

'Yes,' I say.

'Yes?' Elisabeth says.

'But what if I find out I've got a really weird name?' I ask. Elisabeth smiles.

'Like what?' she asks.

'Like Brian Ramsbottom – what if my real name's Brian Ramsbottom?' I ask. I'm not smiling.

'Oh, doll,' Elisabeth says, 'you don't half talk wet sometimes.'

Martha Lost,
Lime Street Station,
Liverpool

The Queen of England,
Buckingham Palace,
London

Dear Queen of England,
My name is Martha Lost and my friend Elisabeth suggested that I write to you, in the hope that you can help me
find my birth certificate.

You see, I need my birth certificate or I'll have to live on
the streets, and if I have to live on the streets, then Lime
Street Station will cease to exist. It's all very complicated,
and if you reply, I'll write again and tell you all about how
I'm the liver bird of Lime Street Station and why Elisabeth
thinks that I could be considered for one of your special
medals.

Anyway, now that you know that it's of national
importance that I obtain a copy of my birth certificate and
because you know people who know everything about
everyone in the whole of England, I am sure that you'll be
able to help me.

As I've said, my name is Martha Lost, but that's not my
real surname. Mother, who is dead now, said that I had to
have the surname Lost because I'm a foundling. And
because I'm a foundling, I don't know my date of birth or

who my parents were, or where I was born, so apologies that I can't help with that information. And because Mother's dead, I've no possible way of finding out the date that I was found or where I was found. I think I might be a little over sixteen years old and I think I might have been born in 1960.

I know I don't have many facts to offer, but I'm sure you'll be able to help. I really do look forward to hearing from you soon.

I do hope that you'll visit the lost property office when you're next in Liverpool. My friend Elisabeth has said that she'll make a double-tier lemon drizzle cake just for you.

With lots of love, dear Queen of England.

Martha Lost

xxx

THE AUSSIE PAPERBACK WRITER GETS HIS TICKET TO RIDE

Word about town is that Aussie Max Cole, 36, is in talks with our very own Beatles expert Graham Kemp, as the mystery of the Mal Evans archive continues to unravel. An unidentified source claims that the Aussie and the contents of his flea-market find are soon to be on their way to Liverpool.

Speculation surrounding the possible contents of the suit-case continues to bubble. Cole claims that he is penning a book based on the findings in the suitcase. However, Cole is also reported to have said that he knows 'nothing about The Beatles' and 'doesn't even like their music'. These reported words have angered a number of people in Liverpool and are said to have prompted the creation of the 'BRING MAL HOME' petition. In one week, over six thousand signatures have been collected, and Graham Kemp's is one of them.

With Evans' ashes still lost, many Liverpudlians are urging the Aussie to 'do the right thing', in the hope that Mal's grieving family will be able to benefit from what is said to be the most valuable Beatles archive to have been discovered.

Unsurprisingly, Cole is reluctant to comment on either the contents of the suitcase or the petition, but we're hopeful that he'll be more forthcoming when he arrives in our city. A spokesman for The Beatles declined to comment.

'Did you read Friday's *Post*?' Elisabeth says. 'About that Aussie keeping all of our Mal's things for himself? What gives him the right to write—'

'Whenever I asked about my once-upon-a-time, Mother would tell the story of the Night Ferry from Paris, about the passengers nibbling on their *oeufs sur le plat* with ham in the restaurant. But all that foreign food made no sense to me. If I asked her for extra detail, she'd shout and she'd say that asking for more was a sin,' I say. I'm interrupting her. I know I'm being rude, but my head's fit to bursting.

'Doll, maybe you need to think less and do more,' Elisabeth says. She's 'frustrated' with me – that's the word she used. It's Sunday, and she wants us to catch a train to New Brighton, have a picnic on the beach and eat ice cream in the heatwave, but instead we're sitting in the coffee bar. The coffee bar's closed today. There are no lights on, there's no music playing, but it's still better than sitting in Mother's parlour. I've a cold cup of tea in front of me. I've been rubbish at conversation, and there's a picnic basket sitting on the counter. I'm wearing one of my fancy dresses – Elisabeth made it for me – it's a red tea dress with little white birds on it. I whistle at the birds, but they don't whistle back.

'Why would anyone want to "paddle" in the sea? Don't you worry about drowning?' I ask.

'It's shallow. I know you can't swim but that's no reason not to—' Elisabeth starts to say.

'I think I've figured out a way around the liver bird problem.

I have to take Lime Street with me,' I say, and then, 'If there's part of Lime Street Station with me, I honestly think I could leave the station. I could go just a few steps at first, then a few more. If it sounds like the station's crumbling, then I could run back in and all would be saved. What do you think?'

'Perfect. It can't fail,' Elisabeth says, and I smile. 'Now—'

'It'll probably take me a couple of weeks to find something to take, something that's essential to Lime—' I start to say.

'Doll, what should be on your mind is finding that birth certificate and National Insurance number!' Elisabeth says.

'I've written to the Queen,' I say. 'Will you post it for me?'

'The Queen?' Elisabeth asks.

I nod and hand Elisabeth the letter. I watch her reading my words. Her face breaks out into the biggest of smiles and then she laughs.

'Perfect,' she says. 'I just know she'll reply. But in the meantime—'

'I've got a plan B,' I say.

I look down at my cold tea and imagine what the sun would feel like in New Brighton. Sometimes I do wonder how I've managed to live almost my entire life in a train station, yet I've never stepped on to a train. But Mother said that stepping on a train was a sin.

'It's time, doll. Let's go and join all them plastic scousers and dip our feet in the water,' Elisabeth says.

I know she means well, but the thought of a crowded train and a crowded beach is making me sweaty.

'In the lost property office, there are lots of shelves,' I say.

'You're avoiding my suggestions,' Elisabeth says.

'There are loads of shelves that are jam-packed full of items waiting to be found. And on that first shelf, you know, on the metal bookcase nearest to the glass front, that's where Mother said that I sat for ninety days,' I say.

'Doll, give over, she can't actually have left you there for ninety days,' Elisabeth says.

'That's what she told me,' I say. 'That's Part Two of my story. I sometimes sit and wonder how many people must've stopped to look at me sitting on that shelf. I sometimes wonder if my birth-mother ever returned, if she ever thought about stepping inside the lost property office and reclaiming me.' I pause. 'I reckon my being abandoned has made me see the world differently.'

'How?' Elisabeth asks.

'Well, every day, I stand by that shelf and look out on to Lime Street Station. I watch people hurrying about, and I wonder if any of them could be my mother, my father, a brother, a cousin. I look at ankles and wrists. I look at the shapes of eyebrows and the way that people walk. I try to recognize the person I've lost,' I say, and then, 'Mother once said that she'd never been told the exact time of her birth and how that somehow connected us, how that was a sign that God had wanted us to be together.' I'd always thought that if that was a sign from God, it was a very subtle one and perhaps he could have made it a bit clearer, like by us both enjoying speaking with French accents or by Mother being a foundling too. 'I don't think she could ever understand just how empty it is in here.' I point at my ribs, mainly because I'm unsure which side my heart's on.

Elisabeth nods, but she doesn't speak. I think she wants me to continue.

'I don't know what it's like to be a child,' I say. 'A real child I mean, without a job and without all the holy water. But perhaps that wishing and perhaps that emptiness of not knowing who I am, perhaps that makes my gift even more special.'

'Honestly, you've lost me now. Help me out here, doll. Have a bash and explain it all proper,' Elisabeth says.

'You once told me I was full of magic,' I say, and Elisabeth nods. 'I have this gift – it lets me connect with items that've been abandoned and lost. But it only works with things that are truly lost.'

'We all know you're fab at finding things,' Elisabeth says. 'You're a right little finder.'

'It's more than that. I've got magic fingers,' I say, wiggling my fingers in the air. 'It's why I sometimes wear gloves. Because, if an item's truly lost and I rub my fingers over it, I can see where and how the item became lost.'

I lift my cup and slurp. Cold tea isn't my favourite, but I keep slurping. I'm too scared to look at Elisabeth. I'm hoping that she doesn't think I'm a nutjob, so instead I'm talking to my magic fingers.

'And that's why you don't like touching people?' Elisabeth asks, and I nod. I can tell that she's taking a moment to absorb all that I'm saying. 'So, you've not got loads of phobias?' Elisabeth asks, and I nod again.

'I never told Mother about my gift. I reckon it would have provided her with that final fact to confirm, without a shadow of a doubt, that I was the Devil's daughter. I couldn't risk her finding out and getting me drowned in the Mersey, like they do with them rats that are found round here. Mother knew people, who knew people, who could have a thing drowned for a few bob,' I say.

'She *was* always one excuse away from having you tattooed with the sign of the Devil on your forehead,' Elisabeth says, and then, 'But, doll, not everyone's lost. You could have a hug or two, every now and then.'

'Are you lost?' I ask, and Elisabeth laughs.

'Don't dwell in the past – it'll give you ugly wrinkles,' she says.

I pull my best ugly face, and Elisabeth laughs again.

'I've been perfecting a sophisticated look,' I say, and then, 'Would you like to be the first to see it?'

*

It's almost an hour until I have to open up, and I've already been for my morning spin, but there's something I want to do before work begins. Even though Elisabeth's told me that the whole of the UK's in the middle of a heatwave, I'm feeling cold, so I reach below the counter and find the scarf and hat that Elisabeth knitted for me. She laughed when I said that I felt cold; apparently, I'd said it on one of the days when the temperature had reached something like thirty-two degrees. It was a record. I asked Elisabeth to describe what the heat felt like on your skin, but she said that it was best I sorted out what I needed to be able to leave Lime Street Station before the heatwave buggered off.

She still made me the hat and scarf though. Even though, Elizabeth told me, this summer is the hottest, sunniest and driest that people have ever experienced, and even though the government has introduced hosepipe bans combined with water restrictions, and even though people have been told to pour washing-up water into toilets instead of flushing, and even though hospital admissions have soared, with loads of people suffering sunstroke and heart attacks, and even though some of the tarmac on the roads is melting and some of the woodlands have been devastated by fires, I've been freezing. So, while the rest of Liverpool was finding a way to stop themselves from melting into a huge puddle of wet, Elisabeth was sitting, roasting in her coffee bar, knitting me a scarf and a hat.

I poke my index finger through one of the holes in the scarf. The wool is bright-red and mismatched, her skill inconsistent. I love Elisabeth, I love my hat, I love my scarf. These are the first items of clothing that have been knitted just for me and that makes them precious. Elisabeth's promised to make me gloves without fingers, when she can find a pattern. I shiver. It's truly cold in the office, even though I'm wearing one of my fancy dresses, two cardigans, a hat and a scarf. We catch the winds from the trains in this box of an office, and we never feel the sun. When Mother worked here, she used to close the door, but I'm not like Mother. I like that the door's always open. I do wonder if the reports of a heat-wave are true. I think I live in my own bubble. Being lost in this lost property office is weird sometimes.

When I'd reached for the hat and the scarf, I'd seen Mother's handwriting. I'd hoped I could ignore it, but my heart's beating and I can't help but reach back down under the counter and pull up a sign. The sign isn't lost, so my mind isn't full of images of Mother. I place the sign on the counter. A single A4 piece of white paper, bold black letters screaming from it, 'NO, WE DO NOT KNOW WHAT TIME YOUR TRAIN WILL ARRIVE. GO AWAY!'

I run my fingers over the letters and smile.

'Been busy, doll?'

I look up and Elisabeth's standing in the doorway, armed with a cup of tea and a couple of slices of toast. 'Breakfast?' she asks, moving to place the cup and plate on the counter.

'You're too good to me,' I say. 'Thank you. I'd forget to eat if it wasn't for you.'

'You've a lot to deal with,' Elisabeth says. 'Stuff your face.'

I laugh and reach for a piece of toast.

'You going to stick this to the door?' Elisabeth asks, picking up the sign.

'One of Mother's,' I say. 'Do you think it'd be OK if I popped it in the bin? Mother hated it when people came in here to ask questions about their trains.'

'You do whatever you want. This is your lost property office now,' Elisabeth says. 'Or it will be when—'

'I help lost things find their way,' I interrupt. 'Including lost people wanting trains.'

'I get those questions too,' Elisabeth says. 'Yesterday, I

must've been asked twelve times in the first hour after opening. At least I could convince a few of them to buy a butty for their journey.' She laughs.

'Sometimes when women come in here I still ask them if they're my birth-mother,' I say. 'I ask it before they've even said what they've lost.'

'I'm not sure that's such a good thing to ask strangers, doll,' Elisabeth says. I nod.

'Wonder how long it took her to make it,' I say, looking down at the sign.

'Best you don't dwell on it too long. It's far more fun to think about happy things, like that young Roman soldier of yours,' she says, and she laughs.

'He's not my—' I start.

'I've seen him sitting on that bench and staring at you,' she says. 'Laters.'

My ten minutes are up. She blows me a kiss and rushes back to the coffee bar to catch the morning rush.

I whistle as I move the sign back under the counter. I'll bin it later; I don't have to decide right now. Being asked questions is the favourite part of my day. The door to the lost property office's always open, and people see that as invitation to come in, to ask questions about the trains, to ask about the nearest toilet, to use a pen, to moan about the state of the train services, to tell me a secret or two. I like all of those questions and comments and secrets. I might make a sign that says 'I LIKE QUESTIONS!' I even like the shouting man who throws his briefcase on to the floor in the office and jumps on the spot. He misses his train to an important meeting at least once every couple of months. He's started to realize that I can't make the train turn around for him. He doesn't mean to be funny.

As I wait for those who need me, I look at my ledger sheet to see which items are approaching their ninety-day deadline.

I've work to do, but today my heart's not here – my mind's someplace else. I look to the floor, to my battered brown suitcase – not too large, not too small. I'm using it as if it were an oversized handbag when I spin around the station every morning. I imagine people think I'm going on holiday. I wonder where they'd assume I'd visit. I'd like to think I look like the type of lady who'd be going to Paris, possibly to study art or to be painted by an artist under the Eiffel Tower. Sometimes I like to speak with a French accent, but not when anyone's around. Lost French people sometimes come in here and ask for directions. I listen to how they say words, then I practise my accent when I tell them to go into the coffee bar and ask Elisabeth. They rarely say thank you. I think French people might be rude. Mother always said that she reckoned I was born from the womb of a dirty French woman. She said I looked French. She said it like it was a bad way to look. I've got a choppy haircut – it was a bob but now it's just above my shoulders – mainly because Mother used to cut it for me, and Elisabeth said that I've got 'magnificent bone structure' and 'doe eyes'. Those words make me ache. I wonder which parent I resemble. I wonder if my father would recognize me if I stood in front of him and whistled.

The spinning is an adventure that I started as a way to explore the station. Every morning for the past two years (apart from the two months following Mother's death), before work I've been getting into character as an ordinary person travelling by train. I put on one of my dressing-up outfits – my favourite's a black polka-dot tea dress and black Mary Jane heels that were found on a train and never claimed. They're a perfect fit, like they were made for me. My fingers showed me the girl who lost them. I saw her changing into a white dress on the train. I saw her fiancé wrapping a sheet around her while she changed – they'd run away to get married. They were laughing; the train's carriage was almost

67

empty. I saw her pushing her dress and shoes under her seat.

After I'm dressed, I grab my battered brown suitcase – the new addition to my adventure – and I spin around the station. Sometimes I stand looking at the departures board, wondering where I'd like to go, imagining buying a ticket and leaving Lime Street Station for ever. Warrington sounds like a magical place. I've heard a couple of the meaner girls who work in the ticket booths laughing at me, but that doesn't bother me. One day there'll be stuff in my suitcase and one day I'll be off on holiday, once I've sorted out a solution to my liver bird responsibilities.

Since Mother's death and only sometimes, if she's there, after my twenty minutes of make-believe I spin over to Elisabeth's coffee bar instead of rushing back behind my counter like I did when Mother was still alive, and she makes me a cup of tea. Sometimes I tell her where I've fantasized about travelling to. Sometimes it's places from books – ones I've read about and then wondered which train I'd have to catch to get there. I plot adventures that'll take me to ask the Wizard of Oz who I really am, or to tend rabbits in the Californian sunshine, or to live in a log cabin deep in the Big Woods of Wisconsin, or to work in a posh Parisian restaurant as a dishwasher, or to visit the gloomy Starkadders of Cold Comfort Farm. But as I sit with my cup of tea, with my battered brown suitcase at my feet, Elisabeth always asks the same question.

'Did you forget to send me a postcard again, doll?' And then we both laugh and I tell her all about the adventure I've planned and which book I've recently devoured. I talk about whether there's an inscription, before I reach into my battered brown suitcase and pass the book to Elisabeth. She always declines the read – she says that books aren't her thing. Music's her thing – music fills her mind with adventure and excitement.

I bend down beneath the counter and stroke my hand over the lid of my suitcase. The image of a baby sitting in the suitcase springs into my mind, but nothing else. I keep trying, but I can't make the image tell me a story. The only flaw, the only clue on the lid of the suitcase, are the initials E. M. G. engraved just under the brown-leather handle. I wonder if they're the initials of my father. I slide one metal catch and the fastener springs up. I slide the other metal catch and the other fastener springs up. Inside, the lining is red, there are no rips, and perfect brown stitching zigzags the silky material. Inside my suitcase is my poster.

It says: 'LOST'.

I've kept the poster very simple – there are no pictures. I have less than six weeks to find answers. My poster has the words: 'MY NAME IS MARTHA. DO YOU KNOW MY MOTHER OR FATHER?'

And then there's the phone number and address of the lost property office.

I'm hoping the person who knows me, that person who sent me the book, will see it and send me another clue.

I take off my hat and scarf, then I step out from the office, armed with Sellotape.

'What you doing, doll?' Elisabeth asks. She's standing in the doorway to the coffee bar, chatting to two of her regulars. One of them's called Clive. He picks his nose, rolls his snot into little balls and flicks them on to the floor in the coffee bar. He's seen me watching him loads of times now; I think that's why he never says hello.

'I'm taking control,' I say. I hold up the poster, and the two regulars have a look at it too. 'Less than six weeks to keep my job and my flat.'

'Go, you,' Elisabeth says, and her smile is so wide I think her face might split open.

I spin towards Platform 6. I stick the poster to the billboard that's right near the entrance to the station's busiest platform. It's a central location, a prime location. I can only hope that the right person will see it.

I return to the office, spinning all the way, and I don't look back.

I wait.

The Roman soldier's there again.

He arrives every weekday, on the 17:37 train from Chester. I know because Elisabeth investigated. I called her Sherlock for days. She drew me a diagram on a napkin as she explained that there's an underground station below the main concourse in Lime Street Station. She said that it's really a single platform. She said that trains run on a loop, taking passengers from Liverpool, over to the Wirral, out to Chester and back again.

Elisabeth told me that from the underground station, the Roman soldier travels up the escalator and out on to the main concourse. It must take him between four and six minutes to march to the benches opposite the lost property office. He doesn't look very comfortable. He sits at a weird angle to allow for his chest armour and the fact that he's the tallest boy I've ever seen. His arms and legs seem too long for his body, and I think he's close to my age, maybe a little bit older. He has a dagger attached to a belt – I hope that it's a real dagger – and his red dress is a little bit too short. Sometimes when he moves we see a flash of his shorts. He never wears socks, even when it rains. His feet are bare within his leather sandals. His helmet is always next to him and his black rucksack sits on the floor close to his legs. He never smiles, he eats butties wrapped in tinfoil, he drinks liquid from a navy flask. He stares at me, whether I'm in the lost property office or in the coffee bar.

After much discussion and speculation, Elisabeth and I have concluded that there are only three explanations. The first is that he is a time traveller, travelling from the time when the Romans were in Chester, and he's not really thought through his disguise for blending into modern-day Liverpool. The second explanation is that he's immortal and was born in Roman times and doesn't have any modern clothes to wear. The third explanation is that he's a nutjob and has convinced himself that he's an actual Roman soldier.

The Roman soldier eating his butties on the bench every day has been going on since the day before Mother died. Sometimes I watch him and wonder what he's lost. Sometimes I wonder if he loves Elisabeth. Sometimes I wonder if he varies the filling in his butties. But mainly I wonder if he knows who I am, because sometimes we stare at each other until I blink and look away. He never looks away first.

Today I wave at him. He looks shocked and part-waves his butty in response. He still doesn't smile. I wonder if he's cold. I wonder why Roman soldiers don't wear coats. I mean I've heard it's always sunny in Rome, but I've read in books that they built loads of walls in northern parts of England and Elisabeth's been to northern parts of England and she's said that it's cold most of the time.

'Why don't Romans wear coats?' I call to Elisabeth. I don't turn to look at her. She's back behind the counter, serving someone, and I'm in the doorway, looking at the Roman soldier. Course, that means I've mainly shouted my question out towards the Roman soldier, but he doesn't answer.

'Don't they wear capes?' Elisabeth shouts back.

'He doesn't,' I say. I point at the Roman soldier, and he stares at me until I look away. I turn to face Elisabeth.

'He waved at me,' I say.

'Who?' Elisabeth asks.

'The Roman soldier,' I say, turning to point at him, just in case she's forgotten that there's a Roman soldier staring into her coffee bar. 'Oh, wait, he's going now.'

I watch as he stands. I watch as he almost topples over picking up his rucksack, and then he smooths down his red dress and leaves the station. He doesn't look at me; he doesn't wave a goodbye. His ears look a bit red.

'Doll?' Elisabeth says. I think she's been talking and I've missed hearing her words.

'What kind of wave was it?' Elisabeth asks.

'A butty one,' I say. Elisabeth laughs, and then I ask, 'Do you think he might be the person who sent me the book?'

'Perhaps . . .' Elisabeth ponders. 'I think tomorrow we need to ask him some questions. Come and keep me company after you finish your shift. We'll come up with a plan and make him a cake.'

'Cake?' I ask.

'Yes, we'll lure him in here with a cake that'll make his mouth water. He looks the type to like lemon drizzle,' Elisabeth says.

'My favourite,' I say. Elisabeth winks. Elisabeth thinks of people in terms of what type of cake they should be. She once said Mother was a pineapple walnut cake with cream-cheese frosting. She once said that I was a butterfly bun and she was a Black Forest gateau.

I whistle as I leave the coffee bar and head back to the lost property office.

Elisabeth's been knitting and humming all afternoon. I've been sitting in her coffee bar reading and whistling. It's been a quiet afternoon, but I love watching her interact with her customers. I wonder if she realizes just how much I learn from her. She calls the men 'John' and the ladies 'queen', but she calls me 'doll', because I'm special. I love the laughter that bounces off the red walls in this place. It's so different to the lost property office. In there I feel cold; in here there's warmth.

Work was good today. I learned how to say 'beryllium' and 'salicaceous' from Stanley, I smiled over two hundred times before I lost count, and I managed to find the owners of two sets of false teeth, one straw donkey and a horsewhip. I didn't charge for either of the sets of false teeth. The couple came in together, holding hands. They'd taken out their teeth on the train and had a little nap. The lady's name was Trisha Toler – the name rolled around in her toothless mouth. I liked her smile. I liked that she giggled and that she whispered the words 'false teeth' with a lisp. I liked that their smiles were gummy. I liked that he let her speak all the words while he held her hand tightly. They should have paid a pound each, but I'll add it to this month's total and write a cheque from Mother's account later.

Now I'm waiting for the 17:37 train from Chester. I'm waiting to see the Roman soldier again. I'm watching from the counter, looking towards the open doorway. I hear the rhythmic click of Elisabeth's knitting needles. I'm smiling. The lemon drizzle cake is wrapped in cling film and sitting on a white paper plate on the counter.

At 17:42 the Roman soldier sits on the bench opposite the lost property office and this coffee bar. He takes off his helmet, puts it next to him, and he bends over, rummaging in his black rucksack. I'm watching him. I haven't noticed that Elisabeth has climbed down from her stool next to the counter. She was next to me, now she's walking to him. She's clutching her knitting needles and her ball of wool.

I watch Elisabeth. I like her confidence. She walks with a wiggle, her yellow stilettos tip-tapping along, her yellow bob bouncing with each step. Everything about her is perfect. She reaches the Roman soldier and bends over to talk to him. I wonder if he's falling in love with her at that very moment. Then she turns, points over to the coffee bar and turns back to him. I watch the Roman soldier; he doesn't smile. He's bending back down to his bag, he's sitting upright, he's reaching for his helmet and standing up. I see how with one hand he flattens the back of his red dress. Elisabeth wiggles in front of him. I notice that when she smiles a wide smile her entire face stretches sideways. The Roman soldier marches behind her. I scurry behind the counter, giggling because I'm excited and nervous and bursting to ask the Roman soldier the best question I reckon I've ever asked. They enter through the open door. In a few strides they've reached the counter.

'Martha, meet George Harris,' she says, and then, 'He likes lemon drizzle cake.'

'Bonjour, George 'arris,' I say. 'Your name! It is almost like ze man from Ze Beatles. I like your 'elmet.' I'm talking with a French accent.

George Harris blushes and puts his helmet on the counter. I think he's going to offer his hand for me to shake, but he changes his mind. I stare at his face. His eyebrows aren't at all like mine. I stare and smile my best smile. I think it makes him a little uncomfortable, as he looks away first. I look to his uniform. I like the detail on his uniform. I can see my eyes looking at me in the armour. Elisabeth bustles about making English tea in bone china cups. She insists that George Harris has a saucer too, and a matching plate for a slice of her moist lemon drizzle cake. She's undoing the cling film. I think she was going to give him the entire cake to take away with him if he'd refused to come into the coffee bar. I'm not sure if George Harris realizes that. George Harris looks a little uncomfortable, perhaps because he's wearing a Roman sol- dier uniform and there's jive music blasting from the jukebox. I'm stopping myself from asking him if he fancies a dance. I'd love to see how a Roman soldier dances. George Harris leans on the counter and wriggles to find a comfortable position. I like him already.

I pull my face into an intelligent expression, ready to ask George Harris my question.

'Are you a time traveller?' I ask. I'm using my normal voice, trying to be normal.

Elisabeth laughs.

'What?' I ask, glaring at Elisabeth. Then I turn to George Harris. 'It's the only plausible explanation.'

'I'm a tour guide, for school kids, in Chester,' he says.

'Ah,' Elisabeth says, 'we didn't think of that, John. I thought you just liked dressing up and were possibly a nutjob.'

'I'm a little disappointed,' I say. I really am.

George Harris laughs, I laugh, Elisabeth laughs.

In the next five minutes, he tells us that he's eighteen, that he has no wife or girlfriend, that being a Roman soldier is his first job, and that he hates being late. I feel that he isn't being as open as I'd like him to be. I wonder if he knows who I am.

When he leaves, I hope he'll visit again.

Later that evening, I'm still thinking about the Roman soldier and practising my whistling. I'm wondering if he could have sent me the book, and I'm wondering if he's seen my poster. I'm standing at the window in Mother's parlour. I'm looking out over the station. It's late, but there are still travellers. I watch as a man and a woman embrace. I watch as he picks her up from the ground and spins her on the spot. I wonder what it'd be like to be lifted and spun. I realize I wonder too much.

Something catches my eye. Something over on Platform 7. I stare out, focusing on the end of the platform, attempting not to blink, because I think that'll mean I get a better look. Platform 7 is one of the longer platforms. The station's footfall is normal for this time of night; people are rushing to catch trains home, to where they belong. All the plastic scousers are hurrying across the concourse to the under-ground station's entrance, hoping to catch the last few trains back over the water. I wonder what the Wirral looks like. I have no idea, but I'm absolutely certain that at the under-ground station's entrance there'll be a clothed white rabbit handing out bottles labelled 'DRINK ME' for those going to the Wirral and currant cake with 'EAT ME' for those returning.

I look at the clock over on Mother's mantelpiece, avoiding Mother's crucifix. I catch a glimpse of Dead Mother in her silver-coloured urn. There isn't a train due to leave Platform 7, so the train that's there must be sleeping. I turn back to the window and watch. I'm sure I see something crawl up from the tracks and on to Platform 7. Its movements are slow and clumsy at first. I think it might be wounded. I think it's a bear, then a dinosaur, then possibly a person. Lit only by lamps at the far end, the silhouette is projected down the platform until it seems to recognize its own image and jumps into the shadows. The jump is clumsy. There's no mistaking that the silhouette belongs to a human; the build and height suggest a man. I watch him move in and out of the shadows, blending into the sleeping train, catching glimpses as he passes by lamps. It seems that he's a tall man in strange clothes – an ill-fitting long frock coat, with a bowler hat perched on his head. It's impossible to tell his age from his movements – not from this distance. His beard seems long – it covers the front of his coat. It looks to be brown and to twist into a point. It seems that a fishing rod is strapped to his back.

I watch him jump with the shadows. I watch him dodge and duck. He appears to trail one leg slightly, sometimes gripping it with both hands as if to hurry the leg along. He's invisible to others, undetected as they bustle and hurry past the entrance to Platform 7.

Two girls wander on to the platform. I want to open the

window and shout at them to run, to shout at them that there's an odd man with a fishing rod hiding in the shadows. I think I hold my breath. I don't move. I'm not brave. I'm crouching on the floor and peering up over the windowsill. I watch as the two girls seem to realize that they're on the wrong platform. One of them laughs and points up at the big number 7. I think they've been drinking alcohol. They're definitely eating something out of brown paper bags.

I watch as the two girls turn around and walk back along the platform. I want to shout at them to hurry up, but I don't. I see the man stepping out from the shadows. I see the girls throwing their brown paper bags with the remains of their snack into a bin. They carry on past the bin, and he steps back into the shadows. He waits for them to continue forward on their journey. It's then that I see one of the brown paper bags float in the air. It hovers above the bin, then sways from side to side, then it jumps into the shadows. The movements are swift. I dare not blink. Then the man leaps from the shadows, his wounded leg still trailing, armed with a brown paper bag and a fishing rod. I watch him weave through the shadows, making his way back to the top of Platform 7.

I jump up and run from the room, down the stairs and into the lost property office. I unlock the door and race out into the centre of the concourse. I haven't even got time to spin.

'Where are you going, doll? I've got you a slice of cake.'

I jump, which interrupts my running. Elisabeth's standing in the open doorway to her coffee bar.

'Do you ever go home?' I ask.

'Baking,' she says, but I'm already pointing to Platform 7.

'There's not a train due, is there?' she asks.

'Can't you see him?' I ask. 'There. Right there, at the end of the platform. That man in a bowler hat.'

77

'Probably just a kid messing,' she says. 'Cake?' She hands me a slice of Victoria sponge on a paper napkin. I look at the cake. Elisabeth always gives me larger slices than normal. My mouth waters. I take the cake from her and continue my run to Platform 7.

'Thanks. Look after the office?' I yell in time with my running steps. 'Back in a sec.'

I'm halfway down Platform 7 when I realize that I've lost him. I can't see him anywhere. It makes no sense. I mean, I know it's dark and night and terrifying, but he couldn't just have disappeared. I stop running. I spin on the spot. I scan the shadows. I move close to the edge of the platform. I lean forward, my eyes scanning left, then scanning right. It's then that I see a flicker of movement right at the end of Platform 7; it's then that I hear the clank of metal. A manhole, to the left of the track – it's moved, it's clanged.

I walk along the platform, tiny steps, my eyes glued to the manhole. My breathing's loud. I try to hold my breath, but instead I cough. I'm not skilled at sneaking. The man knows that I'm coming.

'Hello,' I say.

'Please don't kill me,' I say.

The manhole rattles. I jump.

'Does that mean you are going to kill me?' I ask. 'Because killing me wouldn't be a nice thing to do. In fact, killing me would make you mean.'

The manhole rattles again. I jump again.

I bend down to kneel on the concrete platform. The cold seeps through the white polyester of one of Mother's nighties. Yes, this is the moment when I realize that I am dressed for bed, in a hand-me-down nightie from Mother. It's a million sizes too big. I look down and can see nipple through the fabric. Yet still I lean forward, using my hand to stop the nightie from revealing too much. I watch the manhole quiver.

'Do you like cake?' I ask, and then, 'Elisabeth made it. It's one of my favourites and a great big piece, but I don't mind you having it . . . But you've got to promise not to kill me before I let you have it.'

The manhole rattles.

'Because killing me and stealing my cake wouldn't be nice. And I think you look nice. I like your hat,' I say.

And that's when the manhole moves to one side. I daren't take a breath as two hands reach out and grip the edge, then a bowler hat pops up, then a head, then a body twists out from the hole. Soon, a bearded man is standing tall to the side of the railway tracks, with a too-small bowler hat perched on his head and a fishing rod strapped to his back. His beard is matted with lumps of brown. I hope it isn't poo. He stares at the slice of cake that I'm holding in my hand.

'Here,' I say, holding out the cake. He hesitates, his eyes not moving from the slice. I keep my arm outstretched, watching him staring at it. I look at him closely. I can see how his clothes don't quite fit, and I notice that he isn't wearing any shoes. I look at his face. He looks like he might have a suntan. I wonder if he's been on holiday. Yet not much skin is on show. His body is lost in oversized clothing, his head and face are impossibly hairy. He might be one hundred years old; he might be old enough to be my dad.

'Are you hurt?' I ask. 'Do you like whistling?'

He doesn't answer. Instead, I watch him lift his arm. Slowly. A waft of a sour smell travels up my nose. It's sharp and over-powering. I swallow. I try to hold my breath inside me. The man is smellier than the smelliest thing I've ever smelled. I think he might smell of all the poo in Liverpool. I watch his fingers outstretch. I notice that his fingernails are painted with grime. I place the cake near to the edge of the platform, the white napkin keeping it clean. I watch him wait, a minute or possibly two. Then he leans a little further forward, grabs the cake and lifts it to his mouth.

The way that he devours the cake and the napkin makes me wonder when he last ate. The way that I seem invisible to him makes me wonder when he was last near another human being. The smelly man is animal-like, wild and lost. I like him.

'I'm Martha,' I say. That's the first time that he looks me in my eyes. His eyes are the brightest blue. I think he might have smiled beneath his hairy face. Then he lifts his bowler hat, places it on to the platform, turns and lowers himself back down the manhole. His movements are stiff; his right leg doesn't seem to work very well. The metal clang echoes as the manhole is placed back over the hole. I stay there a minute, possibly five, then lift the bowler hat from the platform. I twirl the bowler hat on two fingers as I spin back to the lost property office.

Elisabeth is behind the counter, sitting on my stool. She's writing something on the ledger sheet.

'One lost cat reported,' she says.

'We're not even open,' I say.

She doesn't look up from the column that she's filling out. 'Although possibly not lost anywhere near Lime Street Station and possibly a rat. I think he might have been bevvied. I noted the description for you here.' She points at the top of the form.

'Thanks,' I say. I don't read the description. I turn to look at Platform 7. I place his bowler hat on the counter, turning it over to look inside. There on the inner rim is a label and written on it in an infantile scrawl: *This belongs to William.*

I run the middle finger of my right hand over the letters. The image of the wounded man jumps into my head. I see him sitting in an armchair, in a dark room. I see him crying. I pull my finger from the label.

'His name's William,' I say.

'Who?' Elisabeth asks.

'The wounded man,' I say.

I turn the bowler hat over. I rub my finger over the smooth felt top. An image of the bowler hat pops into my head – a man, a businessman, worked in the City of London. A proud man, a short-arsed man, how he dressed was important to him. He was on a train, and the train was pulling into Liverpool Lime Street Station – its final destination. He wasn't staying for long. An important business meeting. The bowler hat had been made especially for him; he had worn it only once before. The man was wearing a smart suit, and the bowler finished off his look – a uniform of sorts. It mattered. I can see how he looked around to see if others were looking at his fine clothes. I can see him adjusting the bowler on his head. I can see him waiting to step from the train. I watch. He stepped from the train, the bowler was knocked from his head, someone apologized, the man shrieked. The bowler spun over the crowd. It danced its escape. It reached the end of the platform and fell on to the tracks. It was lost. I can see a manhole cover open. I can see a small boy climbing out from the manhole – his clothes were dirty, he looked grey and sad. He grabbed the hat, put it on his head, and it flopped over his blue eyes. The small boy smiled and leaped back down the manhole. The businessman was not the man that I'd shared the cake with.

'Did you like the cake?'

Elisabeth brings me back into the moment. I take my finger away from the bowler hat.

'I gave it away,' I say, and then, 'To *William*.'

Written by Anonymous to Martha Lost, throughout
The Song of the Lark by Willa Cather, delivered by Drac
the postman to the lost property office

My dear Martha,

*I am truly grateful that you have decided to embark on
this communication with me. I must confess to being filled
with glee when I passed your poster this morning. In order
to establish my 'identity', I must also confess that I am the
coward who sent the book to you so many months ago now.*

*I did hear that the person you called Mother was no
longer with you, and I had considered attempting
communication with you again. Alas, bravery did not come
to me in the way that it should or in a way that I could have
hoped, and I feared that to attempt communication with you
again would add to the anxiety and grief that must have
been accompanying you these last months. Please accept my
humble condolences for your loss and my apologies for not
communicating with you before this time.*

*In answer to your question, I do indeed know of your
father.*

*However, I am sorry to have to inform you that your
father is no longer of this world. He died some ten years
ago. I dislike that I am the bearer of such news, especially
when grief has been part of your young life for the last few
months. It fills me with dread that I must be the person who
enlightens you with the facts surrounding your conception.*

I must speak the truth and advise you that your birth-mother and your father were lovers rather than spouses; indeed, your father had a wife. I can imagine that you must be covered in shock at this very moment, but there is more to this sorry tale.

The story has been told that your father was a piano teacher, some say that he was the best in his village with fingers that could work magic on his ivory keys. I have wondered, over the years, if you inherited his musical gift or magic. Your birth-mother was one of his students, a child. She was a talented musician, she was a lover of books like you. She gave birth to you when she was a mere fifteen years of age.

I apologize for burdening you with these words, my dear Martha. Yet I feel that you must dig a little deeper, for it cannot be ignored that I have indeed referred to a birth-mother.

I long to hear from you.

Yours,

Anonymous x

I look up from the book as Elisabeth dances in, a paper plate balancing on her right hand. 'Only thirty-six days till you're evicted, doll,' she says. She places the paper plate on to the counter. Lemon drizzle cake and a cheese scone.

'How do you know?' I ask.

'Been counting,' Elisabeth says, and I nod.

'Drac delivered this book earlier,' I say, showing Elisabeth the book but not handing it to her. I don't want anyone else to hold it. I want this book to be all mine. 'Someone's written me a letter throughout it, it's like a really long inscription.' I'm smiling the best and widest smile ever, but Elisabeth's not looking at me. She's staring at the book.

'No, who'd do that?' Elisabeth says, like it's a bad thing.

'It's a new book, it isn't lost. It's the most beautiful book ever,' I say. I turn the pages of the book slowly, terrified I'll somehow break the words. Then I open up the book at the first inscription – the letter starts on the inside cover. I read the words aloud to Elisabeth, then turn to the next page; there are more words to read there too. The sender's used the white space, margins, tops of pages, end of chapters. The letter is being told throughout the book, and I uncovered it. Someone's telling me secrets. The book now contains an extra story.

I cry when I read the words written inside *The Song of the Lark* to Elisabeth. I cry for a man I'll never know, and I try to imagine what it'd be like to be a mother at my age. I can't.

Elisabeth listens to the words, and she cries too. She says

that it's desperately sad, then she tells me off for wiping snot on my sleeve, and we laugh.

'I'm going to put up another poster tomorrow,' I say.

'Are you going to ask about your National Insurance number or birth certificate on this poster?' Elisabeth asks.

'Thought I'd best start with some small talk,' I say, and Elisabeth laughs again.

Elisabeth and I have been taking it in turns to keep a watch on Platform 7, either together or separately. We've been hoping to get a glimpse of William. If I'm honest, I've been sneaking a look over at the platform every few minutes all day. I even closed the lost property office twice this morning just so that I could nip up to Mother's parlour and have a proper look out the window. I shut my eyes as I fumbled my way across the room, not wanting to see Mother's too-big wooden crucifix, thinking it might be able to cast a spell and magic me to Hell for shutting the lost property office during working hours. But that window has the best view over the platforms. And after work, before I went for my afternoon tea and natter in the coffee bar with Elisabeth, I took my suitcase and popped William's smelly bowler on my head, before taking a little spin along Platform 7. I didn't get to see him though. Part of me fears that I've imagined him. Maybe that's what happens when you've got no Part One in your life story – maybe you start making up people.

But what kind of person creates an imaginary friend who doesn't wear shoes, smells of poo and carries a fishing rod on his back?

I decided, seeing as Elisabeth was working and George Harris the Roman soldier had been and gone, that I might as well open the lost property office again for a couple of hours extra. I think I was hoping that William would see that the office was open and that he might hand himself in. Because he is lost – no doubt about it. He could be like me. He could sit on a shelf for ninety days and wait to be claimed.

But, of course, that doesn't happen. Instead, the stuffed monkey's been handed in again. I swear I've no idea where people keep finding it, but it's the same one that keeps getting lost and found every week or so. And it's always the same man who claims it. He's always so relieved, he's happy to pay the fee, and I'm always glad to see the stuffed monkey leave the office. I should ask more questions, but when I touch the stuffed monkey I can see it being thrown from a train window on to a platform, and I can hear screaming and swearing. Looking at the stuffed monkey makes my insides wobble.

I've also added another three sets of false teeth and one white stiletto to my ledger sheet. But it's not all bad. I'm sitting at the counter, logging my findings and singing along to the music that's coming in through the open door and rattling through the wall that separates me from Elisabeth's coffee bar. The Beatles are blasting out of the jukebox, and I'm whistling along. Sometimes the room actually jumps to the beat. I like that I can put my hand on the wall and feel the music rushing through me.

A couple of weeks ago there was even talk of a Beatles reunion. Elisabeth told me. She'd read about it in the *Daily Post*. I didn't sleep that night – I was too full of excitement at the thought of being able to actually experience the music that everyone around me spoke about. Because of Mother, it's like our house slept through The Beatles, and the thought of a reunion made me feel things inside that I didn't even know someone like me could feel. Of course, the following day everyone in the station was saying that the news of the reunion was a hoax. I cried for three hours straight when I heard the rumour was a lie. Elisabeth said that meant I was a real fan, not a plastic one.

Mother always referred to The Beatles as 'the Devil's little helpers'.

'Beetles like them dark underground spaces,' she'd say, 'Rats are the Devil's children, and beetles are the Devil's children's pets.' It was all very complicated in Mother's world.

She'd not listen to explanations about The Beatles being spelt differently.

'The Devil can't spell,' she'd say, which I suppose did make sense to me. 'Listening to music by The Beatles is a sin. If a single note or lyric pops in your head, then you'll be one step closer to burning in Hell.'

Mainly because I never left the lost property office – and mainly because on the occasions when The Beatles were passing through Lime Street Station I'd be locked in my bedroom and ordered to sit with my fingers in my ears – I'd managed to avoid the hysteria. I'd even been sent upstairs to our flat if there was any whiff of The Beatles being in the vicinity of Lime Street Station. (Jenny Jones from the kiosk told Mother that George Harrison once sucked her little finger. After that, I was sent upstairs every time Jenny Jones looked like she was headed to the lost property office.)

But since Mother turned into Dead Mother, Elisabeth's been giving me lessons in all things Lita Roza, Frankie Vaughan, Gerry and the Pacemakers, The Searchers, Cilla Black, The Scaffold and The Beatles. Elisabeth adores Ringo. She's got a full-size poster of him in the coffee bar's kitchen. It's splattered with grease now and makes him look like he's got a skin condition, but she kisses him on his greasy-paper cheek every day. Thanks to Elisabeth, I know lyrics and I know dance routines. Elisabeth's spent hours teaching me the Mashed Potato, the Swim, the Twist, the Jive and so much more. She's made it so that I can appear like I belong.

Elisabeth had said earlier that William would come back if

he wanted me to see him again and that I wasn't to take it personally if he didn't.

'Some people prefer being lost,' she said.

I nodded, but really I was thinking that she was saying the most ridiculous thing I'd ever heard her say. Who'd prefer to be lost? No one. Elisabeth talked about how I'd changed and how impatient I'd become. She laughed and said it was a good sign, said it showed that I wanted to be living my life to the full. The sound of her laugh wasn't quite right though, and her eyes were full of sadness.

At seven minutes to eight, I decide to start thinking about what to ask on my poster. By three minutes to eight, I'm worrying that I'll not see William ever again.

It's half eight, the lost property office is locked up and dark, but I'm sitting at the counter and watching Platform 7. I was reading, but my eyes were flicking from the page to the window after every couple of lines. Elisabeth must be close to the jukebox on the other side of the paper-thin wall. 'Hey Jude' is playing – her favourite. I can hear her singing along. The shelf of walking sticks is rattling to the beats of the jukebox vibrating through the wall. The coffee bar must be full. I can hear chatter and laughter. She's having a poetry reading later. She's invited me along, but I don't want crowds tonight.

And that's when I cast my eyes along Platform 7 again and I see the silhouette of a man jumping into the shadows, jumping along next to the sleeping train. I move to the glass door, pressing my face forward so that the tip of my nose rests on the cold glass and my palms leave their mark. I fix my eyes on the spot where I think that I've seen movement, hoping that my eyes aren't tricking me. That's when I see a brown paper bag floating up from the bin. It's clear that William the fisherman is out and about, attempting to make a catch.

I grab the box that I've prepared from behind the counter. I unlock the door, pulling it shut behind me. I move to the doorway of the coffee bar.

'Elisabeth,' I shout, and then again a little louder. She's singing along and slow pirouetting by herself around the coffee bar. There isn't a spare table. Young poets and artists have squeezed around the small tables and into the booths. Some sit on the floor, some stand huddled in corners. Cigarette smoke hops around the room, strangers brush hands. A stab of wishing I could be like them makes me shiver, then it passes. I don't have time to wait for the song to end. I shout her name one last time, but Elisabeth's in a world of her own. She's a princess at her own ball. So I turn and I spin with the cardboard box towards Platform 7, trying not to trip over my feet, because spinning with a box isn't something I've often experienced.

By the time I reach the bin on Platform 7, William's moved to a new shadow, but a whiff of his scent lingers. I stop, letting my eyes dart left and right as I place the cardboard box on the floor. I bend and lift out a bag of Frazzles and a tube of Smarties. I bought them from Jenny Jones's kiosk earlier. It was the first time I'd ever bought anything from Jenny Jones's kiosk. I place them on the floor next to the cardboard box. Then I bring out three pairs of men's shoes and place them in a perfect line. They're all lost property, all lost for over ninety days and were waiting down in the basement, in the storage room, for Management to collect them. No one wanted them. One of the pairs had been thrown in a bin in Lime Street Station, but Stanley the cleaner handed them into the lost property office when he was explaining 'jodhpurs' to me. After touching the second pair, I could see that they'd been taken off on a train from London to Liverpool and left under the seat. The passenger had put on a pair of slippers and forgotten about their outdoor shoes. My fingers told me that the third pair had been found in the toilets in Lime Street Station. These boots had caused blisters the size of small hills and were at least one size too small for the man who had owned them. They'd been a bargain, he'd liked them, but he was going to take them back.

I like the idea that one of these pairs of shoes will keep William's feet warm. The shoes are different sizes, and I hope that one of them will fit William's feet. I hope that he won't be offended. I hope that he'll not pick a pair that's too small for him. I hope that we can be friends.

I move away from the items on the platform, stepping back, leaning against the sleeping train and staying still. I don't have to wait long. The fishing line and hook swing in from the shadows. I watch as the hook tries to attach itself to the heavy shoe. After several attempts, William steps out into the light, then scurries to the goodies on the platform. His sour smell makes me hold my breath again. I wonder if it'd be wrong to ask an odd man if he wants to have a bath in Mother's bathroom. I think about how cleanliness is next to godliness, then I look to see if William has horns or a tail. He doesn't, but I notice that he's dragging his left leg this time. I wonder if both are injured. His face had looked angry, but I watch it alter. I watch a softness come over it. I watch him stroke each of the shoes. I see his hesitation as he looks at the snacks.

'They're all for you,' I say. I don't step forward. I try not to breathe through my nose. 'Didn't know what size foot you had.'

William turns to look at me, his bright blue eyes shining out from his hairy face. I feel his gratitude. He doesn't speak. He picks up the second pair of shoes, brown loafers. They'd been left on the train. I watch him running his dirty fingers across the shoes. A giggle escapes his lips. I smile as the sound of his giggle bounces into me. Then he places them back on the platform and lifts the Chelsea boots – short, plain ankle boots with a low Cuban heel and a pointed toe. These were the shoes that had caused the blisters the size of hills. Elisabeth told me that they were the fashion in the 1960s. I watch William as he sits on the platform, moving his wounded leg slowly, squirming with pain as the injury seems to be in his left thigh.

'You should see a doctor,' I say.

William's eyes shoot to mine. They're filled with fear and scream out no.

'It's OK, it's OK,' I say. 'I've never been to a doctor either. I've never even left Lime Street Station.'

William's eyes stay with my eyes, connecting. I watch as the fear falls away and instead there's recognition, there's understanding. Me and William, we're the same. He switches his focus to the boot, twisting his foot into it. The skin on his foot is black – years of grime and dirt ground into his sole. Then the other foot and the other boot. I watch him stand. I watch him lifting his foot up from the floor and then down on to the floor. The clip-clap sound makes another giggle escape his lips. He moves his hand to cover his mouth, attempting to keep the sounds within. The sound is full of goodness; I think it might be the sound of pure joy. As I watch him, I'm smiling. I understand him. I hope the boots won't hurt him. Then William turns, ready to hide in the shadows.

'Don't forget your snacks,' I say, and then, 'If you come back at this time tomorrow, I can bring you a butty.'

William turns and connects eyes with me again. There are no words. I see that his hands are rummaging in his pockets, and then he bends and places something on the floor. He picks up his Frazzles and his Smarties, then he clip-claps back into the shadows.

I wait – I wait until he's found his safety. Then I bend down to the platform. There, standing tall, is a tin soldier about seven centimetres in height. An old-style cavalryman on his horse – a gift from William. My fingers touch the cavalryman, and an image rushes into my head. A loud noise, a siren. I see a family ignoring the sound. They're eating together at a large dining-room table in a parlour. It's a birthday, William's birthday, a celebration, a knife-and-fork tea. William is six that day. There's a cake; it's going to be a treat. They haven't had cake for such a long time. I can tell the mother and the father aren't relaxed – there's fear. William's crying. The table's set – matching china, crystal glass. William's unable to eat his meal. His father's telling him to be brave. Men don't cry in their family. I can feel that the mother's full of panic; she can sense that they're close. The bombs are close. The buildings are shaking, the lights are quivering. As my fingers stroke the cavalryman, I see the mother stand up and shout at William. She tells him to run down, to hide in the cellar, to hide in the tunnels below their house. William doesn't want to go without his mother. She shouts at him again. He wants to take his box of toy soldiers, his birthday present, from the table. He rushes out of the room, into the hallway, down into the cellar. That's the first time William's felt alone; he's never been without her before. He can't stop the wee escaping into his short trousers.

I lift my fingers from the small toy. The value of the gift overwhelms me, and tears stream from my eyes.

The question that Martha Lost wrote on a poster that
was stuck to the billboard next to Platform 6

Am I right in thinking that Mother was not my birth-mother?

It's 17:42 when George Harris walks towards the coffee bar. I'm excited to see him. I've been standing in the open doorway, watching the billboard and the public telephone box in front of Platform 6 for the last hour. I was hoping to catch a glimpse of the person who'd sent me *The Song of the Lark*. My eyes feel itchy – I may have forgotten to blink.

'I found this,' George Harris says. He's holding a book.

'And bonjour to you,' I say and smile. He walks past me, banging into a plastic chair on the way. He puts the book on a table halfway between the counter where Elisabeth is and where I'm standing at the door. I step away from the doorway and over to his table. I move to the book and trace my finger over the front cover. The reading of it has left white lines on the orange spine; the lines speak of moments. No images are jumping into my head. The title is in black, it covers the orange cover. I look inside – there's an inscription: 'I was an outsider, you welcomed me'. I remember to speak.

'I've not read this one,' I say.

'It's a favourite, you should read it. It's about hope, hope for human nature.' He puts his helmet on to the table. It wobbles a little too close to the edge.

My eyes are fixed on the front cover. 'Thank you for bringing it in,' I say. I look at George Harris, and his cheeks are a pink colour. When he smiles, he has dimples.

'I used to read it every day when I was a teen,' George Harris says.

'You're only eighteen,' I say. 'You're still a teen now.'

'I'm a working man,' George Harris says, but he doesn't smile, and then, 'I liked to imagine the dad was my proper dad. I used to hope that one day he'd turn up and beat the shit out of the one pretending to be my dad.'

I don't speak. I sit down on the plastic chair. George Harris has been rearranging his armour, trying to get comfy on his chair. He's so tall and broad. I think the chair might quiver a little. I think he's gawky. I like that word, and I like George Harris.

'Elisabeth's busy, but I'm sure she'll join us later,' I say. I don't know if George Harris hears, as he doesn't reply, but I catch Elisabeth watching us. She makes a sign for a cup of tea, and I nod. I know she'll bring George Harris one too.

'I think you're practically a giant,' I say. 'Is your mum a giant?'

'I don't have a mum. Dad was all I had. And he liked a drink and he liked robbing houses.' George Harris is talking to his chest armour, his hands clasped together in front of him.

'What happened to your mum?' I ask.

'She got fed up of my dad. She left before I could remember what she looked like,' George Harris says.

'I don't know how to react,' I say. 'I feel like I should apologize to you for you having rubbish parents. Is that the right thing to do?'

George Harris laughs. He looks at me, and I give him my best smile. 'I don't think I know anyone who doesn't have crap parents,' he says.

'Do you know lots of people?' I ask.

'Nah,' George Harris says. 'But I've heard about your mother, was she really . . . ?' He's unsure which word to use. He moves his hands to the table, knocking his helmet over the edge. We both reach for it at the same time, stopping it from toppling to the floor.

95

I smile and then say, 'I've never stepped outside of Lime Street Station.'

'But . . .' George Harris says. 'Why?'

'Mother got a letter ages ago. It said I'd been chosen to be the liver bird of Lime Street Station.'

'Sounds like you're a prisoner,' George Harris says.

'It's an honour, but, if I'm honest, all that responsibility gets a bit too much sometimes,' I say, and then, 'I think I've got a plan to leave though. I just need to find something that's really important to the station, to take with me.' I pause, then say, 'Mother said there's loads of sin in Liverpool. Is there?'

'Sounds like she was a bit of a mental,' George Harris says, and he smiles.

'Basically sin was everything that Mother didn't do. People seemed to either live over the brush or want to pinch pennies off dead people's eyes. I haven't been out there myself, of course, but I think maybe Mother just never saw the good in others.'

George Harris laughs.

'Do you think about your mum?' I ask George Harris.

'I'll never forgive her. She should have taken me with her,' he says.

'Elisabeth would say that she must have had her reasons,' I say.

'She left me with an abusive drunk. She left me with a criminal,' George Harris says, and I nod.

'Abuse comes in different forms,' I say.

'You're wise beyond your sixteen years, Martha,' George Harris says. He's smiling and his dimples are winking. I smile too.

'But what about after Mother died?' George Harris asks. 'Surely you realized it was safe to step outside of the station?'

'I don't understand what you mean,' I say.

'You must realize that Mother was—' George Harris starts to say.

'Sometimes Mother would say that she'd see me penniless and living on the streets if I was naughty. And that scared me – not the living on the streets but the thought of me being thrown outside and then the station crumbling into the underground tunnels. All those lives lost and the whole of Liverpool hating me for ever,' I say.

'I don't . . .' George Harris starts to say something but then changes his mind. His cheeks are flushed. I don't know if I've upset him.

'But the way Mother was – well, none of it was her fault. She did her best,' I say. 'One night, ages ago, Mother drank too many sherries and talked about being taken into care when she was ten. Her mother'd torn out pages of the Bible and stuffed them into her baby sister's mouth. Her baby sister'd been smothered to death, she'd only been six weeks old. Mother'd found her.' I pause. 'She said it had made her study the Bible even more . . .'

I wait for George Harris to speak, but he doesn't.

'She said that God'd sent me to her to offer a second chance,' I say. 'To help ease the pain and guilt of failing her baby sister, to give her the chance to show God that she was strong.'

'I can't feel sympathy for her. She hurt you—' George Harris starts to say.

'You must. I talked to Elisabeth, and she helped me sort it all out in my head. Mother was a product of her own mother's pain,' I say, and then, 'And anyway, George Harris, when you think angry thoughts your face looks like a potato.'

George Harris's face flicks from looking confused to smiling. I smile too, then I pull my face into an angry face, and George Harris laughs.

'But a mother should love her child – that's a natural thing,' George Harris says.

'I was never her child,' I say, and then, 'Do you live with your dad now?' I ask.

'No, he died last year. The booze did it,' George Harris says. 'It's just me now.'

There's an understanding between us. We both nod.

'I think this book deserves a special home. Come with me . . .' I say.

'I have to eat my butt—' George Harris starts to say.

Elisabeth's walking over, balancing a tray with our pot of tea on it and two slices of cake. I hold up my hand to her, indicating that I'll be back in five minutes.

'Eat your butties later. Just this once, George Harris,' I say. I can tell he's about to protest – he likes habit – and so I say, 'Please. I've only ever shared this with Elisabeth.'

On the back wall of the lost property office, on the right, there's another door. When it's opened, there are three steps down to a mini-landing, and from there there are three doors that all have steps down into the three basement rooms. The first door leads to where we store the black bin bags that are waiting for transport to London. The middle door allows access to pipes and boilers and electrics and things that are all needed for the concourse of the train station. That one has 'DO NOT ENTER' on the door and is padlocked at all times.

I open the door to the third basement room. I step on to the top of a metal spiral staircase that twirls down into a room that's ceiling to floor of metal shelves, with a single light bulb hanging from a flex in the middle. I step on to the spiral staircase. My heels clang on the metal, the sound echoing around the room. When I'm halfway around the spiral, I lean over the metal hand railing and pull the thin rope that clicks the light bulb into action. Light fills the room. George Harris remains on the first step of the spiral. I hear him gasp. It's the best sound I've ever heard. I turn and look at

George Harris. His mouth is open and his eyes are wide.

'I collect lost words,' I say, and then, 'I let them have a voice.'

'All of these were lost?' George Harris asks. He's scanning the room, looking at the hundreds of books that fill the shelves. There's even a library stool down there. Elisabeth found it by the side of a road, waiting to be collected with the bins. It's perfect, because I can't reach the top shelves, not even when I'm standing on my tiptoes. The room's a windowless square with books from ceiling to floor all the way around.

'They're all found,' I say.

'Are all of the shelves full?' he asks.

'There's room for eleven more books, depending on colour. I don't know what I'll do when each shelf is full,' I say.

'How long have you been collecting?' he asks.

'Just over eight years,' I say, and then, 'You're only the second person in the world to know about my secret place.'

'You're amazing,' George Harris says, and then, 'But how? How did you keep this from Mother?'

'Mother had a fear of basements, said that the Devil lived in them,' I say.

I don't tell him that Mother said that rats, the Devil's children, lived there with him too and with all of their pets. If Mother ever saw a spider in our flat, her pan of holy water soon drowned it. Mother liked everything in its place, and the basement was the place for everything Devil-related.

George Harris is smiling. I can see his eyes dancing around the room. My rainbow of books is making him happy.

I also don't tell George Harris that the basement was where Mother said I'd almost definitely be sucked alive by the Devil. She said that he'd bite off my body parts, suck the flesh from the bone and then spit the bone out on to Lime Street Station's concourse for all to see.

What made things so much worse, for Mother's basement-fear, was that the lost property office had three basement rooms. If Mother wouldn't step into a basement herself, she absolutely would never step into *three* basements. She wasn't going to take a risk. It was a simple fact that Mother never went into any of the basement rooms, just in case, and for years I was told to stay away, just in case.

'But, how did all the books get here to begin with?' George Harris asks. He spreads his arms out, a wave to all of the books.

'Near the beginning of Part Four, Management started a new system—'

'Part Four?' George Harris asks.

'Of my fairy tale,' I say. 'The part with books. They said that all the lost property that remained lost for more than ninety days should be placed in boxes in the lost property office, and then later in large black bin bags, and put in one of the rooms in the basement. And—'

'Someone had to take the items down to the basement,' George Harris says, and I nod.

'Mother declared, "You're already part-Devil." So the task of sorting the lost property into bin bags and taking them down to the basement fell upon me,' I say.

'Were you scared?' George Harris asks, his eyes locked on me.

'At first, the throwing of the bags into one of the basement rooms was scary. Mother was singing hymns on the station's concourse, I was soaked in holy water, and I did the quickest open-throw-close-door ever,' I say. I'm smiling, and George Harris laughs.

'But Mother soon became bored of that, especially as she spent most of her days upstairs in the flat and avoiding the lost property office. So I started taking a little bit more time opening the door, and after discovering that the Devil wasn't living down here I was keen to explore a little bit more.'

'And that's when the basement became your hideout?' George Harris asks.

'A place where I could escape Mother for a legitimate reason,' I say.

'But how did all these books end up in here?' George Harris asks. He's now at the bottom of the steps. He's running his fingers along the bookshelves. His fingers are skipping – they're like long twigs. There's a Roman soldier in my library.

'I showed Elisabeth the three basement rooms, but it was this room, the room of shelves and the spiral staircase that excited her,' I say.

'I could live in here,' George Harris says. I smile.

'Elisabeth said, "All that empty space not being used, doll." I told her that I couldn't use it because of the Devil, and she said, "You daft nit, it's a perfect space, full of empty shelves that are screaming out to be filled."' I try to do Elisabeth's scouse.

'Was that an Indian accent?' George Harris asks, and I laugh.

'I nearly fell out with Elisabeth over this room,' I say. 'I asked her if the Devil was trying to get her to tempt me, and she laughed. I even asked her to stop and think whether maybe the Devil was trying to trick her into letting him eat me.' I cringe. That wasn't my best ever conversation with Elisabeth. 'But over time, Elisabeth helped me to step into this basement room, filled with empty metal shelves, and over time it became my secret place. Over time, Elisabeth made me question Mother's belief in the Devil.'

George Harris is looking at me. He's smiling but not saying words. His stare is making my cheeks red. I break eye contact.

'It's where all the found books live; it's my library of found books,' I say.

I look to the books. The metal shelves are stacked to capacity with vertical books, every book deserving to stand tall, to be proud. There are shelves and more shelves of wonderful finds. Each shelf on each of the four walls is full of books. The spiral staircase twirls in the centre of the room. I usually sit on the third from bottom step when I read down here, with the light bulb shining down on to the pages. It makes me feel important – a spotlight just for me. But what makes this library extra special, and what makes this library the place where I feel like I belong, is that every single one of these books has been lost. Some of the books are almost new, others are decades old, yet each of them tells its own story when I run my fingers over its cover. The spines of some are broken, the pages of others have corners that are folded over. In some there are notes in pencil or ink, in others postcards and letters to mark pages. The books speak of a journey taken, of a moment in someone's life. There's one that holds a pre-scription for medication, there's another one that has a 'Fi, I hate you, I wish you were dead. Read this and die. Stu x' inscription. The inscriptions are what I read first. Yet, when these books were lost, no one claimed them. I've tried to think of reasons why people didn't try harder to hold on to those moments in their lives. I've spent hours wondering how many of these books were read to the final words before I found them. I've tried to understand why people didn't search harder for their lost book. I guess that losing some-thing sometimes means that people can pretend to forget.

'Each of these books holds four stories,' I say.

'Four?' George Harris asks.

I nod. 'The story of its creation – that one belongs to the author. Then there's the story that's told through its words – that's the obvious one.' I hold up two fingers. 'Then there's the story of the book being chosen or given – books with inscriptions help with that storytelling. And finally . . .' I hold up four fingers, 'there's the story of how the book became lost.'

George Harris smiles.

'Each of these books is my treasure. And loads of these lost items were waiting to be taken in black bin bags down to London before I rescued them all. I found them,' I say, and then, 'I paid for them all, you know, I would never steal.'

'It never crossed my mind,' George Harris says.

'But I lied and said they were claimed when I paid the fee, every single time,' I say. I look to my feet, embarrassed that I told lies. I think about Mother.

'That doesn't make you like Mother. Some lies aren't cruel lies,' George Harris says. I look at him, and his smile makes my belly flip.

'I took them and collected them. Which shelf they were placed on was dependent on the colour of their spine,' I say, and then, 'My library of found books is a rainbow of secrets. And until today only Elisabeth knew of its existence.'

'I am honoured to be here,' George Harris says. He tries to bow, but his Roman soldier armour clatters, it stops his bend and makes him wobble. He grips a shelf to help him straighten up. I giggle, then I look at my library and sigh.

'Too many moments are lost,' I say. 'Sometimes I wish others could listen to the story that each of these books can tell. Not the narratives inside them but their journeys to get to here.'

'How is that possible?' George Harris asks.

'It isn't always,' I say. 'But the inscriptions – they're a secret between the book giver and the book receiver. It's about the journey,' I say.

'Because each journey is a story?' George Harris says.

I nod. 'But not every story has a once-upon-a-time.'

'Mine does,' George Harris says.

'You're lucky,' I say.

'How are you only sixteen?' George Harris says.

'Elisabeth says I've got an old head on young shoulders. But not one with wrinkles,' I say, and then I move to the shelves and start to pull out the books with inscriptions to share with George Harris.

By ten past eight and with Elisabeth's help, I've gathered a small picnic for William. Corned-beef butties, a sausage roll, a slice of pork pie and half a scotch egg. Elisabeth's prepared a cream scone, the top of the scone toppling on a tower of cream. She's placed it on a paper plate, with cling film acting as a scaffold to keep it up straight. She's also given me a flask full of her Italian coffee.

'I don't care if I don't get the flask back,' she says.

'Mother called corned-beef butties dog butties,' I say. Elisabeth nods.

Then I decide. 'Come with me,' I say, and then, 'I want you to see that he's real.'

'Having an imaginary friend's perfectly normal after everything you've been through, doll,' Elisabeth says. She laughs, but I can tell that it isn't a real laugh. 'Yesterday' is pounding through the walls from her coffee shop and into the lost property office. Elisabeth's humming the tune, filling our silence as we pack the items into a cardboard box.

'Please come with me,' I say. I don't need to say anything else. She knows how important this is to me. She realizes that I need to prove to her that I'm not a nutjob.

'One sec,' she says, and she scurries out and into her coffee bar. I carry on arranging the food, whistling along to the final few bars of 'Yesterday'. Elisabeth's back within a minute or two.

'Jenny Jones's holding shop. Let's go meet this young man of yours,' she says.

'Did you see I put up a new poster?' I say, and Elisabeth nods.

'I saw your latest poster. Looks great, but "Am I right in thinking that Mother was not my birth-mother?" isn't going to help with the eviction. Thirty-five days,' Elisabeth says.

'It will. I'm building rapport.' I say 'rapport' in my best Blundellsands voice, and Elisabeth laughs.

I lift the cardboard box, I spin out of the lost property office and over to Platform 7. My spins are slow and understated; I'm trying not to draw attention to us. Elisabeth is clip-clopping next to me in her yellow stilettos. In wide-legged navy-blue trousers and a white blouse with pearl buttons, Elisabeth looks elegant. People watch her walk; men turn their heads to look at her. For a moment I worry that people will be watching Elisabeth and then see William. It was different when I last went to Platform 7. I'm good at being invisible – people don't look twice at me.

'Can you stop wiggling your backside when you walk?' I say. Elisabeth laughs. 'I need people not to be looking at us. William's shy.'

'Oh, doll,' Elisabeth starts.

'You're too beautiful to be invisible,' I say.

'Well, stop your spinning too. You're beautiful when you spin,' Elisabeth says. She stops walking. She bends down and removes her yellow shoes, then she picks them up and runs ahead of me to the platform. I laugh.

It's half eight by the time we reach the end of the platform. I put the cardboard box on to the cold concrete.

'Back here,' I say, moving into the shadows and leaning flat against the sleeping train. Elisabeth follows. She rolls her eyes at me, but she's smiling, so I know that she's not really angry.

Within a minute, we see the fishing line and hook attempting to lift the cardboard box, but of course the box is too heavy and every attempt fails. Elisabeth giggles. I give her a look to tell her to be quiet.

'It's a nervous thing,' she says, lifting her spare hand to her mouth in an attempt to stop laughing. 'What's that smell?' Elisabeth asks. I glare at her to be quiet.

I step forward. 'William,' I say. 'I've brought my friend Elisabeth today. She's made you a cream scone. We hope you like your picnic.' I move to the cardboard box and start lifting the items, one at a time, just raising them up and saying what they are. I can smell William's sour stench. I know he must be near. Every now and then I hear a giggle from the shadows. I'm unsure if it's William or Elisabeth. When I've finished my show and tell, I place all the items back into the box and stand up straight.

'You can keep the flask, John,' Elisabeth says. She steps out from the shadows and folds her arms across her chest. I wonder if she's cold or scared. 'Come on, let's get you home,' she says.

William steps out from the shadows. His eyes flick from Elisabeth to me. He's stepping from one Chelsea boot to the other in a nervous tap dance. His fishing rod is being clutched with both hands. I watch Elisabeth. Her eyes are searching over William, but her mouth isn't twisting into a smile. I don't know if she's angry.

Then, 'William, you can call me Elisabeth,' she says, then she curtseys and twirls.

William giggles. He likes her immediately, everyone does, but I can see he's still nervous about coming closer.

'Enjoy your picnic, William,' Elisabeth says. 'We'll be back same time tomorrow with more.'

With that, Elisabeth starts walking away, her shoes in one hand, and she's wriggling her backside in a totally over-the-top way. I laugh, wave to William and spin after her. We've only taken a few steps together when we hear the sound of Chelsea boots tap dancing on the platform. We turn and look at William. When he sees us looking, he bends down, his right leg not quite bending properly this time, and places another tiny cavalryman on to the platform.

'No, William,' I say. 'They're too precious. Your parents gave them to you.'

And that's when William puts his hands to his ears and begins shaking his head. He lets out a piercing wail. It comes from the soul and sings about the worst loss a child can experience. Before I can react, before Elisabeth can speak, William's taken the cardboard box and disappeared into the shadows.

The lone tin cavalryman guards the platform. Elisabeth moves forward and picks it up. She doesn't speak, and I don't feel like spinning. We walk back to the coffee bar.

YET ANOTHER CASE OF THE FOUND SUITCASE

Word about town is that excitement continues to build surrounding the arrival of Aussie Max Cole with Mal Evans' luggage. It is reported that the suitcase containing one of the most valuable and important Beatles collections ever archived is coming back to Liverpool this week.

The suitcase is said to include hundreds of unseen Beatles photos, signed concert programmes collected by Mal and recording sheets with Mal Evans' name at the top of them. The thought of an archive of this splendour is making this reporter weak at her knees.

Cole, 35, has claimed that recordings discovered in the suitcase include alternative versions of 'We Can Work It Out' and 'Hey Jude', which have yet to be heard in public. But possibly the most exciting highlights of the Mal Evans archive are the supposed reel-to-reel recordings of John Lennon and Paul McCartney chatting, and Beatles recordings sealed in their Abbey Road reel cases. The likelihood of such a find is causing much speculation amongst Beatles' enthusiasts.

But let's not get too excited. This will be the fourth 'case of the found suitcase' in as many months. Rumour around Liverpool is that the ghost of Agatha Christie is already penning a new Miss Marple mystery based on these events.

Yet, perhaps what lends this case credibility is that Aussie

Max Cole is investing his own hard-earned cash in its validation. The man of the hour is said to have taken eight weeks' unpaid leave from his employment, raided his savings and is flying over to Liverpool on his own magical mystery tour to have the suitcase authenticated by our resident Beatles expert, Graham Kemp.

So while the rest of the UK has been getting hot under its collar with the soaring temperatures of this summer's heat-wave, diehard Beatles fans have been fuelling the rumour and belief that *this* suitcase and its contents may previously have been owned by Mal Evans, roadie and confidant to The Beatles.

Evans met his untimely end in January this year, when he was shot and killed by Los Angeles police. After Evans' cremation, his close friend, singer-songwriter Harry Nilsson, agreed to send Mal's ashes back to his family in the UK. Since then reports have hit the press claiming Apple executive Neil Aspinall has made frantic phone calls to Nilsson regarding the failure of the ashes to arrive back in the UK. Lost property offices all over the UK are searching for those missing ashes, desperate to return Mal to his family.

The appearance of the missing suitcase, without the ashes, adds an extra loop to this already tangled mystery.

What do we think? A weird twist in the tail of this tale? Could it be that Harry sent the suitcase with the ashes and both have been lost? Will the ashes soon turn up in a flea market in Australia too? Does Max Cole really hold the most valuable and important Beatles collection ever archived? And what will he do if his findings are discovered to be the real deal?

False alarm or a ticket to fame? Get a move on, Max Cole, your public is waiting.

My weekdays appear to have a routine. I think I like that they do.

I work from eight a.m. until one p.m., and then I go next door and have lunch with Elisabeth. After that, I return to the lost property office – sometimes I do paperwork, other times I work a little bit more or I read in my library or I tidy the flat and make shopping lists of things that I need Elisabeth to get. Sometimes I nip to Jenny Jones's kiosk, and she fills me in on all the gossip in the world. I have a lot of gossip to catch up on. Then it's back to the coffee bar for chats with George Harris when he gets off the 17:37 train from Chester. Sometimes I eat one of his butties. Then, after George Harris has gone, I prepare a picnic for William.

Over the past week, every night at half eight, we've left William a picnic, and every night he's been stepping that little bit closer. He's staying out from the shadows that little bit longer. William likes Elisabeth, and he likes me too. And every night he leaves us small gifts in exchange for the picnic – fragments of china plates, marbles, hair combs, treasure that he's found for us. Elisabeth says that with each gift he's showing us that he appreciates the food and that he doesn't take our kindness for granted. Elisabeth says that's the thing about a person who's been stripped down to nothing, she says that every small thing's a big deal to someone like that. And over this last week, the giggles that have escaped from William's mouth have been allowed to sound; he's stopped trying to push them back inside with his hand.

I like William. I like him even though Elisabeth's said that he's the smelliest man in the whole of Liverpool.

'You're a child trapped in an adult's body,' Elisabeth told him last night, and then, 'And Martha's an adult trapped in a child's body.'

'And what about you?' I asked Elisabeth.

'Me?' Elisabeth asked. 'I reckon you're possibly older than I've ever felt,' Elisabeth said to me. I thought about her words, but then the question escaped before I'd the time to think about it even more.

'How old do you feel?' I asked her.

'I think I stopped ageing when I was fifteen,' she said.

I looked at William and rolled my eyes. William giggled. I giggled too.

'I'm a lost cause,' Elisabeth said, twirling on the spot before breaking into the Mash Potato.

So last night we were picnicking together on Platform 7. I never thought to wonder what the British Rail staff made of us. They never told us to move or to stop. Sometimes I think we might actually be invisible. Perhaps William's given us magic powers, perhaps only those who believe in happily ever after can actually see us. And maybe no one but us really believes in happily-ever-afters. Maybe they just think they do.

In my pocket there's a slip of paper and on it I've written out the days until I'm evicted. Today I crossed off thirty-one, now thirty days remain. Next to the piece of paper, I carry William's tin cavalryman around with me at all times. It's the most precious thing that I own, yet each time that I flick my finger over the tin, I can see the darkness that's been surrounding William. I wish I could make him better.

'Are you two related?' George Harris asks. 'Because you always seem to be together.'

I look over at Elisabeth. She's behind the counter. The espresso machine's steaming away, and she's stacking sugary goodies under her mesh domes.

'She's my best friend,' I say. 'Mother hated Elisabeth from the moment she heard about the opening of a coffee bar, thanks to Stanley.'

'Her boyfriend?' George Harris says, and I laugh.

'The station's cleaner,' I say. 'Mother was horrified. She made us fast for seventy-two hours, praying at every four minutes past the hour to ensure that God didn't miss our important news.'

George Harris laughs. 'That didn't work then,' he says. He's shuffling in the plastic chair, trying to find a comfortable way to sit. He keeps banging the table with an arm or a leg, and I wait for him to settle.

'Mother wrote several letters of complaint and even tried telephoning Harold Wilson to seek his support. Nothing worked, leading Mother to believe that the Devil was *intercepting* her important messages to both the Prime Minister and to God!'

I think about how the coffee bar's windows had been all covered up with newspaper when Stanley told her the 'ungodly news'. Mother grew increasingly concerned about a 'den of iniquity' opening up next door, and when the neon lights with the name 'Lime Street Coffee Bar' went up, she almost exploded. She said something about coffee bars being where the Devil's music was made and how they were places for teenagers to meet up and fornicate on tables. I remember having no idea what she meant. Mind you, I often had no idea.

'The thought of new people being right next door excited me,' I say.

'Because Mother didn't let you speak to anyone?' George Harris asks.

'Exactly! But how could she keep me away from people who were right next door all the time?' I say.

I'll never forget the start of Part Four – it was the day the coffee bar opened. I was kneeling on the stone floor in the lost property office, praying for the souls of the school children in Aberfan but at the same time trying hard not to think about a school and homes being buried by coal slag. Mother had told me all about it, then she told me how everyone in Lime Street Station would be buried alive if I was naughty and even took one step outside. But my praying and not thinking was interrupted by the sound of music as it boomed out. I remember the shelves shaking. I remember walking sticks jumping to the beats. I remember my whole body tingling. Music had never been allowed in Mother's flat. Mother was furious.

'Up, NOW,' Mother shouted. I jumped up, and she gripped my hand and dragged me out of the lost property office. Mother stopped, and I banged into her. She slapped me across the head. The door to the coffee bar was open, and Mother barged in, dragging me behind her. Mother wasted no time. She started ranting, trying to shout over the music. At one point I think she started singing 'I Surrender All'. I stood open-mouthed, my eyes taking in the most wonderful sights I'd ever seen. The place was exotic – it felt like I'd stepped into another country. The Italian espresso machine looked to be full of magic. Steam billowed and swirled from the top of the metal cylinders, and it had those tall levers with black grips to pull down.

'Was everything the same as it is now?' George Harris asks, breaking my thoughts.

I look around the coffee bar. 'Not quite. The walls were as yellow as daffodils back then, not red like now. The table tops were a brighter white. I think they've been replaced since with these ones.' I run my hand over the surface of the table. 'Same

113

red chairs, some swivelled on metal bases then. They were fun. I can still remember walking in for the first time and trying to take it all in. My eyes were darting about; I remember trying so hard to stop my mouth from curling into a smile.' I smile, and George Harris smiles too.

'Sounds to me like a special day,' he says.

I hear my belly rumble.

'Hungry?' George Harris asks. 'Cake?'

'Elisabeth used to say that people would come here and sit all day and then complain their coffee was cold at the end of it. Can you imagine creating somewhere that makes people never want to leave?' I ask.

'She's one of the good ones,' George Harris says.

I look at Elisabeth, but she's too far away to hear George Harris's words.

'Mother never thought that. She hated her from the minute she met her,' I say.

I remember that it started with Mother saying something about how people would pay with their fornication. And Elisabeth saying something like, 'Well, queen. I don't mind them paying for scran with a bit of pot washing, but I draw the line at them paying by shagging on my tables.' I smile.

'What did you think when you first saw her?' George Harris asks.

'That she was beautiful. Her hair was tucked under a blue turban-style hat with a large blue bow on it. Her yellow fringe was perfectly straight like it is now. With thick eyeliner and the longest eyelashes I've ever seen, her eye makeup was like the models I'd seen in glimpses of lost magazines before Mother threw them into the bin,' I say.

I remember that her dress was buttercup-yellow – a mini-dress with a lace collar and matching cuffs. Her legs were long and bronzed, and she stood tall in blue-patent shoes with a high square heel. I remember every little detail. I'd never met anyone quite like her. I still haven't.

'She's quite the looker,' George Harris says. He's still smiling as he looks over at Elisabeth.

'As she stepped out from behind the counter, she removed a blue and white pinny; she placed it on top of the glass display, next to the mesh domes. She was the most beautiful lady I'd ever seen.'

'You're beautiful too,' George Harris says, then his cheeks flush. I smile, but George Harris is looking at his chest armour and not at me.

I think about when Elisabeth removed her pinny. She asked me my name, but I didn't dare speak to her. It was just as well, as Mother had moved next to me. Her grip was tight around the top of my arm, tugging at me to move. I couldn't move. Then Mother said something about no child of hers frequenting Elisabeth's brothel. And I felt so angry that she was being rude to Elisabeth that I blurted out my name.

I remember Elisabeth saying, 'Nice to meet you, doll, I'm Elisabeth.' Then she extended her hand. I didn't shake it. I smiled at her, and she said, 'Can you Mash Potato?'

But that made Mother say, 'She is not going to work for you.' And that's when she tried to drag me out of the door.

Elisabeth said, 'Ah, queen, where've you been? It's a dance . . .' then she nodded at someone, a man I think, then Elisabeth started doing fancy things with her feet. Mother had stopped trying to walk away, but her grip was still strong. It wasn't long before music blasted out – a lady singing about potatoes. Elisabeth was moving her heels inwards and outwards and inwards and outwards. Then her knee was bending and one heel was flicking up in the air, then it was back to the floor and the heels were turning inwards and outwards and inwards and outwards. Then the other foot was flicking up into the air. The top half of Elisabeth's body stood straight and tall, but from her knees to her feet magic was happening. I didn't know people could swivel and pivot and stay upright. It was all happening so quickly, so perfectly in time to the loud music.

'Can you Mash Potato?' I ask George Harris. I stand up and demonstrate the dance. George Harris laughs – it's a laugh that comes right from his belly.

'It's all about swivelling heels and pivoting heels,' I say, dancing the fancy footwork that Elisabeth taught me, to show George Harris what I mean. When I'm finished, I curtsey, George Harris claps. The clap makes his armour rattle. We're both smiling.

Of course, Mother didn't let me stay and learn the dance that day. That first time in the coffee bar, the music was blaring at the same time Mother was attempting to sing 'Rejoice, The Lord Is King'. Mother was possibly volcanic. Then she said, 'Close your ears, Martha Lost, my dear!' And then she shouted, 'CLOSE them! The Devil has moved in next door to us.' Of course the music stopped at that exact moment, the coffee bar went silent and everyone was looking at Mother.

But I wasn't listening to Mother's rants and I wasn't looking at Mother's angry face. I was looking at a jukebox, an actual jukebox. Elisabeth must have seen me looking.

'Do you like music?' Elisabeth asked. She danced a lindy hop around the room. I found myself smiling, and a giggle escaped through my lips.

Mother slapped the front of her hand across my ear – it stung. She pulled me across the room and back out through the doors of the coffee bar. As I was leaving, I locked eyes with Elisabeth. She waved a tiny wave but her eyes looked sad, and I knew she could be my first ever friend.

Back in the lost property office, Mother said, 'The Devil sits in that coffee bar, Martha Lost, my dear.' And just to make sure that I understood the consequences for not closing my ears to the music from the coffee bar, that night Mother hit my bare back nine times with a leather belt and made me sleep on the cold stone floor of the lost property office.

'Do you miss her?' George Harris asks. His question floors me; it breaks my thoughts. I pause.

'Yes,' I say. 'I worry that I'll forget what it is to be truly unhappy and lonely. That I'll take all that I have now for granted.'

Written by Anonymous to Martha Lost, throughout
The L-Shaped Room by Lynne Reid Banks, delivered by
Drac the postman to the lost property office

My dear Martha,
The intelligence that shines from you filled me with
delight this morning. Your poster was precise and offered the
question that I longed for you to ask of me.
As my initial correspondence with you declared, the lady
that you call Mother was, indeed, full of lies. Yet, it must be
stated that an element of the 'once upon a time' that she
rested upon you was, in fact, dipped in the truth. Mother
was correct in that you are a foundling, but you were, in
fact, left in Lime Street Station.
At that time you had breathed alone for three short
months. It is true that your birth-mother left you outside the
lost property office, sleeping in a brown suitcase. It is also
fair to offer that your being left outside of the lost property
office coincided with Mother's personal prayers to HER God
for a sign to continue in this world. It is also a stated fact
that Mother then claimed you as her own and raised you to
the best of her capabilities. She was an older lady, one who
was demonstrably religious. Your birth-mother had
considered that to be a point in Mother's favour.
I must stress that your birth-mother had believed
that she was leaving you with a lady who would cherish
and care for her baby in a Christian way. She was

horrified to discover that this turned out to be incorrect.

I feel the need to reassure you, my child, that Mother was a cruel, vicious lady, yet that she was the product of a cruel and vicious childhood. I must state that Mother's inability to love and nurture was not a reflection of your being, rather it was a reflection of the pain and despair that burdened her mind. Yes, my child, I am stating a simple fact to clarify any confusion or load that may be weighing upon you – Mother was ill.

By this stage in my scribblings, I assume that you desire to know more of your birth-mother, that callous child who delivered you, albeit unwittingly, into the jaws of a vicious monster. Yet I fear that all that I can offer you is the simple statement that your birth-mother abandoned you in the hope that she would be able to return within ninety days and collect you. As you will recall, I mentioned her young age, but I have not detailed that she had run from her own abusive home life. Her relationship with her parents was disturbing and full of guilt.

When her parents discovered that she was with child, your birth-mother was thrown from the family house and left to survive with only the clothes that she wore. She had heard horrific tales of mother-and-baby homes, and she knew that she would not survive life in such a dwelling. Faced with nowhere to turn for help, your birth-mother made her way to Liverpool. I must confess that your birth-mother had initially sought to terminate her pregnancy here in Liverpool, but when faced with the appointment she hid in a corner and sang you a sweet Irish melody. I feel I must inform you that your birth-mother loved you, although I imagine that understanding the concept of such a love that led to abandonment is not one that is easily embraced.

It is true that three months after the birth of her only child, it was with great sorrow and facing a life on the streets of Liverpool, without a home, that your birth-mother considered she had no option but to leave you in Lime Street Station. And from that desperate day you, my darling Martha, became lost property.

I offer no defence for your birth-mother's action, but I can say, without a shadow of a doubt, that her intentions were driven by a desire to protect you. In losing you, your birth-mother ceased being a brilliant pianist and abandoned her love of literature. She removed all pleasure from her life. I fear, with hindsight, that her judgement was misguided and her decisions were full of flaws. Yet, at that time, your birth-mother tried to do right by you.

I trust that you will not be angered by my opinion.

Yours,

Anonymous x

They're standing in front of me, on the customer side of the counter. One of them looks like Humpty Dumpty, all round and shiny. The other is tall and skinny like a wooden ladder. The tall one's gripping a cricket bat, and he's bouncing it off his palm. They both have angry faces. I think they must be lost.

'Did you find that in the station?' I ask, nodding at the cricket bat and picking up my pen to start making notes.

'No, but we found you,' the tall one says.

I look up at him, trying to see if his eyebrows are bushy like mine. I stand and bend over the counter to look at his ankles.

'Thought you'd get one over on Management, did you?' the fat one says, as he waddles to the gap in the counter, turns sideways and shuffles through it.

'You're not allowed behind here,' I say, leaning back on to my stool. 'Unless you really need a wee, and then—'

'Shut the fuck up,' the tall one says. He pushes the cricket bat into my chest. It hurts. I pull in my breath. Sometimes, when Mother hurt me, holding my breath kept the pain inside. I think it might be a bit like pretending to be dead. I don't understand why the thin man wants to hurt me.

'Would you mind stopping that?' I ask, pointing my pen at the cricket bat. My voice is quivering, it is breathy. The fat one is next to me. He smells of beer and dirty socks.

'You've been a naughty girl,' the thin one says, pushing the cricket bat up to my chin. I think he might want to hit my face with it. I think he might want to leave a mark.

'Did the Devil send you?' I ask the thin man. He wiggles his eyebrows a bit and winks at the fat man. I'm even more confused now. 'At first I thought you might be my father, even though he's supposed to be dead, but now I'm really hoping you're not because—'

'We're here to sort you out,' the fat one says. He's poking the fleshy bit at the top of my arm with his stubby finger. He's doing it a million times. I won't look at him; I'm still looking at the thin man. The poking stings.

'Are you my father?' I ask the thin one. I put my left hand in my lap and cross two of my fingers. I hope the answer is no.

'What the fuck?' the thin one says, pushing the cricket bat that little bit harder on my chin. I lose my balance on my stool. I stumble to my feet and take a step back. The fat man's up close now. I think he wants to eat me; I think he could swallow me whole.

'Management aren't happy. They want you out,' the fat one says.

'Management?' I say. I'm listening now, but I'm muddled. 'But I got a letter—'

'You ignored the letter, so they changed their mind. Sent us to sort you out.' The thin one's next to me now too. I'm walking backwards, but soon I'll be at the door to my flat. I don't want to be in my flat with them. I don't like the way they smell.

'They think you're nuts,' the fat one says, and he laughs.

'But I'm sorting it. I'm getting my National Insurance—' I start to say.

'Management don't believe you. They've heard rumours of odd behaviour in this office. They want you out,' the fat one says again.

'But I'm the liver bird of Lime—' I try to say.

'And we're here to help you pack,' the thin one says. He laughs and the fat one laughs. I don't know why they're laughing.

'I've got a suitcase; I can pack on my own . . .' I say.

The thin one raises the cricket bat into the air. He's going to bring it down on my head. I'm going to break into a million little pieces. I scream. I jump to the floor and make like I'm a tortoise. I keep screaming.

'Shut the fuck up,' the fat one says.

I'm not listening; I'm still screaming.

'PETER BARRYMORE!'

I stop screaming. The voice carries on shouting rude words at the two men. I count to sixty, then I turn my head to see who it is. It's Jenny Jones from the kiosk. She's a tiny woman, but today she's a giant, and she's looking like she's going to fight both of them. She's walked through the gap in the counter and is staring at us. Her hands are on her hips and those hands are in fists. She walks towards us. Then I see Drac and Stanley. They're walking through the gap in the counter too. Stanley's reaching into the box of lost hockey sticks. Drac's putting down his bag of letters on the floor, and he's picking up two lost walking sticks. Jenny Jones is right beside me, and she's slapping the fat one across the head.

'What you doing, Peter Barrymore? Does your mother know you like to scare little girls?' She slaps him across the head with each word.

The fat one strokes his bald head. I see that he's not that much older than me. I wonder if he shaves his head. 'Aunty Jenny, man, it's me work,' he says.

'And that *work* is a friend of mine,' Jenny Jones says. She nods at me and I try to smile, but my mouth won't quite turn up.

'Management want her out. They've heard stuff,' the thin one says.

123

'And you can keep it shut too, Gary Baggott,' Jenny Jones says.

'They'll just send someone else,' the fat one says.

'Management have given her twenty-eight—' Drac starts.

'Twenty-nine,' I say. I'm still curled on the floor.

'Twenty-nine more days,' Drac says. He's standing next to Jenny Jones now, and says, 'So why are you here?' He's gripping the two walking sticks, one in each hand, like he's an ageing scouse samurai.

'Management orders. Something about Devil worship in the basement and exhibitionism on the station concourse. They've got someone coming to change the locks in half an hour,' the thin one says.

'Get Elisabeth,' Jenny Jones shouts, and Stanley goes running. And then, 'So you think it's right to threaten a little girl? You didn't think to ask—'

'I've got my letter,' I say. I'm upright now, crawling to the counter.

'What's going on?' It's Elisabeth. Her legs look like sunshine in her yellow Capri pants, but her face is angry. I don't want her to be angry with me. 'Peter Barrymore? What you doing here?'

And that's when Jenny Jones, Drac and Stanley tell Elisabeth all about what Peter Barrymore and Gary Baggott did. And that's when I start crying, mainly because I don't understand why everyone's shouting and why the thin man wanted to hurt me and why Management have changed their mind and want me out of my home.

'But I'm the liver bird of Lime Street Station,' I whisper.

They stop their shouting. Elisabeth and Jenny Jones walk towards me.

'I'm sorry for making you angry. The Queen hasn't replied yet,' I say to Elisabeth.

'No, doll,' Elisabeth says. Her voice is almost a whisper

as she bends down beside me. 'I'm not angry with you.'

'They'll keep sending people,' I whisper.

'She's right,' Jenny Jones says. 'If they want her out, they'll keep sending heavies.'

I see Elisabeth glaring at Jenny Jones, but then she looks at me. 'It's just Management being a divvy. I'll sort it.' She turns to Jenny Jones, 'You stay with Martha and keep your opinions to yourself. I'll get on the phone to London. I'll give them a piece of my mind. And you two . . .' She stands up and points at Peter Barrymore and Gary Baggott. 'You two get yourselves next door and wait there. I've not finished with youse.'

Then, before I can speak, people are moving about and I'm left sitting on the floor with Jenny Jones whistling 'What's New Pussycat?' and filling the kettle with water.

The question that Martha Lost wrote on a poster that
was stuck to the billboard next to Platform 6

Who am I?

Course Elisabeth sorted everything out. She phoned Management, told them about the threatened attack, and told them the police were coming to take statements. Management told her not to report the attack to the police. Elisabeth told them that two strange men threatening to attack a little girl needed to be reported. Elisabeth never mentioned that she knew Management were behind the threat. She talked to them about the 'rumours' they'd been hearing and put them straight about a few things. Elisabeth bet me an iced bun that no one would turn up to change the locks. She was right, but I still got an iced bun.

Peter Barrymore and Gary Baggott came back into the lost property office with Elisabeth and Jenny Jones. Neither of the men looked at me; instead, they spoke to the floor and said they were sorry. Jenny Jones is making them sit outside her kiosk for the next three weeks. They're staying out of my way, but if any heavies turn up during the day, they're going to jump right in and use that cricket bat to protect me. I don't know if that makes me feel safe or not.

Elisabeth said it would be best if I made myself a weapon, for when the other heavies turned up, just in case they slipped past everyone who was looking out for me. She said Management would definitely send someone else in a week or so. She said I should ask my anonymous book sender for my National Insurance number and birth certificate right now, but I've decided I'm not going to do that yet. I just need a little bit longer. I've only had three books, only two wonderful books full of handwritten words, and I just need to find out as much as I can about my past before the anonymous book sender disappears. This might be my only chance to find out who I am. So, instead I made myself a weapon. It's an umbrella with false teeth stuck to the tip, and I've sewn beads, tiny bells and sequins all over the fabric. I think some of the sequins might pop off if I open the umbrella. It's upstairs, under the counter. I'll show it to Elisabeth later.

Right now I'm sitting on the third step up from the bottom of the spiral staircase reading another book that George Harris found. The inscription in this book is, 'I was convinced that you cared little for me, now I have hope that I was wrong'. This time he paid the small fee so that I could keep it. The step isn't the most comfortable of places to sit. The metal is cold through my skirt. I wish I had cushions down here but won't for fear the rats will burrow into them and lay spiders or something like that. My pot of tea is empty, and I'm hurrying to reach the end of the chapter before going to meet William. I don't like to stop a reading session until I get to the end of a chapter.

But that's when I hear knocking. A loud knock, like the knock with a hammer and not the knock with a delicate fist. It seems to be coming from behind the books. I close my book, even though I'm not at the end of the chapter, and I stand.

Knock. Knock. Knock. Knock, knock, knock.

I walk down the remaining steps and stand in the basement. I shuffle tiny steps towards where the knocking seems to be coming from, but then I stop walking.

'The Devil,' I whisper. 'Mother was right.'

Knock. Knock. Knock. Knock, knock, knock.

I take another two shuffling steps and reach the wall of shelves, the wall of books. The knocking seems to be coming from behind the books. I hesitate. The knocking continues

– it's louder, it's more frequent, and it's angry. The shelves are packed full. There's no gap to glance through. These shelves are covered in orange spines. My eyes flick to the spines as I try to recall the four stories of one book with a too long title, but then the knocking makes me jump back into that moment.

I reckon that the knocking is not going to stop, so I start removing some of the books from the shelf. I pile them away from the shelves, close to the base of the spiral staircase and, as the shelves empty, I realize that these shelves are attached to a backing and not to the wall. I try to move the bookcase slightly, just to take a glimpse, just to see what might be behind it. With all my strength, I grip the left edge of the bookcase and try to pull it out. It doesn't budge, not even slightly. My only choice is to remove some more of the books.

I remove all of the remaining books with an orange spine and then half of one shelf of books with a purple spine. The bookcase is almost half full, the path to the spiral staircase is difficult to tread and my fingers are covered in a fine layer of book dust. I sneeze and sneeze again. I grip the left edge of the bookcase with both of my hands. I heave the bookcase forwards a tiny bit. I walk to the gap and peer behind the bookcase. And that's when I see what the Devil has been knocking on.

I see a metal door.

It takes an age to remove the remaining books from the book-case. I've created neat piles of coloured spines. The slight variations in one colour start from faded to bright. The majority of books seem to be a shade of orange, yet it's the purple spines that excite me the most. They're rarer finds, by authors with names that I struggle to pronounce. There are lots of words and names that I struggle to pronounce, but thankfully Stanley never gets cross at my asking. Sometimes I add a French accent to difficult words. It seems to make them roll from my tongue. I wonder if I am French.

There are seventy-five books in here that I've never read and one book in the library that I've read twice – it has two handmade bookmarks in it, two memories to take me back to those reading moments. There are two hundred and three books that I've started but haven't finished. Sometimes I think it's OK to meet characters and then create your own story for them. I know for sure that there are two hundred and three books because I kept a tally, little indents in the fake panel at the bottom of the counter upstairs, but no titles. If a character is killed or hurt in some way and if I'm not at all happy with that, I turn back to just before the events took a nasty twist. Then I reread that paragraph, and then I place the book in its correct position on a shelf. The first time I did that was when I read *Tess of the d'Urbervilles*.

I guess I could have pulled the books off the shelves. I could have pushed them into a huge pile at the bottom of the spiral staircase. I guess I could have muddled them all up and quite enjoyed the task of creating the library again. But it's about respect; it's about seeing their beauty.

When all the books have been removed, I can grip the shelves and pull the bookcase away from the metal door. I'm covered in dust, and I'm full of panic. I'm waiting for a whole load of black rats to jump out. I can almost feel their yellow eyes on me. I can almost feel them waiting to pounce. And, if I'm completely honest, this isn't the first time in the last five minutes that I've considered that the Devil could be a giant rat, and at this very moment my whole body's trembling with the possibility that I might be about to come face to face with him.

With the bookcase moved, I look at the large metal door. It's a perfect rectangle, no patterns, there isn't a sign stuck to it declaring 'THIS WAY TO HELL'. I'm slightly relieved that there's no sign. Instead, there's a round metal handle and a keyhole. Obviously, if there's a keyhole there's a need to bend down and look through the keyhole. My reasoning is that if Hell's on the other side of the door, then I'll be able to see the flames through the keyhole.

And so I kneel down – I'm actually holding my breath – and I move my eye to look through the keyhole. And that's when I scream the loudest scream that has ever escaped from my mouth.

There's an eye looking through the keyhole and right at me. I swear it's yellow, I swear it's the Devil, I swear Mother was right and I'm one step away from having the flesh sucked from my bones. And so I do what I should have done when I first heard the knocking. I stand, I leap over the piles of books, and I run.

I scream as I run up the spiralling stairs, but screaming and stairs both take up a lot of breath, so I'm just panting by the time I reach the top. I run through the lost property office until I'm standing on the customer side of the counter. The clock on the wall tells me that it's almost eight p.m., nearly time to meet William, but as I stand in the lost property office I find myself shaking. I'm not quite ready to join the Devil and his children in Hell; I don't want to spend my days with a giant black rat.

I move with tiny shaky steps to stand with my back to the glass front door. I'm looking in the direction of the door that leads to the basement rooms, but I'm trying to figure out what I need to arm myself. I'm thinking that my umbrella with false teeth, sequins, bells and beads might not be that useful against the Devil. Perhaps either a normal umbrella from the lost umbrella box or a hockey stick from the lost hockey sticks box would be better. I wish there was a lost sword box. Both boxes are on the far left-hand side of the room, near the kettle. I'm not sure if my legs are still working. I put a hand up to my cheeks – they feel hot, and I bet my face is a big red blotchy mess. My clothes are covered in dust and cobwebs, and my breathing's all over the shop. I reckon I'm panting like a poodle, but also I'm hating the thought of the Devil getting his rat paws on the found books. I can't bear the thought of the books feeling lost and alone and discarded again. I've let them down. They'll think I've abandoned them. Yet I'm trapped and I'm grounded and I'm annoying myself. I start thinking about the Devil messing up my piles of rainbow-spined books. I start wondering if he's coming up those stairs and into the lost property office right now. I start wondering if he's about to suck my—

There's a knock on the glass front door behind me. I scream. I dive to the floor. I lie still and pretend like I'm dead.

Seconds pass. I'm holding my breath, too scared to breathe in case my body moves and the Devil figures out I'm pretending. The knocking doesn't happen again, so I reckon I've tricked the Devil, but then I hear a voice. It's a bit muffled – it's on the other side of the glass. I'm lying with my feet touching the glass door and my head's in the centre of the lost property office.

'Doll, what you doing?' I hear.

I stay playing dead; I'm not going to fall for one of his tricks. Mother warned me about temptation and trickery and about just how cunning the Devil can be. But that's when I hear Elisabeth laughing. I swear she's going to wet herself – the laughs are proper belly-rumbling laughs. I've never heard her laugh quite like that before. I can't help but smile, even if it's a shaky smile.

Slowly, I move my head from a 'looking at the floor and being dead' position to the left. It's only a slight move; I'm hoping it'll go undetected if the Devil's trying to trick me, although I'm feeling less suspicious of that now, because I don't think even the Devil could fake Elisabeth's laugh. I open my eyes and have a quick look at the glass door. Thankfully, my hair's fallen over my eyes, so I'm looking through my hair, and I reckon I could still be pulling off the 'being dead' thing. Elisabeth's bent over, she's still wearing her yellow Capri pants and she's laughing like a quilt. I lift my head off the floor, then my arms, and soon I've moved and I'm sitting cross-legged facing the glass. I'm watching Elisabeth hopping around.

She joins me on the floor, in a position that mirrors mine. The glass door's still closed and in between us. Elisabeth hasn't spoken; instead, she's pulling faces. She's happy, she's sad, she's confused, she's surprised, she's angry. She's the best person I've ever met.

'I was playing dead,' I whisper, leaning forward to the glass.

'Why?' she asks. She's stopped pulling faces.

'The Devil,' I whisper, and that's when Elisabeth's eyes change from happy to sad.

'How's about you let me in, doll, and I make you a nice cuppa?'

'Will tea make the Devil bugger off?' I ask, and Elisabeth nods.

And so I stand up, I unlock the door, and I move to let Elisabeth in.

'William,' I remember. I look over to the platform, but I can't see him. Suddenly I'm scared that if I miss this one day, then he might never come back again. He'll be hungry, and I hate the thought of him being hungry or thinking I've abandoned him.

'Don't worry,' Elisabeth says. 'I'll go leave him a slice of lemon drizzle and a butty later.'

But that's when I hear the knocking again. And that's when I scream again. And that's when I see that Elisabeth's mouth is moving and she's saying words that I can't hear and her eyes are looking just about the widest I've ever seen her eyes look. All I can hear is my heart hammering in my head and the echo of my scream going on and on and on and on round the lost property office. It's like I'm some major operatic star, able to hold one note for forever.

But, of course, I stop listening to my heart and my scream echoing, because Elisabeth looks so excited in a good way instead of a scared way. I can still hear the knocking. It's in a pattern – three separate knocks, then three knocks close together. The pattern's being repeated over and over again.

'Morse code,' I whisper. 'The Devil knows Morse code.'

The knocking's that loud that I can hear it up some stairs and in a different room. I look at Elisabeth.

'You hear it, don't you?' I ask. Elisabeth nods, and then I say, 'It's the Devil, he's come for me.'

'No, doll, you're talking wet,' Elisabeth says. 'It's someone knocking to be let in.'

I look at her like she's Soft Mick, because obviously I knew that, but it's the Devil wanting to be let in. She raises her eyebrows at me, and I shrug my shoulders. I've no idea what to do next.

'Where's it coming from?' Elisabeth asks.

'Metal door – behind bookcase – library,' I say. Elisabeth nods.

'Tunnels,' she says. I nod. And then, 'Might be someone from Management. How's about we get us a couple of hockey sticks and go say hello?'

So we do, and the hockey stick I pick up is J-shaped.

I place it on the counter and let my fingers play along the shaft. I can feel how it's been constructed. My fingers find the curved hook at the playing end, they dance along the flat surface on the playing side and then on to a curved surface on the rear side. I lift the stick from the counter and my eyes close. This one's never been played with and it longs to be played with. I can feel the stick's sadness, and I can see the very moment when it was purchased.

I can see a man – he has a black beard, his black glasses are held together with Sellotape across the bridge. He doesn't have a wallet, and his coins and notes are loose in his pocket. He's a father. It's a present, something extra for his daughter. The father's excited about getting it home; it's her birthday the following day. He's in Lime Street Station. He's buying a ticket. He can't get his hands into his pockets because they're holding white plastic bags and the hockey stick. One of the white plastic bags is full of apples and oranges from St John's Market, the other has three pork chops and two rashers of bacon – his daughter's tea, his daughter's birthday breakfast. He puts the white plastic bags and the hockey stick on to the floor. The person in front of him turns to leave the counter; she kicks the white plastic bags. Apologies, scattered items, an apple, an orange, he's bending to save the meat from being squashed. The person in the ticket booth is shouting.

'Haven't got all day,' he says.

The man hurries to get upright. 'Single to Edge Hill,' he says. Then he fumbles in his pocket for some change. He pushes the coins across the counter and waits for the ticket.

'You'll have to hurry if you want to get the 5.10,' the ticket master says, then he pushes the man's change back across the counter.

I can feel the man panicking. Ticket gripped between his teeth, change going in his pocket, he bends down to lift up his white plastic bags while looking up to see which platform he needs. He's forgotten the hockey stick. It's no longer in his view. It's been kicked behind someone who is two people behind him. I don't know if the others in the queue noticed or if they simply don't care. No one seemed to be offering

135

to help. I'm hit with a wave of sadness that no one would help—

'Martha?' Elisabeth breaks my thoughts. I look up.

'Sorry,' I say. I'm full of sadness. But I can't be focusing on my sadness for too long, as the knocking's started again. I swear it's louder. Elisabeth's giggling, and her eyes are full of sparkle.

'Aren't you scared?' I ask, as we're tiptoeing over to the stairs that lead down to my library of found books. I'm so nervous that my teeth have started chattering. Elisabeth's taken her stilettos off – they're on the floor over by the glass front door. I look at her nylon-covered toes and wonder if she's worried about stepping on a splinter.

'Nah,' Elisabeth says. 'When you've had the worst thing imaginable happen to you, there's nothing that can frighten you.'

I nod, but I can't find the right words. I wish I could learn to stop being scared. I wonder if there's a book on suitable responses in infinite situations. I think about what the book could contain and how much I'd love to read it. There'd have to be something about how to deal with—

'Doll,' Elisabeth says. I've stopped walking. Elisabeth's smiling. 'Really? Daydreaming now of all times, you divvy?' she says. I hurry up my step to be next to Elisabeth at the top of the stairs. The light's already on, so there's no need for me to go first and lean over the handrail to pull the rope. Course, Elisabeth goes first, with her hockey stick guiding the way and her other hand gripping the handrail that curves around the spiral staircase. I'm holding my hockey stick in my hand, hoping I don't end up bashing in the Devil's head with a little girl's hockey stick. That would be a bad memory to give the stick. We reach the bottom of the stairs. Elisabeth lets go of the handrail and raises a finger to her lips, telling me to be quiet, because clearly she has no idea that my voice stopped working a few minutes ago. She steps into my library of found books and then she drops the hockey stick on to the floor. It makes a clang. Elisabeth does a commando roly-poly roll forward, avoiding the stacked books and almost banging her feet on a bottom shelf full of green books. The forward roll ends with her lying flat on her back in hysterics, while I stand at the bottom of the spiral staircase, shaking like a loon and clutching my hockey stick.

But it's not long before I'm laughing too, and the more I'm laughing, the more I'm wishing that I'd gone for a wee before we'd come downstairs. I swear Elisabeth's the funniest person I've ever met. Lately, I've been seeing more and more of Elisabeth being jam-packed with happiness. It's like each day a little bit of the sadness that hides in her eyes is falling away. And seeing those bits of sadness fall away makes me happier than I've ever been. I just know that one day there'll be no sadness left inside her.

Elisabeth sits up on to her knees. All of the laughing has stopped.

Knock. Knock. Knock. Knock, knock, knock.

'Hear that?' I ask, pointing at the door. Elisabeth raises her eyebrows, and we both try our hardest not to giggle, which is a little bit ridiculous considering that the Devil or more men with cricket bats might be on the other side of the door.

'I'm going to open the door,' she says, and before I can say anything like, 'DON'T OPEN THE DOOR!', Elisabeth's at the metal door and she's gripping the handle and she's turning it and . . .

'Locked,' she says, and then she's laughing again. 'Looks like neither the Devil nor Management will be popping in for a brew today,' but I'm already halfway up the stairs and pulling out the cardboard box that's on the second shelf on the right-hand side of the lost property office, third box from the left, and I'm already carrying the box back down the spiral staircase and into my library. Elisabeth's still standing at the metal door with her hand gripped on the handle. She turns to look as I carry the box to her and place it at her feet. She glances down into the box and then back to my face.

'Keys?' Elisabeth asks.

'Lost keys. Hundreds of them,' I say.

'The buggers,' Elisabeth says.

'I'll find the right one,' I say.

Elisabeth nods. I sit on the stone floor and lower my hand into the box of lost keys. I let my fingers dance over them. As my fingers play over the tips and tops and tails of the keys, my mind's filled with images. A girl being carried over a man's shoulder, fumbling to turn the key in a lock to a brand-new house as her new husband pretends to joke about her weight; a key on a piece of string around a young girl's neck; a key to a neighbour's house being used when the neighbour's at work; a key to a locker that contains more money than I've ever seen before. Hundreds of images jump around my head. Mother appears with a key for a box I've never seen before. I dwell on Mother's key a little too long.

'Doll?' Elisabeth says. She must have seen my hesitation. I lift Mother's key and place it on the floor. Elisabeth reaches for it.

'Not that one,' I say, before delving back into the box. It's not long before I'm pulling out a key. It isn't fancy, just a simple metal key. An image of the metal door jumps into my head. I hold the key. Elisabeth lifts it from my palm, careful not to make our fingers brush each other.

'That it?' she asks, the key gripped between her fingers, and I nod.

She takes the key and turns to the door. I'm still sitting on the floor, so I can see that the key slots into the keyhole. She's nodding – the key fits. I see her turn the key. I hear a click as she turns the handle. The door opens slowly. I think it creaks. I think I'm holding my breath. As the door stops moving, I look into the empty space, my eyes trying to adjust to the blackness. There are no yellow eyes staring back at me, I can't see a giant rat ready to pounce, there aren't any heavies sent by Management. In fact, I can't see any movement at all. It looks like an entrance to a tunnel, and the blast of cold air that hits me makes me shiver. I stand up. Elisabeth hasn't spoken. I can tell that she's trying to figure out where the door leads to, but I'm desperate to know if there's someone watching us.

'Reckon we should explore?' Elisabeth asks, and I shake my head.

'What's the worst that could happen?' Elisabeth asks. I stand up.

I'm thinking rape, murder, drowning, being buried alive and my face eaten by rats, but I don't say anything, so Elisabeth seems to think this is confirmation that I want to explore. She's turned and she's looking around the library.

'Got a torch?' Elisabeth asks. Her voice echoes around the library and then out into the tunnel. But before I'm able to speak, Cilla Black's voice booms into my library, making me jump and making Elisabeth squeal with delight.

'Oh, doll, I bloody well love this song,' Elisabeth says, running into the darkness.

'Wait!' I yell. I step into the tunnel and make Elisabeth stop running and stop singing along to Cilla Black. The air is bone cold; the dampness seeps through my clothes and makes me shiver. I don't think I'll ever be warm again. The narrow tunnel is cave-like, eerie, echoes of sounds make me tremble.

'What? Don't you know this one? You're my—' Elisabeth starts.

'We shouldn't do this,' I say, and then, 'We shouldn't be here.'

'Where's your sense of adventure?' Elisabeth asks.

'Mother was right. The Devil lives in the basement. He's luring us in with Cilla Black,' I say.

'Doll, listen to me, if the Devil was trying to lure us he'd not be using our Cilla. Cilla's Liverpool's angel.'

'Elisabeth, be serious. Aren't you a little bit frightened?' I ask.

'Nope,' she says, and then she's singing along with Cilla again, and I'm faced with no alternative but to follow her into the darkness.

We turned a corner the moment we stepped into the tunnel, so there's no light guiding us or behind us. Elisabeth's hurrying, and I'm trying desperately to claw the walls and make markers for when we're running for our lives later. Cilla stops and a man's voice booms out.

'Tom Jones!' Elisabeth says. 'I do like a Welshman.'

I don't answer. I'm too busy trying to count steps and leave markers, while worrying about how long we've got left before we're sucked to death by a giant rat. I swear we're in a labyrinth of tunnels and corridors. These tunnels are a sandstone kingdom under the city, lost tunnels hiding passageways leading to unknown places. I touch my nose – snot is dripping from it. There's a heatwave outside, yet down in the tunnels the cold makes my fingertips freeze and my nose drip snot as we walk. I have no desire to spin in these tunnels. The darkness is covering us. I shiver. What if we never see light again? I wonder if we've entered a different world. I wonder if Hell is actually ice-cold and the Devil's really a Snow King. I wipe my nose on my sleeve.

'Use your toilet paper,' Elisabeth shouts. I rummage up my sleeve and pull out toilet paper. I wipe my nose again and hurry to catch up with Elisabeth. My feet are wet, as there's a layer of water covering parts of the tunnels. Water seeps through sandstone, and now it climbs over my toes. I can't help but wonder if it's from the public toilets in the station. The tunnel smells of wee. I can't help but wonder how wet Elisabeth's nylons must be. Elisabeth's singing along to Tom

Jones, and I reckon she's wiggling her backside to the beats of the chorus.

'Music saved me,' Elisabeth shouts.

'From what?' I shout.

'From me, from a time when—' But Elisabeth doesn't finish, because right at that very moment we walk around a corner and into light.

We're in a room. We're in someone's front room, yet somehow we're not. My eyes are adjusting to the light, but at the same time I'm not wanting to blink, as there's a feast of items in front of me and I'm scared to blink in case they disappear.

Bric-a-brac is lined up along the sides of this room; actually, I think it's more like a wider tunnel that's been made into a room. It's a bottle shape; it's at least ten times as big as the lost property office. It's wide at the bottom, where we are, shaping to a narrower neck. I mean there's no door in and I can't see a door out. The sides of the room, I guess they're tunnel walls, have shelving of sorts. So, as well as being lined up against the walls, some items are displayed on crooked shelves. Nothing matches, but there seems to be order. I can see old bottles of different colours and sizes. There are plates and parts of plates – all of them seem to be a blue and white willow pattern. Every item is dirty, muddy, beautiful. There are loads of horseshoes of different sizes, broken crockery that looks like it's been glued back together, and I can spot a few old gas masks too. There are bones, ginger beer bottles, marmalade jars, ink wells, poison bottles, Rose's Lime Juice bottles, Codd bottles – there is too much to see.

'Oyster shells,' I say, pointing at the hundreds of filthy oyster shells piled on the floor, close to the collection of ginger beer bottles.

'A poor man's feast,' Elisabeth says. Her eyes are darting around the room; we're both trying to make sense of what we've found. On the right-hand wall is a faded Second World War air-raid shelter sign. But then the music starts again. It's not in this room, but I can already tell that it's near.

And that's when Elisabeth and I look at each other. Elisabeth raises her eyebrows; I nod. I know that we've no choice but to follow the music to its source. I see Elisabeth is no longer smiling. Neither of us has any idea what's going on. My hands are sweaty from gripping the hockey stick, but somehow my fear's gone. This doesn't feel like the work of the Devil, and I haven't seen or heard one rat since I've been here.

Elisabeth coughs to get my attention and then starts walking forward. I follow. We're not walking quickly, as our eyes are flicking left and right. And that's when I see it. I stop. Elisabeth keeps walking forward. She's heading towards the narrow exit, but I'm walking sideways towards the left wall. I'm walking towards an armchair, a tall lampshade, half of a sideboard and a dining table with one lonely chair pushed under it.

And there on top, sitting on that table, which only has three solid legs, is a doll's house. I reach it without turning to see if Elisabeth's still in the room. The missing leg area of the table seems to be propped up with a broom handle. The doll's house is rectangular in shape, there's no roof but there are lights on inside. There are lights all over this room. I wonder how that's possible, but only for a moment. I'm captivated by the doll's house. I crouch down beside the table to get a better look inside. And that's when I realize, because when I get closer I can see that the doll's house isn't actually a doll's house, it's a miniature replica of Lime Street Station.

Then I look even closer and see that it's not a replica of the whole of Lime Street Station. There's the lost property office, but not the flat upstairs. There's Elisabeth's coffee bar, my library of found books and the tunnels leading to where I am now. Then I can see Platform 7 and the bench outside the lost property office. The attention to detail is breathtaking. The lost property office has the exact number of shelves; there are tiny cardboard boxes with tiny labels. One of them, when I lift it from its shelf, even says 'hockey sticks' on it. In my library of found books, the shelves have tiny books on them and they're all displayed showing their rainbow colours. I just know there'll be miniature replicas of every single book that I have. I don't mind that someone has explored the lost property office and the basement rooms. I like that someone has already been in my library of found books. There's even a silver-coloured door that's open and two tiny figures in the bottle-shaped room. I put the hockey stick on the floor and pick up one of the figures. She's got dark hair in a scruffy long bob, like me; her eyes are brown like mine. I think I should be shaking, I think I should be freaked out, I think I should be screaming and running back to my library and bolting up that door for ever. But what I'm feeling isn't fear. It's admiration, it's gratitude, it's the fact that the minute I picked that mini-me up, I knew who had created her.

I hear a sniff. I turn slightly and see Elisabeth. She bends over the creation, tears dripping into it. She brushes her tears away.

'So beautiful,' she says. She picks up a mini version of herself and moves it into her coffee bar. It's a perfect replica of the coffee bar. She opens a tiny drawer to find miniature knives and forks in it, another has minuscule copies of bills that she's been avoiding.

'How?' Elisabeth asks, but she doesn't require an answer. I turn towards the narrow entry. I nod towards where we have to go. Elisabeth nods back.

'You're not frightened, doll?' she asks.

I put my hand in my pocket and run my fingers over the old-style cavalryman.

*

We enter a new room, yet this is like no room I've ever seen before. The space is vast, possibly twenty-five feet wide and at least a hundred feet long. Huge arches a minimum of sixty feet high offer passage to different tunnels, yet I have no desire to rush to investigate them. Standing at the base of this room I feel like I'm in a palatial underground ballroom. The area is divided into separate sections, yet instead of walls suggesting the divisions there are changes in decor. My eyes flick around. The space is incredible. It's like an open-plan house but I know that it's a tunnel. And I doubt it's ever been cleaned. Above my head hangs the largest mirror-ball I've ever seen. It's been made with fragments of mirror mixed with fragments of coloured glass, and they bounce light around this area of the room.

Ahead of us there's an area with a table, and sitting on that table is an old gramophone. Beside it is an old armchair, and in the armchair sits a man. The man doesn't look up to acknowledge our presence in his home. There's a fishing rod at his feet.

'Bonjour, William,' I say. I'm smiling. Elisabeth's standing next to me. She hasn't spoken a word since we entered. William doesn't look towards me. I don't know if he's angry that we've intruded on his space, such a wonderful space that this man has created over time and with patience.

Where William sits, in that specific segment of the space, is a room filled with furniture and ornaments and photographs. It looks like an old parlour, and it's at odds with the mirror-ball above us. There's a large dining-room table – it's set for a knife-and-fork tea for three people. I gasp.

'What is it?' Elisabeth whispers.

'Where William's sitting, I've seen that room before,' I say.

'How?' Elisabeth asks. 'You've never left Lime Street.'

'In here,' I say, tapping my head, then I take the lone tin

144

cavalryman from my pocket. I can't formulate an explanation, but Elisabeth understands and nods.

'He's built a replica of where he once lived?' Elisabeth asks. I hear her sniff again. 'I'm sorry,' she says. 'The last thing he needs is my pity, but . . .'

I flick my eyes around the other areas. A toilet space, a kitchen, four bedrooms even though he must have only needed one. Yet in the middle of this brilliant masterpiece, of the finest tribute to his parents, there is the wonderful William.

William sits in his armchair. He's pretending that he can't see us. Having visitors is clearly not the norm. He's pretending to read a 1940s comic book, and this hides his face so we can't see if he's angry with us.

I cough.

No reaction.

I shout. 'BONJOUR, WILLIAM!'

William springs up from the armchair. His sour smell hangs in the air. We connect eyes, neither one of us daring to make that first step forward. We are strangers, yet we share so much.

'William,' I say. 'Thank you for this.' I hold the lone tin cavalryman into the air. 'It is the most precious gift I've ever received,' I say.

William doesn't speak.

'I know how important it is to you. I know how it was given to you by your parents just before—'

'I'm William,' he says, as he moves across the room to Elisabeth and me. His smell reaches us before he does, yet as he comes closer I hold out my hand to him. Elisabeth gasps.

'You never hold hands,' she says.

'This is a special occasion. William has a voice,' I say to Elisabeth, and then I say to William, 'And I'm Martha.' I shake William's dirty hand. His skin feels like sand.

'You're the lost baby,' he says slowly. 'I saw you. Being left.'

I let go of his hand.

William turns and points at the large dining-room table, then he turns and points at me, then he turns ever so slightly to point at Elisabeth. His gestures are slow and grand.

'Did you set the table for us, William?' Elisabeth asks, and William nods.

'Well, that's very kind of you. How about we picnic down here tonight?' Elisabeth asks, and William nods again.

'In a Utilitarian age, of all other times, it is a matter of grave importance that fairy tales should be respected.'

Charles Dickens

And so my fairy tale continues. This part occurs in August, still in 1976 and still in a time when giants could be friendly and dragons could be tamed. It's perhaps Part Seven in the story of my life.

Right now I'm standing at the doorway to the lost property office. There's a man using the public telephone box in front of Platform 6, close to the billboard. I can't see his face, just his back, and his luggage is stopping the door to the public telephone box from closing. He's shouting, and his accent's different to any I've heard before.

'Yeah, mate. G'day, Graham. Max Cole reporting in.'

He stops talking. I wish I could hear what the other person is saying.

'Not bad. Just arrived in Liverpool.'

He says Liverpool in a weird way, and then he laughs.

'Long, mate. I've no idea what day or time it is. Wanted to get right in there and book us a meeting though. Best we get the authenticating underway ASAP, yes?'

I look over at Jenny Jones. She's leaning out of her kiosk, watching the man's back too.

'Jenny Jones,' I shout, and then I wave when she looks at me. She does strange things with her hands, possibly the sign for milking a cow, then she points at the man or maybe at the telephone box or maybe even at the billboard. I shrug my shoulders.

'Ace. Ten in the morning OK for you? Shit, just a sec, need to put some more money in . . .'

He drops the phone. It clatters. He's shoving his hands in his many pockets, trying to find some change.

'Hello, hello?'

He's holding the phone with one hand and getting coins from his trousers with the other. He does it. He finds a coin and the slot. I clap my hands together and shout, 'Well done!' but he doesn't turn around. I wonder if I need to learn to shout a little bit louder.

'Sorry about that, was struggling with my coins. I'm half-awake.'

He pauses.

'No, I'm in a phone box, got all my luggage outside . . .'

He pauses. He's turned around now, but I still can't see his face. He's bending down, holding the receiver in the air with one hand, moving his luggage around with the other.

'Sorry about that, so . . . yes, staying at the Adelphi Hotel. Yes, I'll ask . . . SHIT!'

He's trying to bend and twist to look at his luggage while still shouting. He doesn't look at all comfortable.

'No. NO!'

He pauses.

'Can I call you back?'

And that's all I hear. My attention's on Drac, who's handing me a brown parcel and he's got a huge smile on his face.

'Another parcel for you, Martha,' he says, handing over the book-shaped package like he already knows just how precious it is.

'Another one?' I say. I take the parcel, then move to my stool behind the counter.

'Just like the others. Bet it's another reply to that poster of yours,' he says.

Word has spread. Everyone in Lime Street Station's talking about my posters and about Management sending in the heavies. I've had people popping into the lost property office and saying how they're on my side, how they'll help me fight Management. I've been smiling a lot. I know I should be pushing for the details and documents I need to make Management happy, but I'm finally acknowledging what it is to be joyful. I finally feel safe.

Holding the parcel, there's a flutter inside of nerves and of happy and they're both muddled together. Someone has taken the time to read my poster, then to choose a book, and then to write words in the white space available, then to post that parcel and now it's being delivered to me by Drac. I don't want this communication to end, not just yet. I look at the postmark.

'Liverpool postmark,' Drac says. 'Just like the other times.'

I nod. I look at my name and address on the neat parcel. The words are all in upper case, black ink, no clues in the penmanship. I open the parcel. I flick open the book, and my eyes scan over the words as I turn the pages. My eyes fill with tears.

'All good?' Drac asks.

I nod.

'You got what you need to get your gaffer off your back?' Drac asks.

'Not yet,' I say, eyes still on the pages. 'Plenty of time still though – twenty-six days.' My voice sounds bored, but I'm not. I'm looking at the way that the handwriting loops.

'Don't leave it too long,' Drac says, and then, 'I'll be on my way then.' Drac leaves, and I nod.

I watch the words. I will them to dance. I wish that they'd change into something concrete. They know who I am, there's comfort within them. I'm communicating with someone who can help me with my National Insurance number and birth certificate. There's that tiny flicker of hope within my belly. I want to chase it away. I don't want to expect.

I wonder if I'm still lost.

I place my book on the counter. I bend to flick on the gas heater; I've pulled it near to me. It's true that the whole of the

UK remains basking in a never-ending heatwave, yet I rub my cold hands. I try to think about my working day.

Today I must make a decision about an engraved lighter and a dead ferret that appears to have been treated to some taxidermy – their time is up. But first I focus on a lost butterfly.

And that's when he walks into the lost property office.

I feel him watching. I'm encasing a Purple Emperor butterfly, a shy soul, difficult to capture but driven by its need to quench its thirst. I have a book in my library – it told me everything about butterflies. This one was captured, but not by me. My fingers shake slightly as I grip the forceps. This one's male; his female would have been hiding. I wonder how long she waited for him. A steel pin has been inserted through the centre of his thorax, and he would have been stretched out on a setting board – not by me. I try not to think about his past or let my fingers brush against him.

I'm placing him in a dome – cork layers the bottom, glass captures his beauty. The dome has a mirror fragment positioned so that he can see himself. His wings fan with purple sheen, they dance with the artificial light in this office. He's no longer lost.

A man stands by the door, the open door. He's been standing there for a good five minutes, but I dare not turn or speak; for now my focus has to be on the positioning and protecting of this Purple Emperor. It has been eighty-nine days since the butterfly was lost. Today he is found.

The glass dome is secured; I place my forceps on to the counter. That's when he speaks.

'Why the mirror, mate?' he asks. His words are rushed.

I look to him. He's tall, his hair's wavy, black, flopping over his eyes. His eyes are a colour I've never seen before. They're the purest blue, and I'm staring into them.

'It's tragic,' I answer. I return my gaze to my Purple Emperor.

152

Then, 'How a butterfly can never see its own beauty.' Then, 'Are you lost or are you found?'

'Lost,' he answers and laughs.

'No two butterflies are identical,' I say. The Purple Emperor holds my gaze. 'The slight deviations in colour and design are hard to detect, but I see them. Such beauty.'

I place the domed butterfly into my open suitcase on the floor; later I'll let it live in my library of found books. He's a beautiful butterfly and the handwritten words I've just read carry so much more weight: *'For you, my dear Martha, are a butterfly. It pains me that, like the most striking of butterflies, you may never see your true beauty.'*

I now know that whoever sent it must have known about my plans for this butterfly. Whoever sent that book must be watching me, but I still can't narrow down who it could possibly be. It's fair to say that I'll tell anyone who'll listen all about the items that are lost, so my butterfly isn't a secret. Elisabeth once told me that if something has their story heard, then that something can never truly be lost.

I turn and look at the man. I see his eyes and know that he's anxious. He looks a little sweaty and out of breath.

'My apologies,' I say. 'What assistance can I offer?'

'I've lost a suitcase. A really important suitcase, possibly the most important suitcase ever and—' His accent is one I've heard before.

'Did you just use the public phone?' I ask, and he nods. 'You're here on holiday?' I ask, looking at the luggage on the floor.

'Work,' he says, and then, 'Well, research. I write. I flew in a few hours ago. Well, I want to write . . . I've come from Australia. The suitcase contains the key to everything.'

'An Australian writer without his research,' I say, then I pull my most serious of faces. 'Come, sit on my stool and let me see what I can do to help you.'

Written by Anonymous to Martha Lost, throughout
I Know Why the Caged Bird Sings by Maya Angelou,
delivered by Drac the postman to the
lost property office

My dear Martha,

My delight at seeing your poster this morning led me to
take my pen in hand and try to alleviate some of the
confusion and misery that dampens your smile.

If I say that I gaze upon you daily, I wish neither to cause
you fear nor anxiety, more that with my daily visions I feel
that I am able to offer a description of you that is both
honest and insightful.

Your poster asked a simple question of me: who am I? A
question that few your age would voice, an unanswered
question that I fear leaves you confused and alone. Yes, my
dear Martha, it is true that your short life has been
sprinkled with sorrow and pain, but that does not define
who you are. For you, my dear Martha, are a butterfly. It
pains me that, like the most striking of butterflies, you may
never see your true beauty. You are wise, compassionate and
full of good, my child. Your svelte, almost boyish physique is
a gift from your mother; your magic is a gift from your
father.

If I could be so bold, I would offer that you ask not who
you are, or who you may have been, but instead that you
look to your future, to all that you will become.

Yours,

Anonymous x

When I saw a tiny Roman soldier sitting on the tiny bench outside the model of Lime Street Station, I knew that William would be OK if we invited George Harris to meet him. We did. The boys were a little awkward around each other at first, but that's just how we all are. Elisabeth says that we're lost children, which is why social graces don't seem to matter and why we struggle with appropriateness.

Today we're having afternoon tea at William's dining table, instead of a picnic tea. We're all in William's tunnel. He's playing songs by The Beatles. George Harris has stayed past his normal time; he was keen to discover more about William. Now William's talking he wants to tell us everything. I think he just wants to try to get it out of his head. We're sitting around William's dining table. He's acquired an extra chair; it doesn't match. The table's set for four now, and there's even a mended cake stand in the middle of the table. Elisabeth and I spent hours making goodies – egg butties, spam butties, cream scones, fairy cakes, mini cherry pies, cheese scones, boiled eggs and more. Elisabeth brought her own teapot – it's a huge one – and she insisted on bringing clean china cups, plates and cutlery. William didn't seem to mind. I can feel that he's happy we keep coming back. We like to visit him.

I guess, to strangers, we must look like an odd bunch of folk. William in his ill-fitting long frock coat, the bowler hat back upon his head and Chelsea boots on his feet. His brown beard is matted and long, and it twists into a point. He still smells and he's dirty. I doubt he's washed for years. Elisabeth's sitting next to him. She's glamorous. Her hair's always in a perfect bob, she's wearing slim trousers, a black turtleneck, a string of pearls and ballet flats. There isn't a fleck of dust or flour on her. Her clothes look as if they've been pressed on to her, not a crinkle in sight. I've no idea how she stays so perfect, even though she rushes around her coffee bar all day long. George Harris is sitting opposite William. He's dressed exactly like a Roman soldier; he never seems to take off his armour to relax. Then I'm next to George Harris. I'm wearing a red and white rockabilly halterneck dress, a tiny fitted white cardigan and white stilettos. They were a gift from Elisabeth. She made the dress for me, complete with a net underskirt that swishes when I spin. I imagine that if someone happened upon us, they'd be curious. We're a mismatched bunch, a Mad Hatter's tea party, and yet we fit together perfectly.

The conversation is ragged too. Aside from William's difficulties, we keep jumping from one topic to another. I shared *I Know Why the Caged Bird Sings* with them all. I read the handwritten words to them, and when I finished, William clapped.

'She's not been outside yet,' Elisabeth says, in response to George Harris's comment about the heatwave coming to an end. There's a drought now. Elisabeth gave me a radio, and I heard it on the news this morning.

'I'm going to go out soon,' I say. 'I just need a way of taking Lime Street Station with me. And when that's sorted, I think I'll take my little battered suitcase with me and have a wander around Liverpool. I'll pretend that I'm a tourist.'

'Been thinking,' William says, 'what you could take.' He reaches under the table, then sits back upright and places a large lump of sandstone in front of him. It's as wide as the dinner plate and as high as one of Elisabeth's china cups.

'Where'd you find it?' I ask William.

'Tunnels. From far down, very far, the heart of Lime Street Station,' William says. 'Carry it, for outside?'

'Oh, William,' I say, 'you're right. It's perfect.' I have to use both hands to lift the lump of sandstone. I place it on my lap. It's heavy and the weight squashes down on my thighs.

'Don't you think it'll be a bit awkward carrying that around, doll?' Elisabeth says, pointing at my lap.

I smile at her, and she laughs.

'I could help you carry it,' George Harris says. I glance at him, but he's looking at his chest armour and not at me. I glance at Elisabeth, she laughs again, then I smile as I look at the lump of sandstone in my lap.

'The heart of Lime Street Station,' I whisper. 'Thank you, William,' I say, turning to him. 'I'll not put it in my suitcase, I'll . . .'

I look at William, but he's not looking at me. I look at the others. Elisabeth smiles. George Harris smiles too. But William's face looks sad, like his mind is someplace else.

'Where's your fishing rod, William?' I ask.

'Somewhere safe,' William says.

'Fisher King of Lime Street Station,' George Harris says. I laugh, and Elisabeth laughs. William doesn't laugh.

'Other children, they evacuated. Little brown suitcases,' William says. He doesn't want to talk about fishing rods. And then, 'Some women, lots of children. The children were excited. Going on holiday. A farm, in Wales. I wasn't going. Mum and Dad . . . Mum and Dad wanted to keep me. Safe. With them.'

'During the war?' Elisabeth asks, but I don't think William's listening. He's poking the white bread of his egg butty with his grimy finger. Black finger marks stain the bread. I stare. I'm hoping he's not going to eat it.

'Had tunnels under our house. No Jerry bombs would hurt us. Dad had been a sailor. A royal sailor – a Navy sailor. He'd

157

not quite got a medal, but he was a good sailor. Didn't have to fight again. Dad was a war hero. He'd not let bad happen to me or Mum.'

'How do you remember all of this, William? You were so young when—'

'I remember. Found papers, in the rubble—'

'Oh, William,' Elisabeth says, but William isn't wanting sympathy, he's wanting his words to be heard. I don't imagine many have listened. People judge others on appearance.

'I watched – my bedroom window, with nets on. I watched. The family from opposite – Davies – their children, outside the house, with suitcases. There were six children. My friends. Didn't know if I'd see them again.

'Laura and Mary sent postcards. From Wales. I couldn't write or read. Too little. But Mum said she'd help, and I could draw a picture to put in. I was five.

'I waved. Laura and Mary, walking down the street. They didn't wave back. Little brown suitcases and gas masks. They were excited. Going on an adventure. I wanted them to hurry back already.'

'A suitcase like that one?' I ask. I point to the little brown suitcase and the child's gas mask that are on the sideboard. William gets up, dragging his left leg behind him this time, and picks them up. He's still talking.

'One month. Every night Mum filled pots and pans with water. Pots and pans, in case the Jerries came to get us. I drew a picture every day, the first week. For Laura and Mary. Mum said she'd give it to Mr and Mrs Davies to send on. No children, no other ones in our street, anywhere. Mum laughed. Said her and Dad saved me from the pie . . . the Pied Piper.'

'Were there rats?' I ask.

'He doesn't mean it like that, doll,' Elisabeth says, and I shrug.

'One day Mrs Davies came. A letter for me. From Laura,'

William continues, and then, 'It said . . . they were having a nice time. People there spoke a funny language. The air, fresh, and no traffic sound. The only noise Laura heard was a stream, from the mountain at the back of the house where she was. I tried to think what a stream sounded like. Couldn't. I asked Mum, she switched on the tap, she splashed me with the tap water. The letter got wet.'

William giggles. He pauses his conversation and runs his grimy fingers over the gas mask.

'Did they come back?' George Harris breaks the silence.

'They did,' William continues. 'Nothing happened in the month. When the children went away. No bombs on our houses. No one was killed by the Jerries. Not near us. Mum said it was a phone . . . a phoney war. I thought maybe then the war was over. The children came back. The Davies. Mary and Laura, playing on the street again. Mum said I could go out playing too. They told me all about a girl at the farm, said she had blue eyes. Raven hair. Eight, maybe, or nine, and used to give kisses for a penny. Mary and Laura were shocked. I was glad they were back. Everything was normal. Nearly normal. Mum and Dad said a tea party, for my birthday. I would be six. They promised sausages. Dad said he could get some. Under-the-counter ones, sausages.'

'Under-the-counter?' I ask.

'Rationing,' Elisabeth says, and I nod.

'Are you sure you want to continue?' I ask William. I can see that the memory is making him anxious. He's hopping from one Chelsea boot to the other.

'Then, a raid,' he continues. 'A bomb, in Prenton, over the water. One reported cass . . . casualty. Mum heard it was a German maid. People were, people seemed happy. Because the Jerries killed one of their own. Dad laughed and Mum made angry eyes at him. Laura and Mary – back to Wales. Mary was the oldest, she was fifteen. No boys, no sons. When they left, Mary gave me a taxi. A Dinky Toy London taxi, a bit battered, still good. She knew it was almost my birthday. I hugged her. She said she wished I went with them. Mum didn't want a stranger looking after me. Mum said Dad would keep me safe.

'We didn't have much, not like people now. We had things we needed. Nice things. Mum said our china was the best. The best that money could buy. She said we'd use the best plates for my birthday tea party. Just Mum, Dad and me invited. We had each other. That was all we needed. We took care. Care of what we loved.'

Tears are streaming down William's face. Elisabeth stands and takes slow steps to him. She holds out her arms, and William allows Elisabeth to hold him. I watch. He sobs, and Elisabeth keeps him safe.

The question that Martha Lost wrote on a poster that
was stuck to the billboard next to Platform 6

What's my real name?

I call the Adelphi as Lime Street Station's clock chimes into the ten o'clock news. Charlotte answers the phone. She works on reception at the Adelphi, but most Thursdays she has her tea in the coffee bar. Elisabeth says that she's a plastic scouser and a bit of an Anytime Annie in her spare time. She puts me through to Max Cole, so that I can deliver the good news.

'I found your suitcase,' I say.

'G'day?' Max says.

'Sorry, it's Martha Lost, from the lost property office,' I say.

'Martha! Wait, your surname's Lost?' he asks.

'Long story,' I say. 'Whenever I asked about my once-upon-a-time, Mother would tell the story of the Night Ferry from Paris, about the passengers nibbling on their *oeufs sur le plat* with ham in the—'

'But you found my suitcase?'

'God, I'm a quilt, sorry, Max. It's the phone, I panic—'

'Don't worry, darl. You're not a . . . what did you say, a blanket? But – you really found it? My suitcase?' he asks again.

'It's here now. I'm looking at it,' I say.

'That's beaut. You're a lifesaver, Martha, a proper lifesaver,' he says.

'Do you like books? I do,' I say, and then, 'I finished a book last night and it was so good I only went and slept with it under my pillow. I didn't want to say goodbye to the main character. I found myself crying at the thought of putting it on a shelf.'

162

'Books? Nah, to be honest, darl, I can't get on with reading books,' Max says.

'How's that even possible?' I ask. I didn't mean to, but my question was asked in a shout. I really need to remember not to shout at strangers. Elizabeth says it can be a bit off-putting.

'Well, sure, books are nice to look at,' he says. 'It's just that I don't like filling my head with another writer's voice. You see, mate, I want my writing voice to be pure.'

A writer who doesn't like to read – that seems a bit odd to me. I'd always thought writers would love books. Max's explanation doesn't make much sense. I can't wait to tell George Harris. He'll be shocked too. I bet he thinks writers like reading books.

'Other people's words would dilute my creativity,' Max says, and then, 'No writers like to read.'

That makes me feel ridiculously sad. Of course, I don't tell Max that. I don't want to sound like the biggest divvy in the world. It's just that I hate to think about a writer only ever knowing the world that they create.

'It's a lot like me only ever knowing Lime Street Station,' I say.

'Maybe, darl,' Max says. I'm not sure he understands though. I hear him yawn. It's just that books have helped me to travel beyond this lost property office. I'm grateful to the lands that others have created. I don't tell Max my thoughts. I don't want him thinking that I'm mocking him in any way.

When he first reported the lost suitcase, I asked him about when he'd last seen it. He told me that he'd definitely had it on the train to Lime Street Station. I asked if he was sure that he'd taken the suitcase from the train with him. He had no recall, said he'd been awake for hours, he wasn't at all sure he'd collected it from the luggage rack, he'd been distraught. That was why it was so easy to find the suitcase.

'I've started writing other books,' Max says, and I wonder if I've missed part of the conversation. 'This one's different.'

'You're a long way from home,' I say. 'You must really like The Beatles.'

'Can't stand them. I've only recently listened to a few of their songs,' Max says. He laughs. 'I'm more of an Elvis fan.' I laugh. I think he's being funny. 'I've got eight weeks,' he says, 'to make this happen. Used all my savings, took time unpaid off work. This is going to be a life-changer, mate.'

'A life-changer?' I ask.

'Being published, giving up my day job, writing full-time, being rich,' he says.

'Sounds exciting,' I say.

'Too right. That's why you finding my stuff is a proper life-saver. I'm better than so many people who are already published,' he says, and then, 'Sorry, shouldn't boast.'

Then he tells me how he'd found a suitcase full of special items that once belonged to Mal Evans. Elisabeth'd told me about Mal Evans dying in January. She'd cried when she told me.

'There's all kinds of lost Beatles stuff that could be in my case. Paul made a load of films of this holiday he went on back in '66 – driving round France in a false moustache, crazy stuff like that. Never been found. And who was on that trip with him? Mal Evans! I'm telling you, this suitcase is gonna turn out to be a proper treasure trove.'

I hope Max gets his treasure, but something about that story makes my stomach full of sadness. Driving round France in a false moustache is just the kind of trip I dream of when I go for a spin with my suitcase. Mal Evans must have been happy then – only for him to end up so sad later.

'Can I look inside the suitcase—' I start to ask. Elisabeth would be keen to know more details.

'NO!' Don't open it!' Max shouts, and then his voice

softens as he says, 'Sorry, Martha love, but you've got to understand, right, I promised an expert the first look. I can't risk anyone taking anything.'

'I don't steal,' I say. I'm offended.

'Course not. But I gotta be careful. Without the suitcase I'd be lost, mate,' Max says, and I nod, not that he can see the nod.

Finding the suitcase had been easy for me. He'd clearly left it on the train. We have systems. A few phone calls yesterday, and the bag was here as I opened the office for my morning spin. I waited until the ten o'clock chime to telephone him. He's creative; he might not sleep the hours I sleep.

'How old are you?' I ask, and Max laughs.

'Thirty-seven,' he says. 'Why?'

'I thought I should ask,' I say. Max laughs again. I don't really understand why. I wasn't trying to be funny; I was seeing if Mother lied about it being rude to ask a person's age. I still don't know.

He's the first writer I've ever met. I'm trying really hard to play it cool, but I keep thinking about my library of found books and wondering if he'd like to write in there. Then again, if he doesn't read books, it's probably a stupid thought. I hate that I'm not always sure how to behave. I'm hoping that Elisabeth will give me some pointers.

'How about grabbing a feed tomorrow – my treat?' Max says.

'A feed?' I say.

'Food. I'll pop round now to pick up the suitcase, but we could have a feed tomorrow. I'll book us a table downstairs. Be nice to say thank you, mate.'

'I finish work at one,' I say.

'No worries. I'll collect you then, on my way back from a meeting. We can walk here together,' Max says.

I don't tell him that I've never been out to lunch before. I don't tell him that I've never been out of Lime Street Station before. I don't tell him that the station might start crumbling the moment I step outside, or that if it crumbles I'll have to run back inside and go without a fancy lunch. And I know already that I'll not charge him when he picks up the suitcase later. I reach down to the second shelf under the counter and retrieve Mother's cheque book.

I've spent the last hour trying to apply mascara, closing the lost property office, running upstairs to get changed, running downstairs, unlocking the door and trying to apply mascara again. I've been running on a loop. This is what I needed – a reason to test my idea of taking Lime Street Station with me – but my belly's still squirming. I'm not sure if I'm more nervous about going out for food in a fancy place or about stepping outside of my world. I look at the heart of Lime Street Station on the counter, and I send a wish to the gods of the liver birds that this'll work out for me.

Elisabeth walks through the open doorway. She's carrying a paper plate with a cream scone and a slice of lemon meringue pie on it. She's later today. It's only half an hour until I finish work.

'Sorry, doll, been run off my feet,' she says. 'Two cakes – to keep you going until lunch.' She's smiling, but her eyes are looking me up and down. She's detected a change, and I'm waiting for her to ask. Thing is that Elisabeth nipping in with cake each day is part of our new routine – it's been going on for weeks now. We don't ask; we assume. I assume she'll pop in, and she assumes I'll want cake, then later we'll have lunch together. Our lives tick and twist with a clockwork beat. And I like that. I mean I really like that they do. Over the last couple of months, our routine's kept me smiling.

But today's different. I should have told her earlier, but I didn't. I think I thought he'd cancel. I think I thought

I'd bottle going outside. I think I was trying to avoid fuss.

'Do you think meringue's a fancy word? I mean it's proper hard to—'

'I'm going out for food,' I say. I blurt it out and stop Elisabeth mid sentence.

'Out of Lime Street Station?' she says. 'Who with?'

'You know the man who lost his suitcase the day before yesterday?' I ask.

'The man who's old enough to be your granddad?' she asks. I laugh; Elisabeth doesn't laugh.

'He's thirty-seven,' I say. 'He's taking me out for *a feed*. That means lunch.'

Elisabeth looks at the cake she's just delivered, then she shrugs and smiles. I smile too.

'Where's he taking you?' she asks.

'The Adelphi,' I say.

'Bloody hell, doll. He's Lord Muck of Muck Hall,' she says.

'He's staying there,' I say. I'm smiling the widest smile ever.

'His treat or do we need to do a whip-round in the station?' Elisabeth asks. I laugh. Then she says, 'You're stepping outside the station?' I nod. Elisabeth's entire face lights up. I can see her joy. A knot forms at the bottom of my throat. I think I need to cry.

'I'm sorry,' I say, pushing the paper plates back across the counter towards Elisabeth. I'm distracting my tears. 'Today me and the heart of Lime Street Station leave at one.'

'That soon!' she says, and then, 'Shall I help you with your hair?'

'Would you? And putting on mascara's impossible. I keep poking myself in the eye. I've got about twenty minutes,' I say.

Elisabeth rushes next door and she's back with a bag full of goodies before I count to sixty. She steps behind the counter, puts her bag on the floor and starts pulling out items. 'Stay still,' she says, standing next to my stool. 'I'll have you looking like Cilla Black in no time at all.'

I sit and let Elisabeth work her magic, with eyeliner and mascara and blusher and eye shadow. She even sticks on some false eyelashes and all before I've time to worry about stepping outside. She flicks my hair, backcombs and sprays half a can of lacquer on it. After five minutes, she's showing me myself in a mirror, but I don't really believe that it's me.

'A bobby dazzler,' Elisabeth says.

'I can be someone different today, someone who's stepped out of Lime Street Station a million times before,' I say.

'But take small steps, doll. Don't be frightened – nothing bad will happen. The Adelphi's right near,' Elisabeth says. 'And if there's a problem, tell Charlotte to call me and I'll come and walk you back.'

And that's when I see him. I see him from the corner of my eye. I turn my head. I hear Elisabeth. Her sigh tells me that she's seen him too.

We're both looking at Max. He's standing outside the lost property office. His shoes are purple. He's five minutes early. I turn to Elisabeth. She looks worried. She's staring at Max, her mouth all straight, with not a splash of happiness on her face. I grab my coat, then I grab my hat and my scarf from under the counter, then I grab the heart of Lime Street Station. The sandstone needs two hands to carry it.

'It's not that cold out there,' she says, taking the hat and scarf back off me, and then, 'I'll lock up. Don't you worry about little old me.'

I laugh as I run through the counter and out of the door to Max.

'Walk, don't spin,' Elisabeth shouts after me, and I nod.

'I'll come see you later,' I shout to her, and then I turn my attention to Max.

We are going to walk out of Lime Street Station together. He has no idea how momentous this is. I know people are watching me. People are holding their breath to see if Lime Street Station will crumble around them. Jenny Jones is in the kiosk. Stanley's sweeping, but his eyes are on me. Drac's delivering the second post, and even Elisabeth's stepped out of the lost property office and into the centre of the concourse. We've turned right. I'm not spinning; instead, we're walking towards the main entrance. I count the platform numbers with my steps – past six, heading for nine. After passing Jenny Jones's kiosk, I turn and with both hands I'm waving the heart of Lime Street Station at everyone as I go off on my adventure.

Stanley starts clapping. He shouts, 'Go on, girl.'

I see them all stepping forward, following us to the exit. I catch Max's eye. He looks confused, possibly about the heart of Lime Street Station, possibly about the little crowd gathering, and I shrug. I attempt a gurning wink at Elisabeth, just to let her know that I know she's watching me. I wonder if they'll cheer when I step outside.

I reach the exit. It's an entrance too – an open arch. I stop, just for a second, on the station side that's still under the shelter. I think about that invisible line that's kept me inside for all of my life. Max takes a few more steps. He's in the sunshine. He turns and shrugs his shoulders. I smile, and he smiles back, inviting me to step outside, to step into the real world. And I do. Me and the heart of Lime Street Station step away from the shelter of Lime Street Station's roof and out into Liverpool.

And no one cheers and the station doesn't start to crumble behind me. I look up to the sky. Max probably thinks I'm about to comment on the weather; he doesn't know that I'm feeling the weather for the first time, that I'm feeling more alive than I've ever felt before. I want to stand here until my skin turns pink and everyone asks if I've been on a little holiday. I want to savour every second of this first. I want to tell Max, but I won't. I'm ashamed. I'm a little bit too different. This is the happiest I've ever felt.

'Bet you're glad the heatwave's nearly over,' Max says. He's stopped walking and is watching me with an expression that's either confusion or concern that I'm a nutjob. I take two more steps forward, listening for any sounds that could be crumbling.

'Are you putting that rock out here somewhere?' he asks.

'No, it's the heart of Lime Street Station,' I say.

He shrugs. 'Table's booked for ten past. We best hurry, mate,' he says.

And with those words, that first experience is over and we're rushing along the road next to the station. At the end of the road stands the Adelphi. I'm out in Liverpool but still close enough to the station to feel safe.

As we walk, Max talks, and I realize my arms are already aching.

'I've been researching Mal Evans this morning,' Max says, 'about when The Beatles were in Amsterdam for some gigs. Turns out that before their shows, The Beatles hired boats and toured round the canals in Amsterdam. Crowds gathered on the banks – well, you can imagine, can't you, mate? Beatlemania was spreading worldwide by then! Anyway, somewhere in the waving crowd George Harrison spotted a bloke wearing,' Max checks a crumpled bit of paper from his pocket, 'a "groovy-looking cloak". And Mal, proper legend, right, he dived right off the boat and swam to the side! Three hours later, Mal turns up at The Beatles' hotel with the cloak. He'd bought it from the bloke. Can you imagine doing that for someone else? Top bloke or what?'

I can imagine. Elisabeth told me Mal Evans was supposed to be a roadie, really, and drive The Beatles around and make sure their equipment was working, but that he was always doing extra things for them, like getting suitcases full of baked beans to India, or finding cars with extra-wide doors for them to dive through to escape screaming fans, or doing sound effects for their songs with alarm clocks. Elisabeth gets a look on her face when she talks about Mal Evans that makes me think that if Mal wasn't dead, then Kevin Keegan's thighs would have serious competition.

'Can you research anything?' I ask. I'm feeling a bit sick. Walking, listening, carrying the heart of Lime Street Station, taking in everything around me and talking is overwhelming. I stop.

'Too right I can. Research is my thing,' Max says, and then, 'Come on, slow bird, nearly there.'

'I think I need to research about the time I was lost,' I say and keep walking.

'Lost?' Max asks.

'I'm a foundling,' I say, and Max nods. He doesn't ask for details.

'That's easy, mate,' he says. 'All you need to do is search local newspaper archives around the time of you being found.'

I nod, but really I'm standing in front of the Adelphi and wondering if the Adelphi's going to topple forward and swallow me whole.

'Can you believe this place was once seen as the most luxurious hotel outside London? Let itself go a bit now, don't you think?' Max asks.

'I think it's beautiful,' I say.

We've been sitting here for at least five minutes, the heart of Lime Street Station heavy on my lap, but I've been lost for words. I'm absorbing all that's around me. There's a table between us. It's low and on it sits a delicate white-porcelain cake stand, with matching plates, cups, saucers, a small jug of milk, a small dish of sliced lemon, and tiny little bowls containing curls of butter in one and a selection of jam flavours in the others. The tea pot and strainer are waiting to be used.

'You know when we went through the revolving door. You know that room, at the top of the stairs, straight ahead when you walked in?' Max asks.

I nod, but I don't really know which room he's talking about. The lobby was large, overpowering, it was all marble and leather and wood and brass. I think I held my breath as he spoke to Charlotte at the reception desk. There were people milling around, arriving or departing. I'd wanted the ground to swallow me whole.

'That's the Sefton Suite. It's an exact replica of the *Titanic*'s first-class smoking lounge, darl,' Max says, bringing me back to this moment.

'Really?' I say, and Max nods. I can't wait to tell Elisabeth later. I shuffle in my seat, trying to get comfy, but I'm feeling very out of sorts. 'What's the name of this room?' I ask. I want to try to remember everything, so I can tell Elisabeth, George Harris and William.

'Hypostyle Hall,' Max says. 'Bird on reception said it used to be an open courtyard with first-class rooms around it.' He points around, and I nod. The room is breathtaking – a number of huge black-and-white marble columns stretch up high to gilded plasterwork. I look up; the detailing on the plaster is gorgeous.

'Dig in. The pastry chef is spot on,' Max says.

I look at the cake stand of tiny butties and a selection of miniature pastries. I'm waiting for Max to make the first selection; I don't want to make a mistake.

'All the famous people have stayed here,' Max says. 'Franklin D. Roosevelt, Winston Churchill, Frank Sinatra, Laurel and

Hardy.' I think about Stanley and smile. 'Even had a horse staying once – think his name was Tigger.'

'Trigger,' I say. 'I remember Elisabeth telling me. And now they can add your name to the list,' I say.

'Too right,' he says with a grin. 'I'm getting the suitcase authenticated soon, but I was wondering if there was something else you could help me with,' Max says. 'Well, two things, really.'

'I'm only really any good at finding lost things,' I say.

'Perfect, mate,' Max says. 'You've heard about Mal Evans?' I nod. 'And you've heard about his ashes being missing,' Max says, and I nod again. 'Well, I wondered if you'd help me find them? Rumour is they're in a lost property office somewhere in England, and me finding them would be the icing on the suitcase.' Max laughs.

'Do you know when they were last seen?' I ask.

Max nods, reaches into a plastic bag on the floor and hands me a newspaper cutting. I read through the article.

'January?' I say. Max nods, and then I say, 'Shouldn't be a problem at all. Will you help me find—'

'Really? You little beauty,' Max says. 'Do you promise?'

'Cross my heart,' I say, flicking my fingers over my ribs. I smile. 'I'm the little finder.' Max doesn't smile; instead, he reaches for a triangle of cucumber butty and pushes it all into his mouth. I do the same.

Max finishes munching the cucumber. 'The other thing that I wanted to ask,' Max says, reaching for a triangle of ham butty. 'I'd quite like you to show me some of the local sights, mate. Would you have the time to—'

'YES,' I shout, spitting little pieces of cucumber into Max's face before I've considered that I've no idea where the local sights are located. I watch as Max lifts the cloth napkin from his lap and wipes cucumber from his face.

Written by Anonymous to Martha Lost, throughout
A Taste of Honey by Shelagh Delaney, delivered by
Drac the postman to the lost property office

My dear Martha,

*Of all the questions that I suspected you may have, this
was not one that I expected. Yet may I firstly express my
relief and gratitude that you have continued to communicate
with me. Seeing your poster a mere thirty minutes ago, has
filled me with joy. I had feared that the forthright opinion in
my last chosen book may have led to your decision to cease
all correspondence. I thank you, my child, for allowing me
this voice.*

*And so to your question, and it is an unassuming one
today. Your name, my dear child, has always been Martha.
It is the name that your birth-mother chose for you, the
name that was given to her by her grandmother. Martha is a
family name that speaks of generations of strong women; it
was offered to you as a gift.*

*I feel that this is an opportune moment to share with you
a fact that I fear was not communicated in the fairy tale
that Mother created surrounding your arrival in Lime Street.
My dear Martha, when your birth-mother left Lime Street
Station without you, she left a letter for Mother covering a
few simple facts and demands. Your birth-mother left your
full name and your date of birth included in those details. If
Mother had desired to search out your heritage, it would*

174

have been a simple task for her to complete. You exist, my dear child. You have always existed. You bring delight to all who cross your path.

I await the question that I know you long and need to ask.

Yours,

Anonymous x

'For as long as I can recall, Mother told me the story of how I came to be hers. I didn't have a day when I wasn't lost. I believed that I waited ninety days for my birth-mother or my father to collect me. I sat on that shelf for those ninety days,' I say, and I point to the shelf.

'Next to a box of lost scarves?' Max asks. He's leaning against the customer side of the counter. I'm sitting in my usual spot.

'Possibly snuggled over a box of lost false teeth,' I say. 'Mother being the lost property office manager and me being found on the train and then handed to her in this office made perfect sense to me. No one collected me. Nobody wanted me. Mother offered to look after me.'

'Have you got any more of those ginger biscuits, mate?' Max asks.

I bend down to the top shelf under the counter in the lost property office, pull two ginger biscuits out of a packet I keep down there and place them on the counter. Max grins at me, picks one up and starts dunking it in his tea. I'm not sure he's listening, but his teeth are very white and his eyes are very blue.

'Once I asked Mother if she thought my birth-mother was raped. I'd read about rape in one of my books, and I'd not been able to get the images out of my head. Mother shrugged. She said that she had no other answers and told me to stop with my questions, so I did,' I say.

'So you're most probably the product of a rape,' Max says.

I shiver, and inside my belly flips over.

'But Mother lied. Because Mother knew the truth. The documents were given to her. They've been locked away. There's a birth certificate . . . I don't know where yet, but it's the only thing I have to go on. I don't think I'm registered with a doctor. I've never been ill enough to have to go to a doctor,' I say.

'Lucky you,' Max says, and soggy ginger biscuit falls on to the counter.

'So now I know that Mother always knew who I was and it was her choice not to tell me. She let me live in a make-believe world,' I say.

'Make-believe's more fun than real life. I don't understand your problem,' Max says. I wonder if that's because I haven't explained myself very well. He's a writer; he's used to telling stories properly. He only popped in for a cup of tea and to ask for a favour.

'What was the favour?' I ask. I've been talking too much. I've not let him say what he wanted to say.

'Finally,' Max says. 'I know you and that rock of yours showed me some sights yesterday, but do you fancy showing me around some of the city this arvo? It'd be beaut if you could, darl. I've made a list—'

'Sorry, I'm not feeling too bright today,' I say. The truth is that I'd need at least a night to prepare the route I'd take as his guide. I stayed up most of the other night after I got back from the Adelphi, preparing for yesterday's little tour, and that was only ten minutes of walking. 'How about we figure out where you'd like to go tomorrow and make a list?' I ask.

'No worries, mate,' Max says. 'Charlotte said she was free later, so—'

'Did you see my poster?' I ask. My poster's lying on the counter near to him. Max nods; he doesn't ask any questions.

I watch Max's eyes flick from the poster then back to the shelves. I look at the wrinkles around his eyes. He looks tired and I'm not so sure, in this light, whether he's handsome. I wonder if he's worried about finding the ashes. I've never had a boyfriend before. I don't actually know if I've got one now, and I'm definitely not going to ask. Can a thirty-seven-year-old man even be a boyfriend? I can't imagine being thirty-seven – it's really old. When Max leans over, I can see a circle where his hair's thinned and his scalp is pink.

'Want me to stick your poster on the billboard on my way out?' Max asks.

I shake my head. 'No, but thanks. I don't want to break the spell,' I say, and then, 'I have a name.'

'Martha, yes, I—' Max begins.

'That means that I really do exist.'

Max laughs.

'Don't you think that if you name something it leaps into existence?' I ask.

'You playing silly buggers? You're nineteen, mate, you've existed for nineteen years,' Max says.

'Sixteen. And that's not what I'm saying—' I start to say, but I look at Max and see that he's not listening. His eyes are wandering around, looking at all the labels on the front of the boxes of lost things. I stop my sentence before it's finished, to see if he'll look at me to continue. He doesn't.

'Will you put the ashes in a box and write "Lost Ashes" on the front of the box?' Max asks, and he laughs.

'All foundlings have the surname Lost,' I say.

'You said that the other day, you nong,' Max says, turning his very blue eyes on me again, and then, 'You do realize that's ridiculous, don't you?'

I lift my new poster off the counter. It could lead to the answer to a question that excites me. There's the prospect of me having siblings, of there being others who could be my friends. I've put the phone number for the lost property office on the poster, but if I'm honest I'm not expecting a phone call. I don't expect anything, yet I find myself hoping for another new book. I hate that I'll be disappointed if no book arrives. I've lived my life without expectation, yet this search is changing me. I know Management will send someone to get me soon, but instead I imagine someone sitting down and thinking about me for the entire time they search the book for white space and fill that space with words just for me. It's mind-blowing. It's stopping me from asking the questions I know I should be asking.

I look to the phone. It's resting on a stack of newspapers on the shelf below the kettle. I urge it to ring. It doesn't. I feel Max's arm around my shoulder. He's moved to behind the counter. I wonder if he understands what it is to be lost. I want to help him find the ashes. I want to help him be rich and famous and stop looking tired, but mainly I want Mal Evans to find his way home. I think that would make Elisabeth happy too. I don't tell Max that reason; I have a feeling he'll think me a divvy.

'I don't think I've ever met anyone quite like you,' Max says.

I'm curious – people say that a lot. 'Is that a good thing?' I ask. Max nods. 'What did you think when you first saw me?' I ask.

'That you had an interesting face,' he says. He takes a sip of his tea. His arm's still around my shoulder, and his eyes are flicking around the boxes. He's talking into the open space.

'Is that all?' I ask.

'Reckon you're not my usual type,' Max says.

'A type?' I ask, and Max laughs. I don't understand why he laughs.

'Let me help you, mate,' he says. 'I'm brilliant at research.' I'm not sure what he's referring to, if it's the ashes or to help stop me being evicted or to find out who I really am. His arm feels heavy on my shoulder.

'I think Mother has a locked box. I have the key,' I say.

'You think the ashes are in a box?' Max asks.

I turn my face to look up at him. He tilts his head to me and his lips brush mine. My first ever kiss on the lips – a sweep that barely touches. Contact with my lips doesn't make images pop into my head. I'm glad that it doesn't. I hold my breath for a second. I expect my legs to buckle or for him to erupt with passion and throw me on to the counter. Books promised me more than this. I wait. I look at Max, but he isn't looking back at me. His eyes are fixed on a scowling Elisabeth; she's blocking the entrance to the lost property office.

The question that Martha Lost wrote on a poster that
was stuck to the billboard next to Platform 6

Do I have any brothers or sisters?

181

'You missed George Harris last night. He left this for you.' I hear her words, but I'm refusing to look at her. Max made his excuses the minute she walked in; there was no repeat kiss as he rushed from the lost property office the fastest I've ever seen anyone run from here. I wonder if he'll ever kiss me again. I don't think I liked that first kiss, but perhaps they are an acquired taste like olives, and then I flick my thoughts back to Elisabeth.

'Was with Max, I told you—' I start to say.

'Figured,' she says, before I can finish my sentence. She places a worn black book on the counter. 'Said he found it on the train.'

'You're early today,' I say, looking over to the departure boards, then I realize that she's not got any plates of food.

I think she reads my mind – she's weird like that. 'Didn't know if you'd be hungry,' she says. 'Thought perhaps you'd be eating out again.' I look at her. Her face is angry, and I don't like that I've made her fine-looking face less fine-looking.

'I'm sorry,' I say. 'I'm staying in today.'

She smiles. Her whole face changes and the mask of anger falls away.

'I like your face best when you're not angry,' I say.

'You don't like me when I'm angry?' she asks.

'I don't like it that, when I'm not good enough, I make you look ugly,' I say.

'Ugly?' Elisabeth laughs, a proper belly laugh. 'I'm sorry,

doll, I'm just being overprotective. He's forty. He's old enough to be your dad; he should know better.'

'Don't,' I say, and Elisabeth nods. 'Thirty-seven,' I add.

'Ignore me. I'm a mardy arse. I'll make it up to you with an extra-special lunch.'

'Jam butty?' I ask, but before she can answer I'm looking at the book George Harris found and saying, 'Another black one.'

I move over to the novel and run my finger along the white creases dancing on the spine. The cover shows a man chewing a long piece of straw. The cover offers no clue to the story that's exploding inside. The edges of the pages are tainted yellow. I open the novel and inside is an inscription, 'To remind you that I am always thinking about you'. I smile. I wonder who wrote the words. I wonder if the book was lost or left. I hope that the book will be claimed, but if not I know that my bookshelves will keep it safe. My fingers aren't picking up any clues. All I can see is a bookshelf; the book's not saying that it's been lost. I wonder where George Harris found it. I try to remind myself to ask him.

'You'll like that one,' Elisabeth says, snapping me away from the novel. 'So you went on a date?'

I shrug my shoulders.

'We were tourists, me, Max and the heart of Lime Street Station,' I say. 'We didn't go too far, up past the Adelphi. Then up Mount Pleasant, just as far as Paddy's Wigwam, then along Hope Street . . .' I'm drawing my finger along the counter, showing the direction of the route that we took.

'You've remembered all the street names,' Elisabeth says.

'The other night I lay in bed and said them over and over. I was probably saying them in my sleep,' I say. 'I feel alive.'

Elisabeth smiles. 'Small steps,' she says.

I nod. 'I didn't expect it to be so very beautiful,' I say, and then, 'There's a whole world outside of books and Lime Street Station.'

Elisabeth smiles, but not in her eyes. 'This is your once-upon-a-time,' she says.

My face contorts into a scowl, and Elisabeth laughs.

'It's not,' I say, my words stubborn.

'Have you made any progress with Management?' Elisabeth asks.

'Max is going to help me,' I say. I see Elisabeth's grimace.

'I'll bet my arse that he doesn't,' Elisabeth says. 'You can't be relying on him. You've only got another—'

'Twenty-two days,' I say. Elisabeth nods.

'They could send someone any day now. Your mind should be on finding your birth certificate and National Insurance number and not on some spiv who thinks he's the cock of Liverpool,' Elisabeth says, her voice full of anger.

'Please, don't,' I say.

'Sorry,' Elisabeth says. She pauses, and then, 'You know, doll, I only saw him for a second, but he didn't half remind me of an Eccles cake. Have you ever been sick after eating an Eccles cake?'

I shake my head and move towards the kettle. 'Time I brewed up,' I say.

It's fair to say that I've just had the worst day of my life.

I'd promised Max that I'd take him to see 36 Falkner Street, where John and Cynthia had stayed for their extended honeymoon, then he'd wanted to visit 9 Percy Street, where Stu Sutcliffe had lived, and then 3 Gambier Terrace, which was once John's flat, where he'd lived with Stu Sutcliffe and Rod Murray. Max said it was back during the time when The Beatles were being formed, back when they were trying out different names like Johnny and the Moondogs and the Silver Beetles. So Max had told me all about where he'd wanted to go in advance, giving me the time to sit last night and memorize the routes and paths that we'd have to take. I mean it was all in the city centre, all within walking distance from Lime Street Station. I felt confident when me and the heart of Lime Street Station went to meet him at the Adelphi this morning.

Problem was, when I got there he'd decided on a few other places to add to the tour. He wanted to see the Jacaranda Club on Slater Street, because The Beatles had played a few lunch-time gigs there, and Hessy's on Stanley Street to talk about a debt that Brian Epstein had cleared. His requests weren't unreasonable, and for any normal Liverpudlian they'd have been an easy addition to the tour.

But I blew it. I was so full of panic, worrying about how I was going to figure out the new route, that I forgot the old route and ended up getting us proper lost. I guess the worst bit was that I didn't hold my hands up high and admit to Max that I didn't have a clue where I was going. Instead, I kept us walking the wrong way, and we ended up heading towards South Liverpool.

'You sure this is the right way, mate?' Max asked, several times. I kept nodding and walking with my head held high, like Elisabeth had told me to do, even though carrying the heart of Lime Street Station was killing me. I think she called it blagging. After about an hour of walking and not having seen anything on the tour, Max stopped. I didn't realize for a few steps, and then I turned to look at him. His face was one red ball of anger.

'I don't know what your bloody game is, but I've had enough of this shit,' Max said, then he turned and walked back the way we'd come. He left me in the middle of nowhere, my arms aching from carrying the heart of Lime Street Station, and I had no idea what to do next. Eventually, I decided that I had to speak in my French accent and ended up asking for directions seven different times. I was sobbing like a fool each time. I even had to take my stilettos off, as they were rubbing the backs of my heels, so now my nylons are all ripped and they're covered in seagull poo.

All the way home I was thinking about Elisabeth and about how she'd make everything better, but now I'm standing just outside the entrance to her coffee bar. I'm on the station's concourse, people are rushing past me, a man just shouted at me to move. I didn't move. I really don't know how much more rubbishness I can take in one day.

'I've met my fair share of beady-eyed bastards over the years, John,' she's saying. 'I've learned to detect those who are full of shit and he's very much—'

'Full of shit,' George Harris says. Elisabeth laughs.

'He arrives in Liverpool, he's a bit of a spiv, midlife crisis cause he's forty, as good as anyway. He's a chancer, a womanizer,' Elisabeth says, and then, 'Fast bucks, minimum effort – he wants to be the cock of the north!'

'He's getting quite a reputation,' George Harris says.

'Have you been talking to Charlotte from the Adelphi too?' Elisabeth asks. 'She's been getting to know Max a little bit better than our Martha has . . .'

'The bastard,' George Harris says.

Clearly, they don't know that I'm standing just outside the doorway to the lost property office and I can hear everything they're saying inside the coffee bar. They were so absorbed in their gossip, they didn't even notice when I walked past the coffee bar. Elisabeth doesn't expect to see me. She thinks I'm doing the tour with Max and then having food with him. Clearly, there's no way she can know about how Max is furious with me for being rubbish and that I might never see him again. Clearly, she doesn't know that it's taken me two hours to find my way home, that my nylons are ruined, that my arms are aching or that all I really want is a slice of cake and to see her happy face. I can't stop my tears from falling; I want everything to go back to being happy. I don't want Elisabeth to be angry with me, I want her to like Max, I want George Harris to like Max. I want everything to be happily ever after, and I don't even believe in happily-ever-afters.

'He's getting our Martha to work her arse off showing him around Liverpool. The poor girl was up to all hours last night memorizing maps—'

'She's special,' George Harris says.

I can't help but smile even though I'm still crying. I wonder if I look like a rainbow. I smile again.

'Our Martha's bloody wonderful. And she deserves better than that quilt,' Elisabeth says. I laugh, but I don't think they hear, as she continues, 'But really he's got his sights set on finding them lost ashes. And when our Martha finds them, do you reckon he'll give her any of the glory?'

That's when I walk in. Elisabeth sees me straight away. Her cheeks become the brightest rouge I've ever seen.

'Nowt I wouldn't say to your face,' she says, staring at me.

'But you didn't,' I say. Tears are streaming down my face. I reckon my mascara's smudged down my cheeks and I must look a right state. George Harris turns to look at me. Neither of them are sitting down – they've been standing near the door, gossiping about me and Max. Somehow, even though he's at least six feet and five inches tall, George Harris looks like a dwarf when he's embarrassed. He mumbles something about needing some scran and scuttles away to the counter. I watch how his Roman armour shimmers as he walks. He bangs into two empty plastic chairs on his way to the counter and apologizes to both of them.

'What is it?' Elisabeth asks, her voice full of calm and love and everything I need at this very moment. She looks from my eyes to my feet. She sees that I'm holding my stilettos and the heart of Lime Street Station, she sees my toes peeping through my ripped nylons. And even though I want to be angry with her and even though I want to shout at her and tell her that she's being unfair and cruel to Max, I don't. Because Elisabeth's the only person in the world that I can tell about my awful day. And Elisabeth's the only person in the world who can make it all better.

'Come in, doll, give me them.' She takes the heart of Lime Street Station and my shoes. 'Let's get you a cup of tea and a slice of lemon drizzle,' Elisabeth says.

Max didn't get in touch all today, I don't think I expected him to. I mean, he's a busy man. He's paid all that money to be in Liverpool, and he shouldn't be wasting his precious time on a Soft Mick like me. I hope I see him again. I don't expect to, but I think it's OK to hope. I spent this afternoon chasing leads about the missing ashes. I think I'm a step closer to finding Mal Evans. I think they might be in Liverpool. I think I owe it to Max to help as much as I can, to make up for wasting his time and being rubbish at kissing.

I'd been feeling ridiculously sorry for myself, but then about an hour ago a man walked in. He had a black beard, and his black glasses were held together with Sellotape across the bridge. I recognized him instantly.

'You lost a hockey stick,' I said, before he'd even said hello.

'Bloody hell, queen, you're good,' he said, and before he had time to ask any questions, I was handing him his daughter's hockey stick.

'Hope she had a good birthday,' I said, as the man turned and walked out of the lost property office, clutching his hockey stick with both hands and looking a bit baffled. I didn't shout him back and charge him for the find. I'll write a cheque. It felt right to let him go home full of a story.

But right now I'm with George Harris in Elisabeth's coffee bar, and we're sitting at our usual table. We're planning on going down into William's tunnel later. I'm looking forward to spending some time in William's world, just the four of us, away from how chaotic Lime Street Station is feeling.

George Harris has been shuffling to get comfortable in the plastic chair and telling me how the weather's mild for September. He's mainly been talking to his chest armour. He's not wanting to look at me today. Elisabeth's at the counter; the life insurance man is talking to her. He comes weekly for his subs, but lately I've been noticing him in here when he's not wearing his work suit, and it's pretty obvious that he's interested in her. Elisabeth's shaking her head. The insurance man's gone down on one knee. Elisabeth's laughing but still shaking her head. Probably he's asked her out again or maybe he's asked her to marry him. I don't understand why she says no to every man who asks her out. I think maybe she's waiting for someone really special. I think maybe, once upon a time, someone proper broke her heart.

I'm looking at Elisabeth when I speak. 'Sometimes our own stories are the hardest to tell, aren't they?' I ask George Harris.

It's the first thing I've said to him since he sat down five minutes ago. He looks confused.

'But if the story's not told it becomes something else,' I say, and then, 'It becomes forgotten.'

George Harris nods. 'When a story's not told, yes, it becomes something else, but even if it's told it can still be forgotten.'

'How can it be forgotten?' I ask.

'Because not all stories get remembered, and sometimes I don't think people truly listen.'

'I wonder if people have forgotten Mal Evans?' I ask. I look to George Harris, and he smiles.

'Some people won't even know that he existed,' George

Harris says. He's put his butties on the table and is unwrapping them.

'But he played such an important part in The Beatles' success,' I say.

'According to you. Others will say he was merely an employee,' George Harris says, and then, 'Did you know he even signed autographs on The Beatles' behalf?'

'I wish there was a way that no one was ever forgotten and that every person's story was able to be told,' I say.

'I don't think I'll ever meet another quite like you,' George Harris says. 'My granddad used to work with Mal Evans. I remember meeting him once, when I was little. I remember him being a giant, but he was a nice bloke. He patted me on the shoulders.'

'You should talk to Max,' I say. George Harris doesn't reply; instead, he chomps a huge bit of his butty.

'Max is writing about Mal,' I say. 'You should tell him that you met Mal Evans.' George Harris doesn't reply. I think he mumbles something, but he's too well-mannered to speak with his mouth full.

'Do your legs ever get cold?' I ask, looking down to his bare legs sticking out from under his Roman armour.

George Harris swallows, then laughs. I like his laugh – it comes right from his belly and makes his eyes sparkle. 'Mainly after it's rained,' George Harris says. 'But I like marching in the rain, makes me feel like a proper Roman.'

I like George Harris. He understands how my brain works. He has this wonderful knack of finding things that I need or that'll excite me.

He listened the other night. Even though he was eating his butties, he still listened while I spoke to him and Elisabeth about my being a disastrous tour guide. After a while, he said, 'But all tour guides carry maps and guide books.'

'They do?' I asked.

'Of course,' he said, and then, 'It'd be a complete disaster if the tour guide got lost.' We all laughed. My laugh had come deep from within my belly, and I'd ended up with hiccups for ten minutes after I'd finished.

And now, right now, he places an up-to-date guide to Liverpool on the table next to me, and it's even got a map tucked in it. He's not said a word, he's just placed it next to my plate. I lift it up. I flick through it and there are hand-written notes in it about where The Beatles have played and even where they used to hang out before they were mega famous. It's clearly been used before, but when I touch the book no images appear.

'Found it on the train,' he says.

If I could do the whole 'hugging people' thing, I'd hug George Harris. I swear he's amazing at finding things. I wish he'd come and work in the lost property office with me. I wouldn't even mind if he wore his Roman soldier outfit; I could dress like Boudicca. This guidebook must have belonged to a tourist – maybe they left it on purpose, maybe they'd stopped needing it. Sometimes people do that. They leave things behind when they're no longer of use. People do that to items, and they do it to each other too. That makes me sad. George Harris didn't even look excited when he placed the book on the table – it was almost as if he'd not realized how perfect a find it was.

I'm running my fingers over the glossy front cover as I talk to him.

'I feel like the world's opening up for me,' I say.

'Not a once-upon-a-time,' George Harris says, and he smiles.

'No, more that Liverpool's finding me. I think I feel joy,' I say.

George Harris stares at me, just for a second. I think he's about to say something important, but then he changes his

191

mind. His cheeks turn pink, and he's back looking at his chest armour. I flick open the pocket guide to Liverpool and see an inscription written on the inside cover. It says, 'All You Need Is Love'. I smile as I think about how many love stories must have started in Liverpool. I close the book.

'Did you write in it?' I ask, pointing at the book on the table.

'Only a couple of bits,' he says, still not looking at me. 'I saw there was other writing in it, and I happened to know a couple of locations . . . places where Mal Evans used to hang out. I saw they hadn't been marked, didn't think you'd mind . . .'

'Of course I don't mind,' I say, and then I lean over and give George Harris a peck on the cheek. His cheeks flush with red.

'Must be going,' he says, leaping up and almost wobbling to the floor as he rummages for his backpack.

'But we're going down to see—'

But he's already out of the coffee bar's doors.

'See you tomorrow, John,' Elisabeth shouts after him, then I catch her eye and she winks at me. I do my double eye closing and opening wink, and I see Elisabeth laughing.

I turn back to look through the glass front, to see if I can catch a glimpse of George Harris. I don't see him. I wonder when he'll stop feeling lost. I wonder when we all will. I wonder if being lost is more about waiting to be found.

Dear Angela,

Where do I start?

I can't shake how bloody tired I am, everything feels wrong. I worry that my decisions will ruin us. I couldn't even begin to explain when I phoned before. I'm sorry I wasn't enthusiastic about your day.

Is this all worth it? Is it worth the bloody expense? I can't even find my own way around Liverpool, so how am I supposed to discover the secrets from another man's life?

But what else can I do? I reckon I've come this far and we've already risked everything. I must just keep going. We all have to make sacrifices to get where we're going.

You asked where I was up to and what I'd discovered. I hesitated and I'm sorry. It's just that I'm afraid. Already, I'm different here. The answer, now, when I put it down on paper for you, is that since I've started researching I've ended up with more questions than answers. About bloody everything. With each nugget of truth I uncover, I reckon that I expose hundreds more unanswered questions.

But to have it down and to share everything with you, like I promised. This is what I know (or reckon I know):

Mal Evans was part of The Beatles. You already know this. But I've come to puzzle more about the REAL part he played in the band. What was his job? Roadie? What does that even mean? How can such a lowly job result in what happened, what people have said happened anyway, about how important he became to the band members? Is he more important than I thought?

There's a strong suggestion that he was GOOD friends with at least one of The Beatles. But who? George is my best guess, but what about Paul? Wasn't he a sucker for a stray? Didn't he adopt John? But why Mal? The Beatles could have befriended the world, so why did they pick Mal? Because he was a scouser (from Liverpool)? Is that enough? What did Mal offer?

It scares me. I know so little.

What was he like before The Beatles? Was he lost before he met them? It's like his life starts with a meeting in the Cavern Club, as if he's the one who's a Nowhere Man. Is the Cavern the answer? I reckon it always seems to come back to that bloody place. Can that dingy hole really conceal secrets?

Apparently the Cavern Club was used as an air-raid shelter during the war. It was a network of tunnels and rooms, which was accessed by eighteen stone steps from Mathew Street. I found out that The Beatles' first performance at the Cavern was Thursday, 9 February 1961. It was unadvertised and they were paid £5. People say that the gig was a success and they were immediately booked for four lunchtime slots per week, plus weekend gigs. It was one of those gigs that Mal Evans heard when he first went into the Cavern.

And I discovered that The Beatles would often fool around during their sets, telling jokes and even jumping into the crowd. They would also sing jingles from adverts or the theme tunes from kids' TV shows. My first thought was that they were most probably drunk, but they weren't! There was no alcohol served in 1961; the Cavern didn't have an alcohol licence at the time. Apparently John Lennon would often be seen eating a hot dog and drinking a Coke!

But I don't see how finding out that kind of stuff is helping me figure out who Mal Evans was. And what about his bird and his family? What drove him to leave them behind and end up being shot in LA? Does it even matter?

He'd moved to America after The Beatles split up. Why? Was he cut up about it, is that it, or was he running from something? What led to a gentle scouse giant dying so far from home? Is it true? Was he murdered? Did he really carry secrets? If so, what secrets and about who?

I hate that this bloody mystery holds so much hope. I hate that it's got me in its grips. Did I tell you that Mal was forty when he died? Only a few months older than me. Am I running, like him? Is this what blokes do when they're worried about being old? I hate the sadness that I feel when I discover more about Mal Evans – he seemed like a good bloke.

Like I said, right now I've got more bloody questions than answers, but I'm not giving up. No worries about that happening, no turning back now.

Love me, do.

Max

Later, over a picnic tea at William's dining table, I'm telling them about Max and about his research and about the missing urn containing Mal Evans' ashes.

'Someone joked about it being in a dead letter depot, but I reckon they're not far wrong,' I say.

'And it makes sense the ashes should be in Liverpool, because they were sent back to Mal's family. Was the urn logged into your records earlier this year?' Elisabeth asks.

'Not that I can find, and Mother was rarely around, so I'd have dealt with it,' I say.

'I can help. Check the bags – the bags of lost things, in the tunnels,' William offers. 'I'll do it. Finding the ashes will heal hearts. The hearts of Mal Evans' family.' I nod. I can't quite think of a reason why it would have ended up down there, but all leads have arrived back at Lime Street lost property office.

'Where's George Harris?' William asks, looking around the room. I wonder if he thinks that George Harris might leap out at any moment. Sometimes even the smallest of movements make William's smell overpowering. I try not to breathe in until he settles down and stops twisting to look around. I'm hoping Elisabeth will bring up the whole 'getting William clean' thing soon.

'Martha scared him off by trying to snog him,' Elisabeth says. William nods his head, as if that makes perfect sense, and Elisabeth laughs. I don't laugh. I glare at Elisabeth, but that makes her laugh even more.

'I reckon this is what the knights felt like when they were searching for the Holy Grail,' I say.

'Max Cole is no knight,' Elisabeth says. I pull my glaring face at her, but she winks, and I can't help but smile in response. That's when I look at William. Although he's been joining in our conversation, his eyes are full of sad tonight.

'You could do with a shave,' I say. I want to cut the huge chunks of mud, or possibly poo, and rubble from his beard.

'Never learned shaving,' William answers. Then he sighs. Today he's broken and he's lost his spark. I had thought we'd been making progress.

'William,' Elisabeth says, 'you do know that it's OK to be feeling low? You're a child in a man's body. You're just starting to come to terms with the death of your parents. You're finding yourself. I'm sure there's a handsome bloke stashed under all that hair and . . . stuff.' Elisabeth reaches out and lays her hand over William's hand. She gives it a squeeze. William's blue eyes fill with tears. I don't want him to cry. I want to make him happy. I wish we could make him happy.

'The kindness from you . . .' William takes a deep breath.

'You're safe now,' Elisabeth says.

'You're with family,' I say. 'A bit of a weird family full of lost children, but I wouldn't change it for the world.'

'Something bothering you?' Elisabeth asks, and William nods.

'Ash,' William says.

'Ashes?' I ask, my voice full of hope. Elisabeth glares at me. I shrug.

'Do you want to tell us what happened? Did the all-clear siren sound?' Elisabeth asks. William nods.

'After the bombs, people with no house, survivors, had to go to rest centres. The town hall. Bombed-out families. Then Dad said you got "relocated". You went to a new house, an empty one,' William says.

'Yes, I remember hearing something about that when I was little. Folk lost everything,' Elisabeth said. She's still squeezing William's hand. I look at how delicate her hand is, how long and thin her fingers are. Their whiteness contrasts with the grime that is part of William.

'I came out from the tunnels,' William continues. 'I thought Mum and Dad would be in the town hall. Waiting for me. I figured that Dad would know about the tunnels being all blocked, from the Jerry bombs, but he'd know that I was a good digger. He'd know I'd find a way out. I don't know how long it took me.'

'You're a survivor,' I say. Elisabeth looks at me and smiles.

'I climbed out. Dust and sunlight in my eyes, itching. Dirty hands from the tunnel. I rubbed my eyes, the dust scratched them. I cried. I sat in the street. Cried because my eyes hurt. Then I opened my eyes. I saw people, not quite people, bodies, being carried. Doors turned into stretchers. I didn't know where they were going. I wanted Mum and Dad . . .' He pauses, his voice wavering, tears falling even though he's trying so hard to be strong. Then, 'Nowhere looked like it used to look. Broken things, bricks, bits of walls, furniture, clothes, bodies. Too many bodies. I was all dusty. My clothes, covered in soot or dust, in ashes. Inside my mouth too – dust. It stuck to my throat. I worried. Thought I would turn into a wall. But it was a good diss . . . disguise, being grey. I thought I could be invisible. The first time being invisible.'

'But not the last,' Elisabeth says and nods.

'The dust was different dust. Not like anything I'd seen. Not like anything I've seen since. Not like a thin layer on Mum's china that made her tut. This dust was a mix – soot, brick dust, mortar dust, plaster dust. People dust. Dad said plaster in our house, in all the houses then, had horse hair in. The bombs did funny things. They could hit the back of a house, blowing windows and doors in, then windows and doors at the front going out. There was lots of glass – broken glass – on the pavement, on the roads. I looked around. Sandbags, planks of wood, hills made from bricks and walls. Nothing was the same as before.'

'And you were scared,' I say.

'All I was thinking was that the air ponged,' William says. 'I should have thought about Mum and Dad. But then – my name, someone called me. I thought it might be Mum. Grown-up arms came, they were picking me up and hugging me too tight, but the hug didn't feel like when Mum hugged me. It was Mrs Davies. She was sobbing. Not a cry like Mum sometimes cried when she'd argued with Dad. Mrs Davies was crying with her whole body. I wanted her to put me down. I wanted to find Mum and Dad.'

'Did she explain?' Elisabeth asks.

'I think she said, "I'm so sorry," and, "We'll find someone to look after you." But I wasn't listening. Not really. I asked what the stink was.'

'What was it?' I ask. Elisabeth glares at me. I mouth 'What?' but all she does is shake her head and roll her eyes.

'Cord . . . cordite, she said. I think it was from the anti-aircraft guns,' William says.

'How do you know all this?' I ask, and then, 'You're so clever.'

'Books,' William says. 'I find some, sometimes. I know a little bit how to read, from school. And I listened in on people and I practised.'

'You should meet Stanley the cleaner – he's good at helping with how you say difficult words,' I say.

'Anti-aircraft guns?' Elisabeth asks, bringing William back to his story.

'Some clever bloke, he decided to make smoke screens so the bombers couldn't see us. They burnt oil to make the smoke.'

'Did Mrs Davies help you?' Elisabeth asks.

William shakes his head. Droplets of tears fly from his cheeks and one lands in my cup of tea. I watch the ripples in my tea. I make a wish that William will feel better soon.

'I wriggled to get free. Landed on the pavement – it was all broken. I didn't want anyone to look after me. I wanted to find Mum and Dad. They were my family. The only family I had,' William says, but then his voice gets louder. I can hear the anger roaring inside him as he says, 'Another lady came up next to her. She had a black shawl over her head. She said, "Poor little orphan boy," and she was pointing her finger. At me. I didn't know what "orphan" was. She looked like a witch. Then she looked up at the sky and said, "I wonder if Jerry will be over tonight."'

'Oh, William,' Elisabeth says. William's pushed the chair back from the dining table. He's standing up and practically hopping from one Chelsea boot to the other.

'I ran, I jumped over things,' he says. He's jumping on the spot, adding actions to his words. 'I fell over twice. Landed on glass. And brick. My knees were scratched, they were bleeding. I needed Mum. I crawled under a door and prayed to God. I thought God was real then, everyone thought God was real. Mum said people needed God in sad times and scary times. Dad said, "Atheism is a luxury that none of us can afford."'

And that's all he says. He doesn't want us to see the pain that is spilling out from him. He walks out of the room, dragging his right leg this time, and into a different tunnel.

'Better out than in,' Elisabeth says, letting out a deep sigh. Her eyes are filled with sadness, and we're both feeling lost and alone.

'He didn't eat his picnic tea,' I say, because feeding William and making him feel less alone is what I want to do.

'Let's nip upstairs and bake him a cherry pie, doll. I've got a tin of condensed milk he can have with it,' Elisabeth says.

And as we walk back through William's tunnels to my library of found books, I take a little look at William's doll's house. Today I can see me with Elisabeth in her coffee bar. He's got us dancing, and George Harris, in his full Roman soldier outfit, is sitting watching us. I look all around the doll's house, but there's no sign of Max.

I'm practising my whistling when he comes in with a bunch of pink carnations. He doesn't say sorry, he doesn't mention my tour guide failings. Instead, he asks if I'm free this afternoon.

'Just less than an hour left,' I say, holding the carnations to my nose and taking a big sniff. They don't really smell of anything. 'We can explore Liverpool together.' I'd memorized some routes, just in case.

'Graham Kemp phoned me earlier,' Max says, and I shrug. I don't know him.

'The expert, the bloke who knows everything about The Beatles,' Max says.

I place the flowers on to the counter. 'Did he have news?' I ask.

'No, of course not. It'll take weeks. I did explain that to you, darl,' Max says, his voice sounding a little angry, so I nod and say that I'm sorry. 'Anyway, he phoned to say that Rocky Hooper wants to take me out for drinks tonight.'

'Who's Rocky Hooper?' I ask.

'Where you been, mate? He's like some major bloke in your city. He's meeting me under Dickie Lewis at ten. You got any idea where that is?'

I smile – that's an easy one. 'Just across the road from your hotel. You must have seen the statue of the nude man? It's over the main entrance to Lewis's. The sculptor, Sir Jacob Epstein?'

'Was he related to Brian? Put the kettle on, Charlotte,' he

says. I look at him, and he smiles. I wonder if I should correct him, but I don't say anything. Instead, I make him a cup of English tea, and we stand behind the counter and talk about Brian Epstein.

'Lying in bed last night,' I say, 'I tried to count how many times he could have pulled in and out of Lime Street Station, about how hard he had tried to get record companies interested in The Beatles.'

'What number did you arrive at?' Max asks.

'Fell asleep,' I say.

'Mate, I was meaning to ask you about the ashes . . .' He pauses. I wait for a question. He nods for me to answer.

'I will find them,' I say. 'They're getting closer every day.'

'I'll love you for ever if you find them,' he says, and I giggle.

'For ever?' I ask.

'You bet, darl,' he says.

'Did you manage to research anything about me being a foundling?' I ask

Max shakes his head. 'Not yet,' he says. 'Sorry, darl, lot on my plate.'

'I saw that Peter Barrymore fighting a man today, out there, on the concourse.' I point. Max doesn't turn to look where I'm pointing. 'Wonder if Management sent another—'

'What makes Martha tick?' he asks, and then, 'Likes and dislikes – go.'

I pause, thinking what to include and what to hold back. I take a slurp of my tea. 'I like butterflies and English tea,' I say. 'And I like returning lost things. I like stories that don't begin with once upon a time.' Max laughs.

'I'll make a note of that,' he says.

'I like frost, I like make-believe. The word "belonging" is a favourite,' I say.

'Belonging to someone?' Max asks.

'Maybe, but more than that. I like Christmas lights. I like bone china cups, not really saucers though.' Max laughs. I continue, 'I like drawing smiley faces on condensation, I like the battered brown suitcase . . . What else? I like the Eiffel Tower, but I've never seen it. I like the taste of snowflakes, but I've never tasted one—'

'Don't you get snow here?' Max asks. I nod, but Max doesn't ask any more questions about it.

'I like the 17:37 train from Chester,' I say.

'That's very specific. Why that train?' Max asks.

'That's George Harris's train,' I say, but I wish that I hadn't. Max's face changes, and he looks angry. I want to make him smile instead.

'I like talking with a French accent.' I say that one with a French accent, and then I switch back to my normal voice. 'I like the pigeons who live in the rafters. Budgie lives up there too now. I like jam butties—'

'Butties?'

'Sandwiches,' I say. Max nods.

'I like inscriptions in books,' I say.

'You and your books, mate,' Max says. He's smiling his white smile again. I decide not to say the other things I like. I don't say that I like Elisabeth or spinning or whistling or smiling. I don't say that I like my library of found books. I don't say that I like it when someone sits down next to me on the bench opposite the lost property office and the way their weight makes the bench move up and down. I don't say that I like it when balloons float up to the rafters in Lime Street Station. I don't say that I like the sign of the girl on the toilet door, because I think her dress is pretty. I don't say that I like the ticking of a clock or when people cross two fingers to send a wish of good luck. I don't say that I like silence or that I like slurping drinks or that I like the click of knitting needles or that I like the way water feels when it's being sucked down a plughole. I keep all of these things in my head. I keep all of these things inside me because I'm trying not to be me. I'm trying to be mature and older, and I'm trying to make it so that Max likes spending time with me, but not that he likes kissing me. I wonder if I should dye my hair to make it the same colour as Charlotte's hair. I saw Max wink at her when I met him at his hotel.

So instead I say, 'What do you like?'

He doesn't answer immediately. It's like he's really thinking about what he likes and possibly not saying out loud the thoughts as they pop into his head. I wish I'd done that. I wish I'd been all mature and mysterious.

Finally, he says, 'I like Liverpool.'

I don't speak. I wait for him to like more things, but instead he's staring at me and not saying a word.

'And?' I ask.

'And I like the thought of finding those ashes, mate,' he says.

'Will that make you happy?' I ask.

'Too right. That and the thought of me and you getting dirty,' he says.

'Dirty?' I ask.

'Sex,' Max says. I don't know if he's joking. I'm unsure if me allowing a quick brushing kiss over my lips was code for saying I'd have sex. I really hope that it wasn't. Then he says, 'What about your dislikes?'

'Dislikes?' I ask.

'You nong! The things you don't like,' he explains. I laugh. I know what the word means, it's just that I don't think I've ever tried to group together the things that I don't like. I'm quiet for a couple of minutes. Max stares at me the entire time.

'Feeling lost,' I say, and then, 'And ants, I really dislike ants. And I don't like Lent, because that's about giving things up.'

'You don't like giving things up?' Max asks.

'Elisabeth says life's too short to restrict the things you like. She doesn't think it makes you a better person if you give up cake for forty days, not including Sundays,' I say.

'I dunno. I don't really like cake anyway,' Max says. I stare at him. I have no words. I wonder if it's an Australian thing. I can't think of a single cake that I don't like.

'I wish I was short-sighted,' I say.

'That's not a dislike,' Max says.

'I dislike that I don't wear glasses,' I say. 'And I dislike endings.'

'What about happy endings?' Max asks.

'No such thing,' I say. 'Everything dies and that's not happy. I don't think I like autumn or spring, because they're neither one thing nor another. And I don't like chalk drawings.'

'Chalk drawings?' he asks.

'They can be smudged,' I say. 'And I dislike broken promises. And I dislike saying goodbye.'

'What about Mother?' Max asks.

'Mother's dead,' I say, and then I stop leaning on the counter in the lost property office and walk over to the kettle. 'Another cup of tea?' I ask.

'Sure,' Max says, and then, 'And best put your flowers in some water.' I nod. I stop myself from adding that I dislike people buying flowers, that I dislike that the moment they're picked they're waiting to die. Flowers are supposed to speak the language of love, yet all I see when I look at flowers in vases is that they're mourning their approaching death.

It's late now, hours after closing, so really I shouldn't be answering, but someone keeps phoning the lost property office. I reckon that if they feel it's important enough to phone, something like a million times, then really I should make an effort to speak to them.

I answer.

'I'm bloody on my bloody way back, darl,' he says. 'Key bloody witness. Beer . . . I'm bloody outside, darl, I need a bloody piss.'

I hold the telephone away from my ear.

'Have you been drinking alcohol?' I ask.

'What the bloody fuck's that got to bloody do with you?' Max asks. He's shouting, his voice is angry now, and then, 'I bloody need those bloody ashes, Charlotte.'

'Martha,' I say.

'Have you bloody well bloody found them yet, darl?' Max asks, quietly now, but still saying 'bloody' a lot. His words slur together like he's singing.

'Nearly,' I say.

'Nearly's not bloody good enough,' Max says. 'My bloody writing career's bloody over if I don't find those bloody—'

I hear the pips.

'Can't bloody find my bloody change,' Max says. 'I'm bloody outside. I want to have a bloody piss in your bloody dunny. Come on, darl, open the bloody door.'

'Can't you use the public one in the stat—' I start.

Then the line goes dead. I look at the receiver, then I look to the glass front of the lost property office and see him dancing across the concourse. I unlock the door.

'About bloody time,' Max says. 'Grabbed a bloody feed in town. Key bloody witness.'

'You said,' I say. He takes a step towards me, I step back, and he takes a step forward. I think this might be us dancing. I can smell alcohol on his breath. I turn away. I walk through the gap in the counter and to the white door that leads to the flat. It's open, and I point up the stairs to the flat, to the bathroom. He stumbles up the stairs and laughs. He turns. He pulls me to him. He pushes his lips on mine. I scrunch my lips and face. I don't want his kisses. He smells of stale crisps, and he pokes his tongue through my lips. He kisses me and I wriggle him off.

'Use the toilet,' I say.

'Frigid bloody dingbat,' Max says, and then, 'I'm going for drinks now, with bloody Rocky Hooper. You heard of Rocky?'

I nod – we've already had this conversation. I point to the toilet, and he staggers into the room. He leaves the door open; I can hear his wee hitting the toilet bowl. He doesn't wash his hands.

'This way,' I say, as he comes out of the bathroom. I walk down the stairs and into the lost property office. I really want him to go. He walks down the stairs. He pulls me to him and pinches my arms in his grip as he steps back into the lost property office. He kisses me again. It's a heavy kiss, probably a rough kiss. His stubble scratches my chin. I fight him and wriggle away. He licks my cheek and it isn't nice.

'Hold my bloody hand, darl,' Max says.

'You're drunk,' I say.

'You're bloody ugly,' Max says.

'Can I be in your book?' I ask.

'It's not that type of bloody book, you bloody nong,' Max says.

'But can I?' I ask.

'No,' he says. 'Maybe. Find the bloody ashes and I'll tell every bloody one how bloody big a bloody help you were.'

'I'll find them,' I say.

'You'd bloody better,' Max shouts. 'Or bloody else.' I laugh, but Max isn't laughing.

I turn and see Elisabeth in the open doorway. I feel relief. She's there, the door's no longer locked, the sign's not set to closed. Elisabeth looks at me and then she looks at Max. Her eyes are full of anger.

'Think you'd better go,' she says to Max.

'Think you'd bloody best fuck off,' he says to Elisabeth, but he's staggering through the gap in the counter and towards the door. Elisabeth waits until he's out of the lost property office, then she turns and walks away. I walk to the door. I see Max walking a zigzag across the concourse and towards the exit. I stand waiting, hoping Elisabeth'll come back in and talk to me. She doesn't come back in. I don't go to her coffee bar.

Written by Anonymous to Martha Lost, throughout
Great Expectations by Charles Dickens, delivered by
Drac the postman to the lost property office

My dear Martha,
As always, the sight of your poster filled me with both
warmth and affection, yet as I absorbed your question I
must admit to curiosity surrounding the purpose of our
communication. Is it not a fact that you have a deadline for
which you must produce evidence of your identity? When
will you ask about the National Insurance number that you
need so desperately to remain in employment? I fear that
you are maintaining this communication in avoidance of
more pressing concerns.

May I assure you, my dear child, that I have no intention
of disappearing. Indeed, your posters are a delight. They
brighten my days and prevent my peaceful slumber, with the
hope that you'll reply to my scribblings. Can I tell you a
secret? May I? Before I answer your latest query. It is true,
my dear child, that I long to remove the posters and keep
them for myself. I long to rip them from the billboard and
take them home to treasure. I will not, of course, for I know
that you are watching and I know that you have friends who
are waiting to discover this mystery's identity, of the one
who pens these words to you. I do hope that, one day, I can
reveal myself to you, my darling child.

And now to your question, a simple enquiry regarding

siblings who may or may not exist. I can confirm that your birth-mother was not blessed with other children after your birth, that she is alive and that she hopes beyond hope to be reunited with you. Your father, may the Lord rest his soul, had two children with his wife. The children, two sons, are not aware of your existence, nor was his poor wife. It was your birth-mother's choice to protect both your father and his family from scandal, thus he was never informed of her being with child. It is true that your birth-mother's parents knew of her pregnancy, yet they were never informed of your father's identity. I am afraid that, should you pursue this route of investigation, I will not be able to provide you with further details surrounding your father. Your birth-mother chose to protect an innocent family and she would hope that you would find it in your heart to respect her desire.

Forgive me, my darling child, for withholding knowledge from you. I can only hope that you will communicate with me again and that you will understand the gravity of releasing secrets into the world.

Yours,

Anonymous x

'Did I wake you?' I ask.

'No, no worries,' he says. His voice is full of grit, and he coughs. I hear phlegm forming, I hear him spit. 'Hangover from hell.'

'I tried to call you earlier,' I say. I've already finished work for the day.

'Sorry, dead to the world,' Max says. 'It was the best night of my life, mate.' Max starts laughing; I don't quite know how to react. My chin is scratched from his stubble. He'd promised to speak to me in the morning but hadn't called. I'd worried that I'd made him hate me and lost the chance of someone loving me for ever. I'd been unsure what to do. I'd phoned the reception desk at the Adelphi and Charlotte had answered. She'd told me she was seeing him later and she'd tell him I called. I wish I knew how to react to things like this. I've never had a boyfriend before, so maybe this is normal, maybe this is what novels mean when they talk about true love.

'Are we still going out this afternoon?' I ask.

'You're not even going to ask how it went last night?' Max says.

'I thought that if you'd wanted to tell me—' I start.

'Rocky Hooper took me out for a late-night dinner,' Max says.

'What did you eat?' I ask.

'Nightclub boss, owns most of Liverpool, knows everyone, muscles like Cassius Clay and you ask what I ate? You're a bloody nong,' Max says. His voice is angry. He's annoyed that

I haven't asked the right question. I wish I knew what that right question might be.

'Wow, that's amazing,' I say.

'Too right,' Max says. 'He'll want to meet you too . . . after you've found those ashes, mate.'

'I'm getting there,' I say, and then, 'So are we still going out this afternoon?'

'This arvo, too right,' he says.

'I got another book, from Anon—'

He interrupts me. 'I'm looking forward to seeing you, Martha. But . . .' He stops talking. I hear him coughing again.

'You OK?' I ask.

'Feel a bit sick,' Max says. 'Thing is, I really need to tell you something. I really need to tell you something right now.'

I nod to the phone, I hold my breath, I let him speak, I listen.

'I reckon I love you. I don't think I can stop myself,' Max says.

'Thank you,' I say. Max laughs.

'I know there's the age gap to worry about – you being nineteen and me being thirty-seven—'

'Sixteen,' I say.

'But I love you. I've never felt this way before,' Max says.

'Thank you,' I say.

'But I think you need to know I'm divorced,' Max says, and then, 'And I've got two children.'

'Were you once a piano teacher?' I ask.

'No, stop playing silly buggers,' Max says, he laughs, and then, 'My children are precious.'

'Boys or girls?' I ask.

'One of each, but this doesn't change anything between us, mate. We're a team, we're the ashes-finding team,' Max says.

The question that Martha Lost wrote on a poster that
was stuck to the billboard next to Platform 6

Who are you?

Dear Angela,

Liverpool's different from what I'd imagined. Darker? Harder? The city's both alive and dead. Being me isn't enough here and I have to try to be someone else, someone better than me I reckon. Problem is, I keep getting it wrong. I mean, there's one thing lying about my age (it's not like the journos are going to check) and another thing lying about my life with you. I keep making the wrong decisions. I'm an idiot.

Yesterday I headed to the ferry but climbed on the wrong bus. I got off and was lost. I walked for hours. Street after street. On one street I came across bombed-out houses, whole rows of houses missing, like pulled teeth, dark muddy earth in their place, rubbish in the gutters and dirty urchins running wild. But then I turned the corner and I found little gaggles of life, people happy to speak, happy to help, happy in themselves. I looked at each door I passed, wondering what secrets they held.

I know I must start at the start. The Cavern Club's the natural place – after all, that's where it all began. But I'll be honest – perhaps for the first time I hear you say, with that little laugh you do when trying to make a point – the Cavern scares me. I don't know why. I walked past it four times the other day. Up and down Mathew Street I walked, head down like a lost schoolboy. That dark doorway, that hole in the ground.

The place is just a shell now, closed down with its secrets locked inside. So many potential answers gone. I did finally pluck up the courage (after a few tinnies) to chat to one of the bouncers down Mathew Street. He seemed impressed I was from Australia and was happy to talk. He said he didn't know Mal but did know 'of him'. He said Mal had worked at the GPO (that's the Post Office) before getting a part-time job as a bouncer at the Cavern. He did say his boss knew Mal, but I scuttled off like a frightened rabbit when he went inside to fetch him.

So, I've taken the easy way out. I've gone back to before the start. I had to be a sticky beak, dig around, ask questions. I managed to find the GPO building and waited outside until finishing time. Then I followed a few of the guys down the pub. You should have seen me, I was like a real private detective. Just like the blokes you see in the movies. I got talking and after a few bevvies (that's what they call tinnies), I met a couple of blokes who knew Mal. I told them I was writing a book about The Beatles and they seemed pleased.

One of them told me about the first time The Beatles asked Mal to drive them to London. I knew Mal was a roadie, but I didn't know it started because The Beatles' usual driver was ill. Apparently, on the way home, the conditions were bad, with thick fog covering the motorway – think he said it was on the M1. Anyway, the bloke said there was a bang and a stone hit the front windscreen. The glass splintered, making it impossible to see, but, and without stopping, Mal covered his hand with his hat and punched a hole in the glass. Turns out Mal was forced to drive two hundred miles with only the kerb of the motorway as guidance, while The Beatles lay in the back with only a bottle of whisky for warmth. Can you imagine how cold Mal was? But he kept going. He was like me, Angela, he didn't give up without a fight.

I also met an old GPO bloke who used to play darts with Mal on a Tuesday night. Turns out Mal and his future wife met and fell in love at a funfair at a place called New Brighton. It's a seaside resort on the other side of the water – that's what they call the Mersey, the water. Like it's the only river in the world or something. You see, Liverpool sits next to this flat grey monster of a river. You can see land on the other side, sticking up across the water. The Wirral, they call it. New Brighton's at the top of the Wirral, one toe in the Irish Sea. Turns out it's a popular spot with scousers (people from Liverpool) in the summer. They like to hop on the ferry, then catch a train and spend the afternoon eating ice cream, paddling in the sea and walking on the prom. Remember that song, 'Ferry Cross The Mersey'? We heard it at that dance last year? The DJ was an English guy.

I reckon I need to see New Brighton. Get a feel for it, so to speak. It's the kind of thing a writer does when they're trying to get into the mind of their characters. They're at the end of a heatwave here, so I might go and catch the last few drops of sunshine. I'll go on the ferry. You can go under the water in a tunnel, but it's for cars only. I reckon the ferry would be more authentic and that's where I was going yesterday when I got lost.

Another fact. It turns out Mal had a son not long after getting married. A boy by the name of Gary. One bloke remembers him as a 'lively little chap'. I don't think this is important, but it made me think about our Stephen.

I got to wondering if Gary was proud of his dad and then I got to wondering what Stephen must think about me being on the other side of the world. I hope I can make him proud. It's just the promise of money mixed in with some beer, it's not a good combination but I'm trying to make something of it. The people seem to expect something from me too. Does that even make sense? I reckon I'm playing a part here in

216

Liverpool and my public want me to behave in a certain way.

I know we'll be OK though, because you and me are solid, aren't we?

Love me, do.

Max

I've been trying to think of a way to talk to Elisabeth about Max being divorced and about his kids and about him saying he was in love with me. Thing is, though, every time I start formulating the sentences in my head, I can't make them sound any good. I can't make them sound like I'm not being a divvy. Elisabeth's due to pop in any minute now. She said before that we'd have a butty together and a catch-up. I look to the door and I see her talking to a man in a suit outside on the concourse. They keep looking over at the lost property office. The man in the suit looked angry at first, but now he's smiling. Elisabeth's stroked his arm twice, and she's doing a fake smile. I've no idea what she's up to.

Elisabeth walks towards me. I'm staying behind the counter, and the man stays where he is, but he's watching Elisabeth as she does an extra wiggle just for him.

'Brass from London,' she says, almost in a whisper.

'You what?' I ask.

'Management, from London. He's turned up to give you a bollocking but nipped in the coffee bar first for a bacon butty.'

'Is he going to hit me with his briefcase?' I ask. 'Am I going to be sacked?'

'You will get sacked if you don't hurry up and give them what they want,' Elisabeth says.

'I'm trying,' I say. 'Still got . . .' I pull the slip of paper from my pocket, 'seventeen days.'

'Doll, you've got yourself a pen pal and you're having a

laugh,' Elisabeth says, and then, 'But this is serious. They need to know your National Insurance number. You need to be paying your stamp or you'll be going down the fab of the nab to sign on.'

I laugh. The situation isn't funny, but I swear Elisabeth makes up these phrases.

'Fab of the nab?' I say. Elisabeth nods, then she turns around and looks at the man, then turns back to me and whispers, 'Serious face on, now.'

The man in the suit walks into the lost property office and behind the counter. I pull my face into a serious expression. He's standing next to me. I'm sitting on my stool. I reach down to pull up my umbrella with the false teeth, sequins, bells and beads attached to it. I see Elisabeth shaking her head; her eyes are saying 'NO'. I put my weapon back under the counter.

'Martha Lost, I presume,' he says.

I think he's waiting for an answer, but I'm not really sure what he's asking.

'Yes, sir,' I say.

'Martha, we have a problem. I'm up on other business but decided to nip in myself and have words with you face to face,' he says. 'Because the happiness of our workforce matters.'

'Would you like a cup of tea?' I ask. 'Or maybe a set of false teeth?' I hear Elisabeth stifling a giggle. I hadn't meant to be funny. It's just that while he was talking, I couldn't help but stare at his mouth, and I noticed that he was missing two of his bottom front teeth. I wasn't being cruel, it just made sense for me to ask if he wanted to rummage around in the lost false teeth box.

'No,' he says. I'm not sure if it's a no to the tea or to the false teeth, so I put the kettle on just in case.

'Martha, this office has the top finding rate of all of our lost property offices. This office over-performs, if I'm entirely honest, and we have no doubt that this is down to your hard work. I am assuming you received a letter from us?' he asks. I nod.

'She did, and she's been worrying about it ever since.' Elisabeth jumps into the conversation. She's moved to this side of the counter too.

'Worrying?' the man in the suit says. I wonder what his name might be. He looks like a John, but I decide not to tell him that. By now I've forgotten his question, so I nod at the kettle rather than the man in the suit.

'Did you enter the country illegally?' the man in the suit asks.

'I'm not sure,' I say. I turn from the shelf where the kettle is and then I switch to my French accent. 'I might be, see I arrived 'ere on a train from Paris when I was—'

Elisabeth interrupts. 'What Martha means is that since the death of her mother, God rest her soul, Martha's had a lot to deal with. She has not been able to locate her birth certificate or her National Insurance number. Martha's mother put them somewhere for safe keeping and we are trying to locate them.' Her voice is different. She's talking Blundellsands, trying to impress Management.

'You just need to ask for a replacement,' the man in the suit says, but his eyes are looking confused.

'I know, she's just been a bit . . .' Elisabeth starts, then she whispers, 'lost, since her mother died. But I'll tell you what, John—'

'Your name's John?' I ask. I'm smiling, and my serious expression's gone.

'No, it's Simon,' the man in the suit whispers. His eyes are darting between Elisabeth and me.

'And since you sent those two men to attack her—' Elisabeth starts.

'I did nothing of the sort,' the man in the suit says.

'I have a signed statement off each of them, John, detailing that you told them to "get her out" and "use whatever force necessary",' Elisabeth says.

'I can assure you that—' the man in the suit begins.

'She,' Elisabeth points at me, 'was threatened with a cricket bat. You,' she points at the man in the suit, 'accused her of Devil worshipping. She was found on the floor—'

'I was being a tortoise—' I begin, but Elisabeth glares at me to be quiet.

'And since that day, she's been living in fear. She carries a weapon with her at all times,' Elisabeth says, and I flick my eyes to my weapon under the counter. I think it needs a name. 'She's sixteen years old,' Elisabeth says.

'It was never my intention—' the man in the suit begins.

'Anyway, John,' Elisabeth says. I giggle. 'I will give you my personal reassurance that Martha will get all the details you require within the next four weeks.'

'She requires additional time? That's another twenty-eight days,' the man in the suit says. 'By our calculations, she has seventeen days remaining.'

'How about we split the difference, John? Let's say twenty-one days and we'll forget all about how you paid two blokes to attack her? Oh, and let's not forget about the other two heavies you sent even though we had an agreement,' Elisabeth says, and she winks at the man in the suit.

'Other two?' I ask. Elisabeth smiles at me.

'I really don't think—' the man in the suit begins.

'And I'll throw in a couple of slices of cake too,' Elisabeth says. 'You look like a man who'd enjoy an iced bun.'

The man in the suit smiles. 'OK, OK. She's got twenty-one days, starting today, or we won't be paying her wages,' the man in the suit says.

'You can't—' Elisabeth begins.

'I think you'll find that we can. Birth certificate and National Insurance number within twenty-one days or else—'

'And we have your assurance that no other heavies will turn up?' Elisabeth says.

'You do,' the man in the suit says.

'Or I will go to the police,' Elisabeth says.

'Are you going to sack me?' I ask.

'You're leaving us with no option,' the man in the suit says. 'Unless we get those details, you will lose both your employment and your home, Martha. The others are talking about reporting this even higher.'

I'm listening, but I'm already distracted.

'Do you have a book in your briefcase?' I ask, looking down to his black leather case on the floor.

'Yes,' he says. I look at him. He smiles.

'Are you nearly finished with it?' I ask.

'About halfway through it. I have a spare, just in case I do,' he says.

I smile. I like him.

'Are you divorced?' I ask.

'Yes,' he says.

'Any kids?' I ask.

'Two boys,' he says. 'They're everything.'

'I'm sorry,' I say, 'for making you come all this way.'

'Twenty-one days, Martha,' he says.

'Excellent,' Elisabeth says, 'we got there via a slight detour. Now, Simon, about your iced bun. I'm assuming you prefer one with sultanas?'

222

THE BEATLES ARE BACK IN TOWN?

Word about town is that there's been a surge in Beatles memorabilia being sold around the city this last week. From sweaters, caps, scarves and flags, The Beatles are having a major moment.

Perhaps this is due to that bubbling rumour that the band is re-forming. But let's not get too excited – after all, this will be the seventh 'The Beatles are back in town' report in as many weeks.

Man of the moment, Max Cole, was even spotted wearing a white 'What happened to Mal?' T-shirt earlier today – an interesting addition to the memorabilia range. The 35-year-old Australian looked dapper in the new garment that was inspired by his recent suitcase find.

Seen walking through our city centre with nightclub owner Rocky Hooper, Max was unavailable for comment. Meanwhile, it's strongly rumoured that Max Cole is soon to announce the whereabouts of Mal Evans' ashes, a find that will ensure he has the key to both our city and our hearts.

Later I'm with George Harris and Elisabeth, and we're down in William's tunnel. William's not quite himself again. He seems nervous and looks unhappy. I haven't been able to tell any of them about Max having kids or how I want him to stop kissing me, but that I quite like the idea of him loving me for ever. I haven't been down here for days. I miss being down here, but everything feels different, everything feels odd. I want to talk about it, but the mood isn't quite right. I think I'm angry at them all. I think I'm angry because I need them to make me feel better and none of them are even trying. Instead, we've all noticed that William is full of anxiety.

So I ask him, 'What's wrong, William?'

He doesn't reply; instead, he makes himself look busy, sitting cross-legged on the floor and sorting through a crate of new finds. He doesn't even acknowledge my words. I think he might be sulking. Elisabeth and George Harris have been spending time with him without me. I don't know what I've been missing.

I'm sitting at the dining table with George Harris and Elisabeth. I look at Elisabeth, and she rolls her eyes.

'Would you prefer us to go?' I ask, and that's when William lets out a horrific wail of a sound. I cover my ears with my palms. I look and see that George Harris and Elisabeth have too.

'What is it?' I ask, when he's stopped wailing. I climb down from my chair and kneel on the floor beside him. The floor is cold and dirty. I think about rats.

'You're going to leave me,' William says.

'What?' I ask.

'I heard the man. He said you were going to have to leave,' William says.

'No, that won't happen,' Elisabeth says, but William won't look up from his crate of treasures.

'I hid in the day. Dark places, alleys. At night I went back underground,' he says, and then, 'I looked everywhere for Mum and Dad. I went back where I thought our house should be. I didn't know if it was the right place. Everything was different. Too much dirt. Too many buildings all crumbled on the floor. I had my battered Dinky Toy London taxi and my toy soldiers. I was wearing my birthday dinner clothes. Short pants, they were grey, and a wool jersey. I had a belt. It was my favourite, was my belt. It was elastic with a buckle that was an S shape – the buckle looked like a snake. All the boys had the S belts. But mine was special. To me.'

'William,' Elisabeth says. But William doesn't want to hear what Elisabeth has to say.

'Where our house was, I saw Mr Davies and the man from the next house, Mr Peters, carrying a body on a front door. Mr Davies saw me. I thought I was hiding. Mr Davies was good at seeking. He said Mrs Davies was looking for me. He was sorry, about my parents. He said they were nice folk.'

'I won't leave you,' I whisper, but William isn't listening. He doesn't want my words, not yet.

'Mr Davies said to Mr Peters that it was no place for a lad. He said my parents should have sent me with the other kiddies. I hated him for saying that. I asked if the Jerries were coming again. Mr Davies called them Square-Headed Bastards. He said they'd be back.'

'That must have scared you,' Elisabeth says.

William nods. 'I didn't understand what Mr Davies and the neighbour said about Mum and Dad. They didn't stay for more chatting. They were carrying a dead person. I could see the hand. I thought it moved. I screamed and ran back underground.

'Oh, William,' Elisabeth says, 'you must have been so very frightened.'

William nods. Tears are now dripping into his crate. 'I heard a lady say there were massive, no, *mass* graves. But if you were a family, you could get one just for your family, if some of them were dead. After some more days in the dark places, I figured that Mum and Dad had been killed by them Jerry bombs. I was little. I couldn't get them a grave to be a family. I don't know where Mum and Dad are resting. Their bodies. I didn't say goodbye. I hid and I waited.'

'I can help,' I say.

'No, I don't think you can,' William says, and then, 'Some bodies didn't get found, ever. But if you were gone for a long time you got press . . . presumed dead. I'm presumed dead. I don't exist now. I used to hide in tunnels because I thought if they'd made a mistake, with Mum and Dad being dead, then that's where Mum and Dad would come looking. Not here, but the tunnels under our house.'

'But they never did?' Elisabeth asks.

'No, they went away, like you all will . . .' William stands and runs from us, trailing his left leg. He runs into his tunnels, into his safety.

'But I won't ever leave you,' I whisper. I wish that he could hear me.

Then I hear him shouting, 'Max is married,' and I look up to see both Elisabeth and George Harris glaring down at me.

'Divorced—' I start to say.

226

Written by Anonymous to Martha Lost, throughout
Pride and Prejudice by Jane Austen, delivered by
Drac the postman to the lost property office

My dear Martha,
I fear that I may have revealed my identity to you. Did I
imagine your eyes upon me this very morning? I fear that
your enchanting poster caused me to stop in my tracks and
stare at the words that you had formed into a question. I
fear that I caused travellers to alter their strides to Platform
6. Were you watching, my child? Do you no longer seek to
know my identity? Do your words seek a deeper response?
Do any of us truly know who we are?
Yet still you asked. Yet still I contemplate. Who am I?
Are you asking that I give up my name to you? Do you
really wish to know the answer? Will my identity make my
words have less weight? Would a face to a voice or a name
to replace 'anonymous' alter the facts that I offer to you, my
child? Why do you seek a reveal before you have collected
the information that is needed in both your professional and
personal worlds? What if I reveal my identity and you no
longer wish to communicate with me? Would that not
mean that you would lose your home, your income and
your employment? I fear you have not considered the
consequences of this reveal, at this time, my child.
Yet I can offer an answer of sorts. My child, all that you
need to know is that I am your greatest admirer, that I am

lost, that I hope that one day we will be tangible friends. I do not seek to cause you harm, my very purpose on this earth is for your protection. Is that all that you require? Have I answered your question, for now? For Martha, I am the keeper of secrets, I am the Pied Piper, I am misplaced. Who am I, Martha? Who do I want to be? Sometimes, I fear, our own stories are the hardest ones to tell.

One day, my dear child, I will sit and I will tell you the story of my life. My promise to you is that my story will not commence with a 'once upon a time'. My life commenced the day that I met you, it commenced with the day that I learned how to love.

My darling Martha, today you have asked me a question that has shaken my very core. To reveal myself to you at this moment in our communication would prevent the answers to questions that are pressing. Time runs short for you, my sweet child. When will you ask the questions that demand answers I can give?

I await your question,
Anonymous x

I'm sitting at the counter in the coffee bar. George Harris has just arrived. He drags a stool over, and it grinds on the lino floor.

'Lift it, John!' Elisabeth shouts. George Harris's cheeks turn pink, and I continue to speak.

'It wasn't like it was in a romantic moment,' I say. George Harris places his stool near to me. He smiles and balances on the seat. 'It wasn't even in a heated debate. It was this afternoon. He was making me a cup of tea in Mother's kitchen.'

'He?' George Harris asks, placing his helmet on the counter.

'Max,' Elisabeth says, rolling her eyes at George Harris.

'We were looking at his research. I was sitting in Mother's parlour. Did I tell you Elisabeth took away the crucifix?' I ask. George Harris nods.

'Gave it to Jenny Jones at the kiosk. She likes a good crucifix. Daft biddy said it'd bring her good fortune,' Elisabeth says. She pours George Harris a cup of tea as she speaks.

'Lucky Jenny Jones,' George Harris says, and Elisabeth giggles.

'We'd spread out his research notes across the floor and were trying to make sense of the mystery,' I continue. 'He was shouting to me from my kitchen. He called me by his ex-wife's name.'

'What's his wife's name?' Elisabeth asks.

'Ex-wife,' I say and sigh. 'Angela.'

'What did you do?' George Harris asks.

229

'Nothing,' I say. 'I didn't know it was her name until he rushed into Mother's parlour, cup of tea forgotten, and started apologizing. I wasn't really bothered; he's called me Charlotte loads of times.'

'He's an arse,' Elisabeth says.

'You promised,' I say, and Elisabeth rolls her eyes again. 'I listened to what he had to say. He sat near me on Mother's sofa, and that's when he told me how they'd met. He smiled when he spoke about her,' I say.

'You didn't stop him?' Elisabeth asks.

'I let him talk,' I say, and then, 'But when he finished talking, his voice turned angry and he said, "Why are you so frigid? How long's it going to take for me and you to get dirty?"'

'Did you punch him in the face?' George Harris asks, and his cheeks are flushed.

'No, I put a finger to my lips,' I say.

'Why'd you do that, doll?' Elisabeth asks. I see her connecting eyes with George Harris and shrugging her shoulders.

'I wanted him to stop talking,' I say. Elisabeth laughs. 'But then he said that if I loved him, I'd help him find the ashes, but . . .' I stop talking. I turn and watch as Elisabeth races from the coffee bar and out on to the concourse. I look at George Harris, but he's already up and rattling as he moves towards the doorway in his Roman armour.

I run to the doorway and stand next to George Harris. I look right and see that Elisabeth is standing in front of Max. Max is with Charlotte. Elisabeth's face is bright red, and she's clenching her fists to her sides. She looks like she's about to pounce. They're just past the coffee bar, opposite Jenny Jones's kiosk. Elisabeth has stopped them walking. They must have been heading for the exit.

'Oi, Max, you massive arse,' I hear Elisabeth shout. I've never heard her outside voice before.

I step out on to the concourse. I watch. Max turns, he sees

me, he walks towards me. Charlotte stays where she is. I see that she's watching. Max reaches me, he walks right up to me, he kisses my lips, and then he leaves. No plans, no promises, no words. I don't know if I'll see him again, and I don't even know if I want to.

'I'LL SWING FOR HIM,' Elisabeth is shouting. I look to her and see that George Harris is holding her back, but my eyes flick back to Max. He's walked past Elisabeth and reached Charlotte. I watch them walking towards the exit. I see that they're holding hands.

The question that Martha Lost wrote on a poster that
was stuck to the billboard next to Platform 6

Do I have a National Insurance number?

Dear Angela,

I'm now at the beginning. Not the beginning of Mal, that remains a mystery, or the beginning of my story, that happened with the suitcase, but the beginning of THE story. The Cavern Club, still! Before the Cavern, Mal's life is a void. There's nothing, just shade. There was nothing solid, nothing to let me get under the skin of Mal. It's almost as if he's a made-up character in a novel.

Did Mal Evans even exist?

At times, I wonder. But he must have. I've spoken to people who met him! First-hand accounts. Primary sources! Yet the lack of information is a worry. I can only trust the facts. My story must be facts. It's facts that sell.

To what I uncovered:

As you know, I tracked down Mal's old job. Turns out he used to work for the GPO, I've already told you that. I spoke to a few blokes. Everyone remembered Mal, but no one really knew what he actually did. They all said the same thing – basically a huge, gentle bear of a man.

You remember the old bloke who played darts with Mal? Well, I met him for a second time. It was coincidence really. I'd popped in the pub for a bevvie (tinnie) and there he was, sitting proud as Punch at the end of the bar. I bought him a drink and he told me a new story. He'd remembered it after we'd spoken. He was hoping he'd see me again. Fate? Too right!

It turns out that Mal had bought a house when he'd got married. The old bloke had used his van to help Mal move a sideboard from his old gaff to his new house. The two of them had heaved it from the road and into the front room. Mal's bird had been standing, hands on hips, watching the whole thing but not saying a word. The old bloke even remembered the address. Hillside Road in a place called Mossley Hill.

The old bloke was quick to tell me that Mal was pretty strapped for money from that point onwards. Price of a mortgage and family, I reckon. Is that important? Liverpool's not a rich city. I don't reckon anyone I've met, apart from Rocky, has any real money. Good honest folk, looking to get through the week so they can get to the footy on a Saturday and down the pub on a Saturday night. One old bloke joked he liked nothing more than 'a beer and a scrap' on a Saturday night. Was this what Mal was like? I don't reckon so. I reckon Mal was different. I just seem to be getting these feelings. Perhaps it's some kind of writer's insight.

Anyway, the old bloke had one more juicy fact. He held on to it deep into the night. I'd almost given up on him as a source. I must have bought him a skin full of bevvies before it spilled out all at once, just like he'd been holding on to it and couldn't keep it in any longer:

'I know the first time he saw The Beatles, you know,' he said, cigarette hanging from the side of his mouth. 'Is that important?'

'Could be,' I said.

'Well, not much to it really. Big Mal comes in here one Tuesday night for the usual game of darts, but that night he's different. He's full of it.'

'How?' I said.

'Well, it turns out Mal had popped into town on his dinner break. He used to do that. Go into town and walk around. I can't remember why. Anyway, on this day he told me he noticed this little street he'd never seen before.

234

Mathew Street it was called. No little street now, centre of the bloody universe now. But in '61 it was in the arse end of nowhere. Well, he told me he'd walked down and stumbled on this place playing music. A club. The Cavern, he called it. Now, there's something important you need to know about Mal.'

'What?'

'Mal was a big Elvis fan, and I mean big. He loved Elvis. He knew all the words to "King Creole". You know Elvis?'

I nodded. I knew I was on to something. I reckon writers get a nose for this kind of thing.

'Well, Mal had heard this music. Rock music, he called it. He was wanting to know more, so he paid a shilling and went inside. You know who was playing?'

'Elvis?' I said. I knew the answer, of course, but I didn't want to get in the way of a good story.

'Elvis? Why would Elvis be playing in a grotty club, in the middle of Liverpool, in the middle of the day? It makes no sense. No, not Elvis, The bloody Beatles, that's who. And that's the first time he clapped eyes on them.'

I wrote the conversation down on a scrap of paper at breakfast next morning. I knew it'd be important.

But like I said before I left, I want to do this properly. I want to get into the head of Mal and I am – I'm living that rock and roll lifestyle. It's not like people don't know about you and the kids. But they're mainly interested in me and the suitcase. They can't get enough of me and you know how shit I am at saying no.

And the more I'm saying yes, the more I'm discovering! Just last night I heard that there's a connection between Mal Evans and Elvis. And, yes, I'm back talking about Elvis again! Why couldn't I have found a suitcase that once belonged to the King of Rock and Roll?

So, it turns out that during the 1965 America tour, Mal had the chance to meet his idol but rated it as one of the biggest disappointments in his life. The big day was 27 August 1965, at Elvis's mansion at 565 Perugia Way, Bel Air, LA.

Apparently Mal was excited about the meeting and had made an effort to look good. I mean, too right, meeting the King – bet he was over the moon! He sent his suit to the dry-cleaners, picked out a nice white shirt and put on a tie.

The entourage arrived at 11 p.m. and were greeted by Elvis in his circular living room. Apparently the conversation was a bit awkward at first, until Elvis said something like, 'If you damn guys are gonna sit here and stare at me all night, I'm gonna go to bed.' With the ice broken, it wasn't long before guitars came out. As the guitars arrived, Elvis asked if any of them had a pick (that's a plectrum).

Paul said something like, 'Yeah, Mal's got a pick. He's always got a pick. He carries them on holiday with him!' Mal went to grab a pick from his pocket, only to find they'd been removed by the dry-cleaner! Mal ended up breaking plastic spoons to make one, there was nothing else for it.

Apparently Mal felt it was one of the greatest regrets of his life. There was <u>nothing</u> he would have liked more than to have given Elvis a pick and then framed it after the King had used it to play guitar! There was a no-picture rule for the meeting, of course. But there's persistent rumours that a tape of the 'jam' was made. If that's true, would Mal have known or had it? It would be priceless! Could that tape be in the suitcase?

I need you to know that whatever I'm doing now isn't the real me. Folk around here don't know me like you know me. You understand, don't you?

Love me, do.

Max

It's three days before he calls.

He tells me how he's been busy, how he's been sleeping through the day and meeting people at parties at night. He tells me about drugs he's taken and alcohol and how everyone's making excited sounds about the contents of the suitcase. He tells me how a couple of the smaller items have come back as memorabilia, reproductions that Mal Evans could have picked up as souvenirs during the travels.

'But it's nothing to worry about,' he says. He's talking quickly, the words are rolling from his mouth and blending together. 'Some of that stuff's gonna be pure gold, mate, because Mal, he was at the centre of everything. After this one gig in New York, I can't remember where it was, but I've got it written down somewhere . . .' His voice is muffled, like he's put his hand over the receiver.

'You still there?' I ask.

'The Beatles went back to a hotel and smoked marijuana with Bob Dylan,' he says. I don't think he's listening to me; it's like he's talking to himself. 'And Mal was there, mate, of course he was, at the centre of everything like I am now . . . So then I found out, Paul McCartney, he gets the urge to write down his thoughts, darl, cause it was like he was thinking for the first time ever. He badgered Mal, asking him for a pencil and paper. Mal had them . . .' Max pauses. I don't know if he's waiting for me to comment. I don't speak. 'Top bloke, always carrying stuff like that around with him – and he might have kept those notes, Paul's thoughts on the universe. In fact, I bet

237

he would have. Mal was a writer at heart, like me. Missed out on a lot of stuff not putting himself first though. Did you know that Mal never had enough money, mate? He got stuck in economy on the flight to the US too, till the band found out—'

'Is Charlotte your girlfriend?' I ask, and Max laughs.

'That slut?' he says, and I cringe.

'I thought—' I start.

'You think too much. You're the only bird for me,' he says. I don't smile.

'Have you loved lots of women?' I ask. I hear his breaths into the telephone.

'No, mate, I was happily married,' he says, and he laughs.

'I mean, since you stopped being married,' I say.

'No, you nong, you're my first love since—' The telephone line isn't good. Loud music plays over his words. I can hear people shouting and I can hear women giggling.

'Max,' a woman's voice says. She makes the 'a' sound far too long. I don't like her.

'Who's that?' I ask.

'No one,' he says.

'Where are you now?' I ask.

'Rocky Hooper's,' he says. 'You can be happy but still tempted. And I wasn't calling for any of this shit. I thought you liked Mal. Guess I was wrong to think you'd be interested.'

'Sorry,' I say.

'What's happening with those bloody ashes, darl?' Max asks.

I watch the pigeons in the rafters. I watch them fly down close to a traveller's head. The traveller squeals. I laugh. I look for Budgie, but I can't spot him.

'What's so funny? Is that Roman soldier there?' he asks. I look at the clock; it's not quite time for George Harris to arrive.

238

'Soon,' I say.

'I don't want you talking to him,' Max says. I hear the woman giggling again. I hear her calling his name again.

'He's my—' I start to say, but the pips sound and Max says, 'Shit, no change. Find those ashes, all right, darl?' and then he's gone.

Elisabeth comes in just as I'm putting down the phone. I'd left the door open for her. She stays on the customer side of the counter.

'More trouble in paradise?' she asks.

'Having a boyfriend's a bit weird,' I say.

'Hmm . . .' she says. 'I don't see the point, doll,' she says. 'All the heartache when he goes away. You know he's shagging that Charlotte.'

'He's not,' I say, and then, 'Anyway, I'm living.'

Elisabeth nods. 'You need to be finding your birth certificate and—'

'Fifteen days,' I say. 'I'm working on it.'

'You're being selfish. It's upsetting William,' Elisabeth says.

'I don't mean—' I start to say.

'I just wish you'd understand that not all lost things are as they first appear. Living doesn't have to be this crap,' Elisabeth says, and then she turns and walks out of the lost property office.

Written by Anonymous to Martha Lost, throughout
Stranger in a Strange Land by Robert A. Heinlein,
delivered by Drac the postman to the
lost property office

My dear Martha,

*I can but assume from continued communication by
poster that you remain unaware of my true identity. I must
confess that this surprises me somewhat. I believed that you
had seen my reaction to your last poster, yet perhaps I was
mistaken.*

*As days had passed since your last communication with
me, I feared that you had decided not to create another
poster. I hope that I am communicating to you my utter glee
at seeing your QUESTION this morning, just as I hope that
all is well in your world.*

*My child, you do indeed have a National Insurance
number. It was issued by the Department of Health and
Social Security. Your NI card was sent to Mother. I can only
assume that you have not searched Mother's items since her
death, for I know that such a search would result in answers
to many of the questions you dare not voice. I have arranged
for a temporary number for you, until you are brave enough
for that search. The number is TN O5 02 60 F.*

*The authorities were aware that Mother was not your
birth-mother. You were registered as living in the flat above
the lost property office, with an aunt caring for you and*

home-schooling you. My darling child, you have always existed, there was never reason for you to hide. The simple fact is that there was an agreement between your birth-mother, via her solicitor, and Mother. It is true that your birth-mother's identity was never given to Mother, for dread when thinking what Mother could do with such clandestine facts. Yet, close to your sixth birthday, your birth-mother's solicitor contacted Mother and has kept in monthly contact with her since that time. That is why your National Insurance number was sent to you, at the lost property office, and was addressed to you using your full name. Have you never considered why it is that Mother claimed you had no surname? Did you truly believe that all foundlings were without a surname?

I realize that concerns about your abandonment smother the memory of your birth-mother, yet I offer this to you in the form of additional evidence to acknowledge that she has been following your progress for a number of years. My dear child, I feel, as we approach our final communication and you may never again allow voice to my words, that I must inform you that there were birthday cards sent every year. Your birth-mother never forgot the day that she catapulted you into this dreary world. There were letters and Christmas cards too.

There will be official documentation within Mother's secrets, if you so desire to seek more answers. Will you seek, Martha? Will you search or will you remain lost, my dear child? Now that I have given your National Insurance number to you, all that remains is for you to enquire about your birth certificate. Yes, Martha, isn't it time that you sought your full name, the identity of your birth-mother and, even, the date of your birth?

The clock continues to tick, dear Martha, you are running short of time. Will you ask the question? Will you

241

search within Mother's secrets? I fear I know not what you will do next, but know this, my child, know that I long to support you and move forward on this journey with you.

Do not fear me; I do not seek to harm you. I await your final question.

Anonymous x

The question that Martha Lost wrote on a poster that was stuck to the billboard next to Platform 6

Do you have a copy of my birth certificate?

I'm back from my outing in time to see George Harris and Elisabeth heading into the lost property office. By the time I reach the glass front, they've locked up and I can see the door to the basement rooms has been left open. They must be heading down into my library.

'Wait for me!' I shout, banging on the glass. I place the heart of Lime Street Station on the floor and scramble in my oversized handbag to find my key. Elisabeth appears back in the lost property office. She smiles as she unlocks the door.

'Hello, stranger,' she says. 'Where you been all day?'

'The Wirral with Max,' I say, and then, 'I think I love Mal Evans.' Elisabeth laughs.

'Can't argue with you about Mal, doll, but I wish you wouldn't bother with that Max. He's . . .' Elisabeth starts, but she stops herself. She sighs and smiles. 'You know, doll, our Mal was even head of Apple at one point, till they gave him the boot. Never knew what they had in him. I'll tell you more over tea,' Elisabeth says. 'Come on, George Harris and William are waiting.'

I place the heart of Lime Street Station and my handbag on the counter, and then we hurry down the spiral stairs, stepping carefully over the piles of books on the concrete floor.

'I really need to figure out some new shelving,' I say, as we dash through the open doorway. Since finding William in the tunnels, the door has remained open. He's welcome in my home. In fact, I guess there's an argument to say that we live in the same home. I like that.

As we turn the corner, William and George Harris are standing next to the doll's house, next to the miniature replica of our piece of Lime Street Station. George Harris is bending over; William's been showing him something.

'I moved here before Martha arrived,' William says.

'When I arrived?' I ask, and they both turn to look at me. George Harris smiles.

'Hello,' George Harris says, and I wave. His face is happy. 'I hear you've got a National Insurance number,' George Harris says, and I nod.

'Yes,' William continues, and we all turn towards him, 'before Martha. Someone started building where our house used to be. Cement came down into the tunnels, loads of cement. To fill them. I ran. I brought what I could carry. I went back twice, brought more stuff. But on the third time there was nothing left.'

'This stuff was in your parents' house?' George Harris asks. I'm looking around the room, thinking for the first time about how such a little boy could have managed to carry proper large items.

'It's taken me ages to find all the right stuff. To make the rooms just like they were when Mum and Dad . . .' William stops talking. There aren't tears, but there is a definite quiver in his voice. Elisabeth walks over to him. She hugs him. I think she might hold her breath when she hugs him.

'William,' I say. William pulls back from the hug and looks at me. 'I think your tunnel-home is the most beautiful thing I've ever seen.'

William smiles – a real smile – and his blue eyes twinkle. Elisabeth moves her arms from his shoulders. I see her hand gripping William's hand. She is giving him her strength.

'I had to go overground after the cement came. I lived in back alleys,' William says.

'How did you find these tunnels?' George Harris asks. I

look to George Harris's hand and see a miniature Roman soldier sitting on his palm. It's tiny in his huge hands. I smile.

'I was walking. Near the North Western Hotel, it was the middle of the night,' William says, breaking my thoughts, 'and a policeman stopped me. I was going to check my things – I'd put all my special things in a hole behind Lime Street Station. To be safe. Used to check that it was still safe every night. The policeman put his hand on my chest to say stop. He pointed his truncheon down towards the road. Black rats, lots of them, were scurrying, scuttling across the road. There were hundreds of them.'

'Where did they come from?' I ask, giving a shiver.

'Policeman told me they came from cellars and tunnels. He said the rats did the same walk every night. He said the rats were off down St John's Market, for the fresh food being delivered,' William says.

'St John's Market was a fascinating place then,' Elisabeth says. 'Food rationing had finished. You could get everything and anything.'

'I didn't care about that though,' William says. 'I had no money for buying stuff. Just ate scraps, things that didn't need money. The policeman never asked me how old I was or what I was doing out in the middle of the night. After he walked on, I went into the North Western Hotel. Very quiet, in the shadows. I went into the cellars, and that's where I found the door to these tunnels.'

'Then what?' George Harris says.

'I've been down here ever since,' William says.

'And the rats?' I ask. 'Did you ever see the Devil down here?'

'The Devil?' George Harris says.

'Mother,' Elisabeth says, rolling her eyes.

'Black rats are buggers. I'd switch on a light, and they'd be on my bed. I'd blink, and they'd be gone. I thought they might be . . . that I might be crazy,' William says.

'That's what they do in my library,' I say.

'Have you talked to them?' William asks, and I shake my head. 'We live in the tunnels together. We have a deal. They leave me alone, and I don't try to catch them in cages and drown them in the Mersey. That's what other folks did, that's what them folks in Lewis's did. They put the lady rats in cages, to try and trick the men rats in too. The men rats fell for it. They'd climb into the cage to be near their lady rats, then those folks at Lewis's would give them cages to a man. They'd pay him, and he promised to drown them. He didn't though. I watched him letting them black rats go. Down one of the tunnels. They'd run, run very fast, getting away safe. But then the silly buggers came back again. The next night. Back in Lewis's for scraps again. Getting caught in cages again,' William says.

'Some people don't learn,' Elisabeth says. She's staring at me. I shrug, and she rolls her eyes.

'Rats had a thing or two to learn. Me, I learned from them. I learned how to stay still in shadows and how to move quick, in a blink,' William says.

Dear Angela,

*A clear, brilliant blue sky hung over me today, flecked
with just the occasional white cloud, but still I experienced
what has been one of the saddest days of my life.*

*This arvo, we travelled out of the city once again and
headed into South Liverpool. To be precise, we headed to
Menlove Avenue, the site of John Lennon's mother's death.
John was just seventeen years old when his mother died.
He'd been brought up by his aunt and uncle, but as he grew
into a bloke he'd wanted to be closer to his mother. He'd
'rediscovered' her and had been building bridges.*

*Menlove Avenue is a strange road; it's what's called a
'dual carriageway'. Houses line both sides of the avenue,
many with red roofs and black and white exteriors, but a
bank of grass, dotted with sad-looking trees, splits the four
lanes of traffic into a two and then another two.*

*On Wednesday, 15 July 1958, John's mother was talking
to her sister at the side of the road. After the conversation,
she walked part way across the road, waited on the grass for
a moment and then started to cross the other two lanes. She
was hit by a car driven by an off-duty policeman. She was
dead before she arrived at the hospital.*

*We stood for a long time at the side of the road today,
looking at the exact spot she had died. I sobbed like a child.
People walking past looked at me like I was a madman, but
I didn't care. I wasn't even crying for John or his mother.
Afterwards, on the way home, I convinced myself I was*

crying for Mal, but I wasn't; I was crying for me, for you, for the kids. I was crying for what's been and is now lost.

I'm sorry, Angela, I'm bloody sorry. I reckon Liverpool's brought out the worst in me and I'm not proud of the way I've been behaving, but all that's going to change. I promise I'm going to make it up to you. I reckon our life's going to be bloody amazing from now on. We'll be rich and happy and popular, just you, the kids and me. I'll find a way to get you over here and that'll make everything right again. You always pull me back on the right path.

What would I do without you, Angela?

Love me, do.

Max

Today I'm supposed to be working but I'm actually on my way to the Adelphi; Max is talking about his suitcase find to a local journalist. They're talking about the uncovering of some more of the items not being authentic. Max thinks that the items still have worth, as they were clearly collected by Mal Evans during his travels. Max said that Mal Evans travelled the world with The Beatles. That they went to places like the Netherlands, the USA and even the Philippines (although that one didn't go to plan, what with The Beatles getting in trouble with the President, and armed guards attacking Mal). Elisabeth offered to cover my shift for me; she got Jenny Jones from the kiosk to cover for her. I thought it'd be nice to go along with Max and watch him being interviewed. I thought it'd be a nice surprise.

I spin into the Adelphi, clutching the heart of Lime Street Station with both my hands. It's still overwhelming, it's still bustling with those who arrive and those who depart. I look at the reception desk. Charlotte's behind it. I spin over.

'Hello, Charlotte,' I say.

'Hello, Martha Lost,' she says. I don't like her. She looks me up, she looks me down. 'Can I help you?' she asks.

'I'm just going to pop up to Max's—' I start.

'Mr Cole is entertaining a journalist in his suite and doesn't want to be disturbed,' Charlotte says.

'I understand,' I say, 'but can you phone up and tell him that I'm here.'

Charlotte tuts. She picks up the receiver, dials Max's room

number and then turns away. I strain to hear what she's saying. I lean over the reception desk, still clutching the heart of Lime Street Station, and she takes two steps away from the desk. I hear her giggle. It's a sound I've heard before, when Max called me. She covers the receiver with her hand and turns back to talk to me.

'Max says,' she begins, and I notice that she's stopped calling him Mr Cole, 'that he's busy all morning and that he'll call into the lost property office before you close.'

'Can you tell him that I've got Elisabeth to cover and I can stay with him—'

She turns away again. She lifts the phone back to her ear, uncovers the mouthpiece and speaks, then she turns back to me and says, 'He says that he's sorry, but he'd prefer to do this one on his own.' She giggles again and then puts down the receiver. I don't move.

'Is there anything else?' she asks, and then, 'Don't worry, love, Max was fine when I left him this morning.'

'Max said that you're a slut,' I say, and then I run out through the revolving doors, clutching the heart of Lime Street Station close to my chest, allowing the doors to do three full circles of me running in them before I spin out to the top of the Adelphi's steps.

I look across the busy road; people are rushing into Lewis's. I wish I was feeling braver. Instead, I look up to the statue. Mother used to rant about it. Elisabeth said it was commissioned to represent Liverpool's rebirth after the ravages of the Blitz. The statue's a naked man, locals know him as Dickie Lewis. He towers over Ranelagh Place, he's attached to Lewis's department store. I read a book that talked about him being on a ship, defiant and proud. Mother used to say that he poisoned the mind of any who looked upon him. I look up to see Dickie Lewis. I juggle the heart of Lime Street Station to balance between my left boob and my left elbow, and I salute his naked brass penis. That's when I decide to sneak up to Max's room.

I walk back to the revolving doors and spin into the Adelphi again. I don't glance over at the reception desk. Instead, I keep my head up and hurry over to the stairs. I'm attempting to look confident and efficient amongst the hustle and bustle of guests, I'm pretending that I belong in the Adelphi Hotel. No one shouts my name, no one stops me, so I take the stairs two at a time until I reach the third floor.

I pause outside Max's room. I'm panting and bent double, clutching the heart of Lime Street Station to my stomach. I can hear male voices, so I stand up straight, put my ear to the door and listen.

'So, what can I do for you, Rocky mate?' That's Max's voice.

'Listen, lad, I've sorted funds and one of mine's been looking into flights. Reckon we get them here within a week.' That must be Rocky Hooper. His voice sounds like sawdust.

'That's beaut! Are you sure, Rocky? Don't want you out of pocket.'

'Give over. I told you, it's a loan, soon you'll have bags of the stuff.'

'You're a bloody gent, Rocky.' Max sounds happy. I balance the heart of Lime Street on my leg and raise my hand to knock, but then I pause again.

'It's only right she should be part of this.'

She? Max's daughter's coming to Liverpool! I'm filled with excitement at the thought of meeting her and showing her the sights. I think she might become my best friend, even though I'll almost definitely be her stepmother one day and every book I've read has told me that stepmothers are evil.

'Too right. And it'll keep me on the straight and narrow.'

'From what I've been hearing, you've been well and truly

getting your end away. That Charlotte being up the duff is bad news.' I can't help but wonder if 'up the duff' means that Charlotte's in a mood with him. I hope that my being Max's girlfriend hasn't upset her and made her shout at Max.

'Mate, do you think she'll say something?'

'I'll sort it. You can trust me.'

'With my life, mate, with my life . . .' With each word, the voices are getting nearer. They're heading for the door. I turn, clutching the heart of Lime Street, and run to the stairs. I hear the door open, but I don't look back.

Of course, it only takes me a few minutes to get back to the lost property office, especially as I spin all the way. By the time I get to the open doorway, I'm bent double and gasping for air, the heart of Lime Street Station's at my feet.

'What you doing back, doll?' Elisabeth asks. She's sitting on my stool behind the counter.

'Didn't want me there,' I say, and then, 'And that Charlotte's a right one.'

'It's just cause she's shagging Max,' Elisabeth says, and then, 'You do know what shagging is, don't you?'

I nod, but then I say, 'But how can you be so sure?'

'She's Jenny Jones's neighbour's niece. Apparently she thinks she might be in the pudding club,' Elisabeth says.

'I'm not going to cry,' I say, and then, 'I might have just called Charlotte a slut.' Elisabeth giggles, then she says something about going next door and getting us a slice of cake.

The telephone rings. I jump, then rush to answer.

'Bonjour. Lost property, Martha Lost speaking, can I help you?' I ask.

'G'day,' he says.

'I think it's possible that I magic you into my life,' I say. 'Like I talk about you so much that you're finally forced to pick up your telephone and call me.'

'I always want to speak to you, darl,' he says.

'You've been thinking about me?' I ask.

'Too right. I always think about you when I'm talking about Mal's ashes,' he says. 'Charlotte said you seemed upset,' he says. 'The thing is, darl, it's just that I didn't want the journalist to ask who you might be. I was protecting you. I didn't want the journalist thinking you were my ex-wife, then you'd have to be a friend, an acquaintance, a nobody.'

'Is Charlotte in the pudding club?' I ask.

Max doesn't respond. I hear him sigh.

'Max?' I say.

'If you'd been here when the journalist was, she'd have been able to see my longing for you,' Max says.

'I think I know where the ashes are,' I tell Max.

'You little beauty,' he says. 'Tell me everything . . .'

MAXWELL'S SILVER WEDDING BAND!

Word about town is that Max Cole might not have that ticket to riches that he'd very much been riding on! My sources claim that at least ten authentication reports on items from his suitcase have come back with a big fat thumbs down.

But let's not write that suitcase off just yet. Credited with playing bass harmonica in 'Being For The Benefit Of Mr. Kite!', seen hitting the anvil in 'Maxwell's Silver Hammer' and stated to have played tambourine, added handclaps and recorded backing vocals in 'Dear Prudence', the possibility that Mal Evans had original recordings in his possession is very real. So fear not, Beatles fans, there's still hope for those all-important recordings.

This reporter was thrilled to be invited up to a suite at our very own Adelphi Hotel, where Rocky Hooper and Max Cole were generous with their time and cream cakes. Relaxed, sipping champagne and stuffing his face with a cream cake or two, Mr Cole showed no hint of anxiety regarding whether he'd backed a fake. Squashing the bubbling rumour that Max Cole had found love in Liverpool, the thirty-four-year-old father of two was quick to point out that he'd been happily married for the last fifteen years. Be still your beating hearts, ladies, this one's taken, but Rocky Hooper remains the most eligible bachelor in Liverpool and I can report that he's looking for love. You heard it here first!

Man of the moment Cole was reluctant to discuss the feedback he'd had regarding the rest of Mal Evans' archive, but the gossip is that the results will be back within the next couple of weeks. This city's got its champagne on ice, ready to celebrate.

Obviously, I asked him for an exclusive, and the cheeky Aussie gave me a wink that made my knees turn to jelly. I can tell you now, ladies, Mrs Cole is one lucky lady.

Elisabeth walks into the lost property office, and I see that Jenny Jones is hovering in the doorway. Jenny Jones is still small and fat, but today she's looking orange. Jenny Jones looks exactly like an Oompa-Loompa.

'Hello, Jenny Jones,' I say.

'All right, queen,' Jenny Jones says.

Jenny Jones never comes to visit me in the lost property office, so I say, 'Have you lost something, Jenny Jones?' Jenny Jones shakes her head. Elisabeth slides a copy of the *Daily Post* across the counter to me.

'Page nine,' she says.

I turn the pages. I know when to stop, as a smiling picture of Max and Rocky Hooper stares up at me. I run my fingers over Max's smile. I smile too.

'Seriously, doll,' Elisabeth says, 'get a grip and read the column.'

I read the words – I skim over them really – and then I stop.

'He doesn't even like cake,' I say. 'Do journalists always make things up?'

Elisabeth shakes her head, and Jenny Jones looks cross.

'Martha,' Jenny Jones shouts from the open doorway, 'the arse's married.'

I look at Jenny Jones. I'm wondering what she's talking about, so I read the article again, then I shake my head.

'It's a mistake,' I say, and then, 'He's got kids, but he's divorced and he's thirty-seven.'

257

'The sooner he leaves, the better,' Elisabeth says.

'Poor Charlotte's in a right state,' Jenny Jones says.

'She's not a very nice person,' I say.

'She's heartbroken,' Jenny Jones says. 'That cock found out she was pregnant and now he won't have anything to do with her.'

I don't know what to believe. I like Jenny Jones – she sells chocolate – but she's full of gossip. I don't know what I think about Max. I love Elisabeth, and I want to make her happy.

'I guess being "up the duff" means the same as "being in the pudding club"?' I ask, and Elisabeth nods. That gives me a bad feeling in my stomach. Probably not as bad as Charlotte's stomach feels though.

'What you going to do?' Elisabeth asks.

And at that moment, it all feels very clear. 'Keep my promise and then say goodbye,' I say, and then, 'Because I want Mal Evans to find his way home.'

'But, doll, you need to look after you,' Elisabeth says.

'I've written to Management, given them my National Insurance number. I just need my birth certificate,' I say. Elisabeth smiles. I pull the piece of paper out from my pocket. 'Eleven days,' I say.

Written by Anonymous to Martha Lost, throughout *The Edible Woman* by Margaret Atwood, delivered by Drac the postman to the lost property office

My dear Martha,

At last, you ask the question that will end this form of communication. I fear that this will be the final time that I take my pen in hand and try to alleviate some of the confusion and misery that dampens your smile. I fear this will be the final book that I send to you, my dear child.

The answer to your question is a simple no. It must be said that I do not have a copy of your birth certificate. The humble reason for this is that I have your original birth certificate. My dear child, have you still not realized my identity? Do you still seek the answer to who I am?

I am your birth-mother, Martha. I will deliver your birth certificate, I will hand the piece of paper to you and, if you desire, I will answer all the questions that are bursting to be spoken. If you have no words for me, my dear child, I will walk from your life and leave you in peace.

But know this, my Martha, being able to communicate with you over these last few weeks has filled my heart with longing. I have lived with regret for sixteen years. How this story ends is within your control.

Anonymous-still x

The phone rings. I'm tempted not to answer. It's five to one, and I'm expecting Max to arrive. I still haven't decided whether I believe him or the *Daily Post* about his wife. Elisabeth says the *Post* never lies, and I did promise her I would say goodbye to Max, but I dislike goodbyes more than almost anything.

'Bonjour, lost property, Martha Lost speaking, please bear in mind that we close in five minutes—'

'It's me,' Max says.

'Hello, me,' I say.

'Sorry,' Max says.

'What for?' I ask.

'I'm going away, mate,' Max says.

'What about your daughter?' I ask. I want to add 'And Charlotte', but even thinking about that gives me a bad feeling in my stomach again.

'My daughter?' Max says, and then I remember that I'd been eavesdropping when I learned she was coming. I don't even know for sure if the arrangements were finalized, and I can't let Max know about my listening at the door to his hotel room.

I change the subject. 'Where?' I ask.

'The Lakes, leaving this arvo. Turns out I've a long-lost relative and—' Max starts.

'Can I come? I've never been to the Lakes before, and I've heard—'

'No,' Max says.

I pause. I wait for him to offer a reason.

260

'I've never been on holiday before,' I say.

'Shame,' Max says, and then, 'Maybe next time.'

'How long will you be gone for?' I ask.

'Ten days,' Max says, and then, 'Have you found those ashes yet?' He pauses. 'I've only got a couple of weeks left in Liverpool. If I don't find them, my life'll be over. I've put every penny I've got into this, I've even had to . . .' He sighs, then, 'Listen, trust me. It's serious, darl, can't be putting all my eggs in one basket. I owe people . . .'

I don't speak.

'Martha?' he says, and then, 'Hello? HELLO?'

I still can't trust myself to speak, and Max must think that he's got a broken line. I hear the pips, but Max doesn't insert any more money. I don't put the receiver back on to its cradle. Instead, I twirl the cord around my finger, hoping that Max will suddenly appear on the line again. Snot is dripping from my nose as tears stream from my eyes.

'Martha?' I don't turn; I know Elisabeth's there. I know how she feels about Max, and the last thing I need right now is an 'I told you so'.

'What's wrong, doll?' Elisabeth asks. I wonder if she'll grow bored if I don't answer, I wonder if she'll turn and leave me.

She doesn't. She's next to me, staring at me. I turn to her, phone still in my hand.

'Max?' Elisabeth asks. I nod.

'He's gone away for ten days. Didn't want me to go with him,' I say.

'His loss,' Elisabeth says. 'You don't smile as much as you did before Max came on the scene.' She pauses. 'Did William find you?' Elisabeth asks. I shake my head, and that's when Elisabeth says the one thing that could make me feel a million times better. 'He thinks he might have found the ashes.'

*

261

Elisabeth has to get back to finish off the lunchtime rush, but I can't wait. I lock up. I go down into my library and then through the metal door into William's tunnels.

I find him next to his doll's house.

'Have you found them?' I ask. I'm too excited to say hello.

William turns and looks at me. His face is stretched into a smile. I don't even mind when his sour smell travels up my nose.

'This way,' he says, and his Chelsea boots clip-clop past me and back into the library of found books. He climbs the spiral staircase, and I climb after him. He's no longer dragging a leg. Then, at the top, he walks to the entry to the first basement room where all the black bin bags waiting to go to auction are stored. He stops at the door. I think he's asking for permission to go in there.

'Sure,' I say, and William turns the door handle, flicks on the switch and walks down the seven steps into the room. I stay at the entrance to the room and whistle a bit while I wait. I'm thinking about rats and wondering if William actually knows where he's supposed to be looking. All I can see is a sea of black bin bags piling high all over the room. William's bobbing up and down, disappearing and then appearing again. I've checked all my records and ledger sheets since January, and I've no recording of an urn full of ashes being lost. A Tupperware box of ashes and a plastic bag full of ashes were both claimed, but no urn has been documented.

'Are you speculating?' I shout down to William. He doesn't answer. 'Bonjour, William?' I say. He still doesn't answer. I have little choice but to step down into the basement room.

I'm three steps down when I see him. He's standing on top of and surrounded by black plastic bin bags, with his right arm stretched up to the ceiling. I look to his grubby hand, and that's when I see it. An urn.

'Is it?' I ask, and William nods. 'You sure?' I ask, and William nods again.

'They'll heal hearts,' William says. His voice is calm.

I'm in the basement now, kicking aside black bin bags. William's walked forward and handed me a piece of brown parcel paper. I see the name 'EVANS' just below an American stamp. 'But how?' I ask.

'In a suitcase,' he says, pointing to the mound of black plastic bags.

I don't take my eyes off the urn. I can't believe that it was here all along, that it was lost under the lost property office. William must have spent hours and hours searching. He must have made this his own personal quest.

'Can I hold it?' I ask. William nods again and passes it to me. The minute my fingers touch the urn I can see it being handed to a man. I can hear the words, 'Send Mal home,' and I can feel the depth of his grief.

But I shake that off. I squeal and do the Mash Potato on the spot. William laughs. I wish he would spin me off the floor, like excited people do when they meet each other off trains.

'I need to tell . . .' I start, but then I remember that he's gone away.

'Tell Elisabeth?' William says. I smile; he's right.

'Come with me, William,' I say. 'I'll treat you to a cup of tea and a slice of cake.' But William shakes his head. He doesn't do going into public places.

'How about I bring you some cake into the tunnel?' I say, and William nods. 'I won't be long,' I say, as I hurry up the stairs, out through the lost property office and next door to the coffee bar.

Elisabeth's watching me as I hurry through the door, both my hands clutching the urn. She's watching as I put it down on her counter. Then she looks at the urn, then she looks at me. I nod, and Elisabeth squeals. She jumps up and down.

'You did it, you little finder!' Elisabeth says, her voice full of pride and love.

'It was William,' I say. 'I promised I'd take him cake and a cuppa, can you—'

'Yes. But what now? Mal Evans' family will be thrilled,' Elisabeth says.

'But Max is away,' I say.

'No, he's not gone yet,' she sighs. She rolls her eyes and then says, 'He's being interviewed on the radio right now.'

'He can't be,' I say.

'If you hurry down to the radio station—' Elisabeth says.

'I'll catch him before he leaves for his holiday,' I say. I'm fit to pop with excitement. I'll hand Max the ashes, I'll see happiness, then together we can return Mal Evans to his family, and Max will love me for ever. I don't want to kiss him or anything like that. I just like the thought of there being someone out there who'll love me for ever.

'But I don't know the way,' I say.

'Quick,' Elisabeth says. 'Take this slice of chocolate cake to William.' She hands me the cake on a paper plate. 'And tell him to show you the quickest way through the tunnels. He'll get you there.'

I smile, and I think I giggle. I grab the paper plate and the urn and run back the way I came and down to the tunnel. The relief that I don't fall over and drop the urn or cake before I find William makes me squeal, and, of course, William's waiting for me beside the doll's house. I look at his model. I count the little people; there's still no Max.

'Cake,' I say, handing him the plate. 'But I need you to get me to the radio station really, really quickly.'

'Max?' William asks, frowning.

'I need to catch him before his holiday,' I say. 'He's going away any minute!' and then I hear Elisabeth shrieking from the library of found books.

'I'm coming too.'

William starts laughing, and I can't help but laugh too, as I see her running into the tunnel, carrying her white stilettos and the heart of Lime Street Station.

'You tell Max, then Mal Evans gets to go home and hearts will be—' William starts to say.

'Max will want—' I start to say.

'Max can take a walk till his hat floats,' Elisabeth says. 'Mal Evans is going home!' Elisabeth's voice is high-pitched. I've never heard her quite so excited. She holds out the heart of Lime Street Station, and I swap it for the urn.

'How the hell do you carry that round Liverpool all day?' she says, and I smile.

'This way,' William says, and then he starts running. We follow his sour smell, his Chelsea boots clip-clapping echoes as he runs, neither of his legs dragging.

We emerge from the tunnel on the corner, right next to the radio station. Elisabeth climbs out first. William giggles as he pushes her backside through the manhole. William doesn't climb out. He tells us that he'll wait there for us, that he'll watch. I pass the urn and the heart of Lime Street Station out to Elisabeth, then I hold my breath as I kiss William on the cheek. I say thank you before he pushes my backside out too.

Elisabeth's standing slipping her grimy feet back into her stilettos and holding out the heart of Lime Street Station to me. We're both covered in dirt. I know that I smell of sweat, and Elisabeth has William's dirty hand marks on her backside.

'How do I look?' I ask.

'Gorgeous,' she says, then she laughs. 'Doll, believe me, he'll only have eyes for these ashes.'

I laugh, although I'm not even sure if that's the reaction I should be having, but none of that is given another thought as I see him. It's only a glimpse, through crowds of shoppers, but I can see his head. I recognize his profile.

My heart actually flips, or perhaps it stops beating, or maybe it beats double-time. I'm wondering which it is when Elisabeth whispers something.

'What?' I ask, looking at her lips in the hope that she'll form the words again. But then I remember Max is there and that I have the heart of Lime Street Station in my hands, and I start running through the crowds. I'm dodging, not spinning, saying sorry as I bump people. I'm uncoordinated – running in crowds is a new experience. My running is flat-footed and my fleet slap off the pavement. I try to weave through the crowd, and I hear Elisabeth calling my name, but I need to reach Max. I need for him to see that I'm the best little finder, and I need him to love me for ever.

But then I stop. Because I've reached a gap between shops and I can see that Max has stopped too. He's far enough away for me to blend into the crowds; he's near enough for me to be able to see what he's doing. I don't call his name. Elisabeth stops beside me, urn in her hands.

'What a cock,' she says, and I nod.

'Cock,' I say.

Max is standing with a child holding his left hand. A girl, she's blonde, probably nine or ten, she's smiling. There's a boy there too. He looks a little older, maybe almost a teen, and he's not holding a hand, he's pointing to a building, and they're all looking up to the rooftop. It's Max's right hand that bothers me. That hand's being gripped by a woman, by a blonde woman who looks very much like a taller version of the little girl. I know that she's the mother of his children. I know that she's his wife.

'He lies,' Elisabeth says.

'About far too much,' I say.

'Let's go,' Elisabeth says. 'Let's take Mal back to the lost property office and make a plan. It should be about Mal's family now – that's what he lost through being with The Beatles. He wouldn't have cared about being the centre of attention or about having a crowd of fans for himself. He was always the one holding back the crowds,' Elisabeth says. She's looking at the urn, and she's in a world of her own.

'You know, doll, the last time The Beatles performed, that rooftop gig in '69, that only worked because of Mal. The crowd was looking at The Beatles, but Mal was holding back the police. He was all about letting The Beatles have their moment. George had insisted Mal turned the amps back on, even though it meant Mal had to deal with four policemen. Much good it did him.' She pauses. She kisses the urn. 'That was the last time Mal got to be the protector; everyone went their separate ways after that. No matter how good a fixer Mal was, he couldn't make it last for ever.'

I nod, but I'm back to looking at Max. 'Is that Rocky Hooper?' I ask, pointing the heart of Lime Street Station towards the other man who's with them. Elisabeth looks up, she nods, then she looks at me.

'You OK?' Elisabeth asks.

'No,' I say. I know I'm crying. I don't think I can remember how to stop the tears.

'Let's get you home, doll,' Elisabeth says. She strokes her hand down my arm. I feel her warmth through my blouse. I shiver.

'The Adelphi, reception speaking. How can I help you?' she asks.

'Max Cole's room, please,' I say, using my Blundellsands voice.

'Can I ask who's calling, please?'

'Martha Lost,' I say.

'I'm sorry, Martha,' she says. 'Max isn't staying with us at the moment. If you'd like to leave a message, I'll be sure that he gets it after his short break.'

'Charlotte?' I ask.

'Yes,' she says.

'Are you lying?' I ask.

'Yes,' Charlotte says.

'Are you pregnant?' I ask.

'Yes,' Charlotte says.

'Is it Max's baby?' I ask.

'Yes,' she says. 'I'm sorry,' she says, but I don't think she is sorry.

'Will you tell him that I called and that I need him to contact me?' I ask. I end the call and turn to Elisabeth and William. They're standing right behind me. William is in the lost property office. This isn't like him, usually he hides, but today I know that he's here to protect me. The love I have for him and for Elisabeth is making me feel like I'm going to pop open. But that feeling is interrupted by a banging on the glass front door to the lost property office. I turn to look; maybe I expect to see Max.

I see George Harris. It's not even four o'clock yet, let alone 17.37. Elisabeth goes to unlock the door.

'I came as soon as I could,' George Harris says. He's out of breath. He's trying to bend over, but his chest armour's making that difficult. Elisabeth points for him to join me. He walks through the gap in the counter, banging into a shelf on the way. I wonder if he's been running – a Roman soldier running through Lime Street Station. He nods to Elisabeth, he smiles at William, then he asks, 'Are you OK?'

'How?' I ask.

'My friend Martin works in Woolworths in Chester. I phoned him, and he went in search of our Roman soldier,'

Elisabeth says. 'I figured you'd need us all this afternoon.'

And that's when I can't stop the tears. My knees become floppy, and I crumple to the floor. I curl into a tortoise again. It's ridiculous really, I must look ridiculous. I have all the love I've ever wanted and needed right here in this lost property office, but I'm covered in sadness. I don't even think this is about Max, not really, it's more that my time with Max took me away from spending time with these three amazing people, away from my true and only friends. It's more that I trusted him, that I invested in him, that he's made me feel like I'm unlovable, that no one will ever love me for ever, however good a finder I am.

Elisabeth sits on the floor beside me; she's stroking my back.

'When you're ready,' she says, 'we're going to make a plan. And that plan is going to involve that beady-eyed bastard not getting his hands on Mal's ashes.'

'When you're ready, Martha,' William says.

'I don't think we should leave her tonight,' George Harris says.

'George Harris!' Elisabeth says. I hear her voice from my curled-up ball, and I know that she's winked at him. She's cheeky. The others are laughing. I can't help but uncurl myself and move so that I can see their faces. They're all smiling – I mean their eyes are full of concern, but they're all fit to burst into giggles.

'Did she wink?' I ask George Harris, and he nods. And that's when I laugh too. I laugh so hard that my belly aches and the tears that fall from my eyes are lucky tears. When the laughter stops, I say, 'I need answers.'

'We'll get them,' Elisabeth says.

Elisabeth's genius plan was decided on an hour ago, and now we're all – even William – sitting on Mother's cushions, on the floor in Mother's parlour. William is shifting about on his cushion, leaving skid marks of grime with every move. Dead Mother's in her silver-coloured urn on the mantelpiece. I've put Mal next to her in his urn – maybe Mal can talk some sense into her. Elisabeth nipped out before and came back with a bottle of whisky and four shot glasses. Now she's pouring the liquid into the glasses.

'Looks a bit like wee,' I say.

'Your wee is that colour?' George Harris asks. He's smiling. He's still not taken off his Roman soldier uniform.

'Are you cold?' I ask him.

'No,' he says, but I can see tiny goosebumps all over his arms and legs. Before I think about it, I run a finger over his flesh. George Harris jumps and contact is broken, but not before I see a young George Harris hiding in a wardrobe.

'Whenever I sit in Mother's parlour—' I start to say.

'Doll, this is your parlour now,' Elisabeth says. I smile. 'Here,' Elisabeth says, handing me a tiny glass. 'Drink this in one.'

I take a sip. The liquid makes my mouth hot. I cough and splutter. I need water. I need not to taste anything like that ever again. They're all watching me. They're all laughing at me, but I don't mind at all. I love that my parlour's filled with happy.

I turn and look at William. Budgie's flown in through the little gap in the window. He's landed on William's shoulder. William stops laughing. He's staring at the tiny bird.

'He likes you,' I say. William smiles. He's not moving his body at all.

'I don't want to hurt him,' William says.

'You know what I think,' Elisabeth begins. She's had three shots now. 'I think it's about time we spruced you up, William.'

'We love you William,' I say.

'But you really stink,' Elisabeth says, and then, 'But if you'd let me spruce you up . . .'

William doesn't say anything. He keeps staring at Budgie. I wonder what they're both thinking.

'That's a perfect idea,' I say. 'You can have a bath. We can get some clothes from the plastic bin bags in the basement room, wash and press them. George Harris can show you how to shave, and Elisabeth will cut your hair.'

'I reckon you're handsome under all that grime and hair,' Elisabeth says, and William smiles.

'Right, quick, he's smiling,' Elisabeth says to us. 'George Harris, you go and look in the basement for clothes, Martha can run a bath, and I'll nip next door and get everything else we need. '

'What should I do?' William asks, mainly to Budgie.

'You stay right there, William. We're not letting you out of our sight until you're less hairy and not quite so brown,' Elisabeth says.

The question that Martha Lost wrote on a poster that
was stuck to the billboard next to Platform 6

Please, can we meet?

'Some day you will be old enough to start reading fairy tales again.'

C. S. Lewis

And so my fairy tale continues. Part Eight's heading towards October, still in 1976 but no longer in a time when houses were thatched with strawberry laces and monkeys were chased by unicorns. My world's a little less full of strange and a little less grimy too.

And right now it's been two days since William was discovered under all that hair and dirt.

He looks amazing. He's clean-shaven, he's been scrubbed, and the clothes that George Harris found fit perfectly. He's got a range of clothes now, from jeans and jumpers to a dinner jacket and dickie bow. I wrote a cheque and paid the fee for it all – a little thank you for him finding Mal Evans. Of course, William insists on wearing his Chelsea boots and bowler hat with every ensemble, and he's been changing his clothes several times a day. But the thing that's brought me the most pleasure is seeing William walk around Lime Street Station, out in the open, not hiding at all, raising his hat to say a hello to people and even popping into the coffee bar as a surprise for Elisabeth. I heard her squeal through the wall, and this morning they spent an hour jiving.

But now Elisabeth and William are in here. They've come to report back on what Max's been doing while I've been working this morning. Part of Elisabeth's genius plan is to have him followed.

The phone's ringing. Elisabeth answers. She places her hand over the receiver. She mouths, 'IT'S MAX,' and shrugs her shoulders to ask if I want to speak to him. I nod.

'Bonjour,' I say.

'I miss you, mate,' he says.

'Where are you?' I ask.

'Lakes,' he says.

'Where?'

'I don't know. What's this, a million questions?' he asks.

'So how's the weather?' I ask.

'Probably the same as you've got,' he says, then, 'Listen, I've not got long, but I wanted to check up on your progress.'

'Progress?' I ask.

'Mal's ashes, mate,' he says.

'Yes, loads of progress,' I say, and then, 'We found them.'

'What?' he asks.

'Found them. Elisabeth heard you on the radio, and we hurried to get to the station before you left.'

'You've actually found them?' he asks. I can hear that he's smiling. 'Bloody hell, I could kiss you. You little beauty!'

'Yes, but you're not in Liverpool,' I say, 'and you're only back a few days before you leave for Australia. So we thought it best I just return the ashes to Mal's family.'

'WE thought that? Who the fuck is this WE?' Max shouts.

'We thought it'd be—' I say.

'You're shagging that Roman soldier, aren't you?' Max shouts.

'No, Max,' I say. I'm trying to sound calm, but my blood's bubbling and any minute my head's going to pop open and everything inside of me's going to explode out. 'I am not *fornicating* with George Harris. But I do think that your wife is very beautiful.' Then I slam the receiver down before he can shout at me any more. It's like the receiver's burned my fingertips, and I jump backwards. I turn to look at William and Elisabeth. They're both staring at me, neither saying a word. I watch as they turn and look at each other, and I watch as huge smiles spread across their faces.

Then I watch as William nods and Elisabeth starts to clap and shout, 'Bravo! Bravo!' And then, somehow, I'm laughing, even though I'm shaking, and even though I want to cry I find myself doing curtseys and giggling.

Of course, George Harris walks in while I'm doing my fifth dramatic curtsey. I almost topple over as I try to pretend, mid curtsey, that that's not what I'm really doing. George Harris raises an eyebrow, and William's laughing so much that he's hiccupping.

'What are you doing here?' I ask. 'It's not 17:37.'

'Said I was sick, wanted to see how you were,' he says. He walks through the gap in the counter to stand next to us.

'Max called,' I say.

'She told him about the ashes, then as good as told him to arse off,' Elisabeth says.

'I'm proud of you,' George Harris says. He stares into my eyes, and my belly does a tiny flip. Then he turns to the others, 'So, what do we know?'

'Charlotte, Little Miss Anytime Annie, has poked a safety pin through her nose and she's saying she's a punk,' Elisabeth says.

'He wasn't divorced,' I say. 'I never would have let him kiss me if I'd known.'

'I know,' George Harris says to me. 'A safety pin?' Elisabeth shrugs her shoulders and rolls her eyes. I smile.

'Apparently, it was Rocky Hooper who suggested Max fly over his kids and wife,' Elisabeth says. 'They're expecting the big reveal about the suitcase in a matter of days, and Rocky Hooper thought it'd be good for Max's wife to be here too.'

'But he said he spent all his savings on him being here,' I say, and then, 'More lies?'

'That part might not be a lie,' William says. 'Rocky Hooper's funding their trip. He's given Max an advance on the suitcase money.'

'Max said he'll pay it back when the sale's complete,' Elisabeth says.

'He's selling the suitcase?' George Harris asks.

'Only when it's all authenticated,' William says,

'But shouldn't Mal's family have a say?' I ask.

'Finders keepers,' William says.

'What I don't understand,' George Harris says, 'is what Rocky Hooper gets out of all of this?'

'That's easy,' Elisabeth says. 'He'll be expecting Max to give him a wad of cash from the sale, and he gets all the glory of being Max's bessie.'

'I would never destroy a family,' I say. I wish that I could scrub the inside of my mouth and take away the taste of Max.

'That's over now. None of this is your problem any more,' Elisabeth says.

'Max can dig his own tunnel,' William says.

'Do you mean grave?' George Harris asks. William winks at George Harris.

'What we really need to do,' I say, 'is get the ashes back to Mal's family.' I think about the urns on the mantelpiece.

'And get you a birth certificate,' William says, and I nod.

DO YOU WANT TO KNOW A SECRET?

Word about town is that the buzz and mystery surrounding Mal Evans' ashes has reached the best possible conclusion. You'll remember that Mal's ashes had been reported missing, after our postal system failed to deliver him home. Evans met his untimely end in January this year, when he was shot to death by Los Angeles police. Yet this week, Mal Evans' family stepped forward to report an anonymous delivery of his ashes to them.

That's right, folks, Mal Evans is home!

Course we're all dying to know who the hero of the hour might be. Who was it that made the anonymous delivery? Why is that person hiding from us?

So, dear anonymous finder of Mal's ashes, this city will embrace you close to their hearts. Let us see your face! We are holding our collective breath.

An unexpected twist in the tail of this tale! Max Cole is yesterday's news, while our city wonders if the hero who found Mal's ashes will step forward and take a bow.

'Quick,' Elisabeth shouts, sticking her head round the door of lost property office, then she turns and rushes back into the coffee bar. I turn to look over my shoulder, in case she was shouting to someone else. Of course, I'm the only person in here, so I grab my keys from under the counter, lock up and nip next door.

Elisabeth's sitting; William's next to her. He's wearing his bowler hat, and he smells of talcum powder. They've got a radio on the counter in front of them. They're both leaning in to listen.

'What are you do—' I start to say.

'Sssshhhh!' William and Elisabeth both shout, neither turning to look at me. Elisabeth stretches out her arm, and her hand tells me that I'm to sit next to them. I've absolutely no idea what's going on, but I'm curious. William pulls a stool around so that I can sit in between them. All of this is done without taking their eyes, and I guess ears, away from the radio.

'For those of you just tuning in, we are joined today by the city's very own Beatles expert, Graham Kemp, and Australian Max Cole. If you haven't heard about the Mal Evans archive by now, then maybe the heatwave really did fry your brains. The city has been hot for this topic for the last few months.

'And today, live on this show, we're going to reveal the findings of the authentication. Now, Max, is it true that you've no idea what the findings might be?'

'Too true, mate! I haven't slept all night,' Max says.

I hear Elisabeth tut. I'm biting the skin around my fingernails.

'Some would say you're brave to be choosing to receive this news live on radio,' the presenter says.

'Liverpool's been great to me; it's time I gave a little something back,' Max says.

'Does that mean that if the contents of the suitcase are revealed to be authentic, that you'll be leaving some of the items in Liverpool for us?' the presenter asks.

'Too right, if you pay enough,' Max says, and he laughs, Elisabeth tuts.

'Remind us all, Max, how did the suitcase fall into your hands?' the presenter asks.

'Bought it in a flea market, close to Melbourne back home. Paid around twenty pounds in your money,' Max says.

'And what was it about the suitcase that attracted you in the first place?' the presenter asks.

'It had loads of stickers on it, seemed well travelled, and I fancied myself a look inside. When I opened it up and saw all the Beatles stuff, I reckoned I was on to a winner,' Max says.

'Are you a Beatles fan?' the presenter asks.

'No, mate,' Max says. 'I do like Elvis though.' Max laughs.

'And, as I said, we've also got Graham Kemp in the studio. Graham, you're the man with all the news, right?'

'That I am, John, sealed in this envelope,' says Graham.

'Shall we get to it right now?' the presenter asks.

'Tremendous!' Graham says.

They all stop talking. There are muffled sounds, probably the envelope being handed to someone and someone else opening it. And then, 'This is it, folks, the moment we've been waiting for. I reckon we need a drum roll.' There's the sound of palms slapping a desk.

'I can reveal,' Graham begins, 'that the contents of the suitcase were found to be replicas, fakes and, in one case, a badly recorded jumbling together of different radio interviews with John Lennon and Paul McCartney.'

'Fuck,' is the only thing I hear from Max, as there's a smashing sound, mumbled shouts, and the presenter cuts to play 'Hey Jude'.

Elisabeth switches off the radio, and we all bend our bodies back to straight.

No one speaks.

'Anyone taking orders round here?' Someone breaks our silence. We don't turn to look at him.

'No,' Elisabeth shouts. 'Bugger off! Go find a jerker who'll serve you!'

'A what?' I ask.

'Should have just told him to go down the pub, shouldn't I?' Elisabeth says, and that's when all three of us start laughing. Not the poor man who's wanting serving, just me, Elisabeth and William, bending over and laughing like drunken fools. If I'm honest, I don't even know what I'm laughing at, but we carry on like that for several minutes after the customer's long gone.

'What'll he do now?' I ask.

'Go home, most likely,' William says.

'Best place for him,' Elisabeth says, and I nod. I'm actually not sure whether we're talking about Max or about the customer who was told to bugger off, but I nod anyway. Inside, I'm feeling sad for Max, and I don't really understand why.

Bang. Bang. Bang. Bang. Bang. Bang.

I'm not quite awake. Bang. Bang. Bang. Bang. I jump out of bed and pull my dressing gown tight around me. I tiptoe forward in tiny steps, but the bang, bang, bang, bang makes me hop.

'Go away!' I shout. I think it might be Management. I think

they might be about to kill me and hide me in a black bin bag in the basement.

'Martha, it's me,' William says, and I rush to unlock the door to my flat.

'I've found Max,' he says.

'William,' I say, 'we've already solved that mystery. Max is married, he's in the Adelphi.'

'He's in my tunnels, and he's hurt. Come,' William says.

I grab a pair of stilettos, because they're the only shoes I can see.

'Quick!' William shouts. He's already back down the stairs into the lost property office and probably heading down through my library of found books.

I hurry, shoes in hand, pulling my dressing gown across as tightly as possible and tying the cord with a knot. I run down the stairs into the lost property office and then down the spiral stairs into my library and out through the metal door into William's tunnels. William has lit the way. He's waiting for me beside his doll's house.

'Put your shoes on. The tunnels aren't nice where we're going,' William says, and I slip on my heels.

'The heart of Lime Street Station, I'll—' I start to say.

'No need,' William says. 'Tunnels all link to Lime Street Station.'

'How did you find him?' I ask.

'Heard crying, thought it was an animal . . .' William says, and I nod, but William can't see as he's already racing ahead along the tunnel, and I'm running to keep up with him. The tunnel's damp, cold and stinking of sewer. I'm unsure whether I'm shivering or my body's preparing to throw up the slice of lemon drizzle cake I had for supper.

'How far?' I ask.

'Along here,' William says.

I'm wrapping my arms across my chest as I run after him,

wishing I was wearing more clothes, wishing that Elisabeth was near me. The tunnel stinks. I didn't think there was a worse smell than William before he was cleaned up, but I was wrong. I keep stopping and gagging. I'm too scared to touch the walls. They're a mismatch of red bricks, thrown together, curving up and above me as I run. I think the rats are running with me. I think about them running over the bricks too. William's fast; he's no longer broken. I'm struggling to keep up. And with every step I run, the coldness covers me. This is a cold that has never been warm. These tunnels are full of cold that cannot be warm; this cold is lost.

'William,' I shout. My voice booms around the tunnel. William doesn't answer. He isn't talking, and his silence is making me anxious. I run faster. I don't know what I'm going to find. I'm running along tunnels that are muddled in construction. Some wide sections, several tight sections, in and out and in and out – I'm weaving underground. Deeper and deeper, the sense of all that is missing grows stronger with each step I run. I duck down, narrowly avoiding a ledge. My running slows as I step into a tighter corridor, and I stumble along the tunnels as my eyes try to adjust. I am not having fun. I cross the fingers on one hand and wish for light; I cross the fingers on the other and wish for Max to be alive. There is no good down here in these tunnels, only sad and fear and poo. I'm covered in cold. My shoes will be covered in poo. I try to run, but I'm lost.

'Over there,' William says. He's stopped, and I nearly run into him. He's pointing to a pile of rags below an open manhole. Fragments of light fall on to the rags. I rush to them.

'Max,' I say. 'Max, can you hear me?'

'Martha?' he asks.

There's light shining in from a streetlamp somewhere above. Max's face is covered in blood, his right eye's all puffed up and there's a cut on his forehead, but he's still alive.

'Need to get him back to the station,' William says, and then to Max, 'Can you stand?'

Max nods and then screams out in pain.

'Small steps, stick your tongue out,' I say.

'Why?' Max asks.

'In case you swallow it,' I say, mainly because I can't think of anything else to say and mainly because I'm completely out of my depth. And to make this about as bad as it can get, at that very moment the biggest and blackest rat I've ever seen decides to sit on my foot and stare right up into my eyes.

I scream and run in circles shaking my foot. I don't think I'll ever feel clean again.

Somehow, we get Max back to my flat. I hated that we had to walk through my library of found books, but it was the quickest route and I was struggling to help hold him up without touching him with my fingers, on top of manoeuvring along the tunnel in my heels. I hoped he wasn't concentrating on his surroundings.

Now Max is sitting on the sofa in my parlour. He seems to be recovered – just a few bruises, some cuts from the fall, maybe concussion. I'm keeping an eye on him for a few more hours. I'm bathing his wounds in salty water, and we're not talking to each other. Max is watching everything I'm doing. His staring's making me want to leave the room and perhaps catch a train to Paris. He's been here a couple of hours already. Even William got bored and left us alone. Clearly, the lack of conversation made him feel uncomfortable too.

'I'm sorry, mate,' Max says. 'I can't give you what you want.'

'What I want?' I ask.

'Too right. Commitment, a child, for ever,' he says.

'You have that with your wife,' I say, and then, 'And you're wrong. I don't want any of that with you. I did think it might

285

be nice to have you love me for ever, but I don't think that any more.'

'You're just saying that because you can't have me,' Max says.

I stop padding his wounds with cotton wool. I move back slightly, along the sofa, and I take a really good look at him. And then I laugh.

'When I was little, I wondered if I'd missed a train. I wondered if all the people I should love were on that train out of Lime Street Station,' I say.

'I don't understand,' he says.

'Sometimes I let myself think that if I'd caught that train, then maybe I'd have parents in my life now,' I say.

Max doesn't answer.

'The thing is, Max, that train,' I say, 'I know that you weren't on it.'

'Too right and that's a good thing,' he says, and then, 'I've come on a train *into* your life, darl. Look at our story. Look at how fate brought us together and look at the amazing end we'll have, mate.'

'End?' I ask.

'The ashes,' Max says. He's looking at the silver-coloured urn on the mantelpiece. 'This is my chance to get the money I need to pay Rock—'

'I don't understand,' I say, because I don't. Max must not have seen the *Post* recently.

'Mal's family are bound to pay a bit for the ashes, and I owe Rocky,' Max says.

That's when Max pounces. He's up and grabbing Dead Mother from the mantelpiece.

'Mother!' I shout.

'No use shouting for Mummy now,' Max says. 'The fucker's dead.' Max is standing in my parlour, both hands holding up Dead Mother's silver-coloured urn above his head.

He thinks the urn's a trophy. He looks like a proper quilt.

'You arse,' I say, and then, 'You're holding my dead mother in your hands.'

Max looks at the urn and then back at me.

'You're a bloody liar,' Max says.

'Mal's back with his family. Dead Mother's been on that mantelpiece since they burnt her,' I say.

I can see Max is thinking about my words. He's been in my parlour enough times to have seen her before.

That's when Max throws Dead Mother on to the carpet. Then he jumps at me, knocking the bowl of salty water from my hands. His body weight hits me as I try to move off the sofa. I fall to the floor, my head hitting the corner of the coffee table on the way. Max falls on to me, his weight squashing me. I try to wriggle out from under him, but he grabs my wrists in one of his hands and pulls them together.

'Get off,' I yell.

His lips are at my ear; his breathing is fast.

'Think you're clever, don't you?' Max asks. 'Well, I'm going to take what I want from you, you dirty prick-tease.' His voice is full of venom, and his tongue flicks into my ear. I keep wriggling, but the more I move, the more his grip tightens around my wrists.

'GET OFF!' I yell again.

With his spare hand, he pulls my dressing gown apart. The knot of the belt stays tight, but the towelling robe's open, revealing my white nightie.

'Slut,' he says. I know that he can see my nipples through the white nylon.

'Fuck off,' I say, but that makes him even more angry.

'Nice girls don't say fuck,' he says, and he rips my nightie by pulling the neckline down. The ripping sound echoes around the flat, and pain springs from the back of my neck where the material's fought to stay intact. He can see my nipples. I look at him, and he licks his lips.

'Why are you doing this?' I ask, fear and anger fuelling my wriggle, as I refuse to stay still for him.

'You've ruined my life,' he says, then he flicks my right nipple with his middle finger. Pain rushes through me. And that's when he sits up, pulling my wrists in front of me, his weight heavy on my pelvis. And that's when he starts undoing his belt. He's struggling, he only has one hand to use, he daren't let go of my wrists.

'No,' I say.

'This is what you deserve, you dirty bird,' he says. His pants are down, and I can see his penis. I don't want to look at it. He's straddling my waist, pushing my arms back above my head and shuffling his penis towards my face.

'And what do you deserve, big man? Someone like me?'

I let my eyes look, part of me terrified I've lost the plot and started hearing voices. I haven't. George Harris is there, in my parlour. He's a Roman soldier, he's six foot five inches, he's a giant of a boy. He can see my nipples, and he can see Max's penis. George Harris is holding the dagger from his belt. I wish I'd asked him if it was real.

George Harris raises the dagger in his left hand and steps towards us. He's standing tall. He's the bravest boy I've ever seen. Max lets go of my wrists and climbs to his feet. Before Max can play the big cock of Liverpool, George Harris swings his right arm, his fist catching Max across the bridge of his nose. Max falls back to the floor, holding his face, blood seeping between his fingers and on to my carpet. I can still see Max's penis. George Harris stands like a tower then moves over to Max.

'You've broken my nose, you fucker,' Max says.

'Have you had enough?' George Harris asks.

'You're welcome to my sloppy seconds,' Max says, holding on to his nose.

I catch George Harris's eye, and he smiles at me. He knows Max is lying; I don't need to say the words.

'Someone downstairs wants a word with you,' George Harris says, then he grabs the collar of Max's shirt and drags him from my parlour. Max's penis waves goodbye.

I don't know what to do. I'm shaking. I need Elisabeth. I need William. I need George Harris. I need to know who they've gone downstairs to meet. I crawl through my parlour, my nipples pointing to the carpet, I crawl to the top of the stairs, and I listen. I don't recognize the voice.

'Trying to rape one of our little girls,' the voice says.

'No, Rocky, mate. I wasn't,' Max says.

And then I see George Harris looking up at me from the bottom of the stairs. 'Go back to your parlour, Martha, please,' he says, and I do, because at this very moment George Harris is my hero.

I can't sleep. George Harris is in my bed, still fully dressed in his Roman soldier armour. I said that I wanted to sleep on the sofa. I needed to make my peace with this room. I needed to lift as much of Dead Mother as possible from the carpet.

William was here last night too. He was downstairs in the lost property office. He was the one who'd phoned George Harris after we'd found Max, and it was his decision to let Rocky know where Max was hiding. William said that he'd seen something in Max's eyes, that he'd watched enough angry men from the shadows to recognize the look. Elisabeth hadn't answered when William had first called her house. He said that he'd try her again after he left, even though it was after three in the morning. And now I know where Elisabeth is. I guess William managed to wake her. It's five a.m. and she's sitting on the bench opposite the lost property office. I'm watching her from the window in my parlour.

I leave the parlour and go down into the lost property

office. I don't flick on the light. At first she doesn't seem to notice me. I stand very still, in front of my stool, behind the counter, watching her. I like to watch Elisabeth. She fascinates me; she makes me smile. Yet today she looks different. She's fiddling with a thread on the pocket of her tweed jacket, then twirling a lock of hair around her finger, then biting a finger-nail, then back to the thread. She's upset, I can tell. I feel sick. I've made her this unhappy. What if she's decided that I'm just too much bother to be next door to? What if she's here to tell me that she's closing down her coffee bar, that she's moving away and I'll never see her again? I know she's fed up with me. She's annoyed that I didn't sort out my birth certificate and National Insurance number straight away. I've upset her, I've upset William, I've let George Harris see my nipples, and I've made George Harris see Max's penis.

But it's the thought of never seeing Elisabeth again that fills me with fear. I want to hide, not to open up today, maybe hide in the flat all day and pretend I've got measles or cholera, or both. I can't lose Elisabeth.

I'm in slacks and a T-shirt, as I felt I needed to cover up my nipples from George Harris. I'm shaking. I wish I was wearing a jumper. I'm about to creep backwards, but that's when she turns and sees me, and, before I can pretend to be a statue, she's making her way over to me. Elisabeth's not smiling. Her face is full of worry, so I smile at her to let her know that I'm OK, that she shouldn't move away and that I won't be any more bother. I don't think my smile looks real.

She's at the glass front door. 'William called me,' she says. 'Are you all right?'

I nod. 'George Harris saw my nipples,' I say.

'I know, doll,' Elisabeth says. 'Did Max hurt you?'

'George Harris saved me,' I say. 'He sleeps in his Roman soldier armour.'

'Only when he's on duty,' Elisabeth says. 'Love's like that.'

'He loves his job,' I say, my hand on the glass pane.

'He loves you,' Elisabeth says, and then, 'You going to open up?' And that's when I realize that we've been talking through the glass. I lean over to the lock, fumbling to fit the key into its hole.

'You've got news, haven't you?' I ask, watching Elisabeth while trying to get the key to fit. She nods, and I'm covered in sadness.

'Can I come in?' she asks. 'I'll make us both a cuppa?'

I open the door, and Elisabeth walks past me, through the gap in the counter. She's carrying a paper plate, and there's a slice of lemon drizzle wrapped in cling film on the plate. She puts it on the counter. She puts her handbag on the floor beside the counter. She walks over to the kettle. There's still water in it from yesterday. Elisabeth flicks on the light switch. I notice that there's blood on the floor, on my side of the counter. I think about Management and hope no one reported the disturbance last night. Neither of us speak as the water boils. I stand in the gap in the counter, next to the cake. Neither of us speak as she makes the tea. Elisabeth's humming a Cilla Black song, but today it isn't making my heart sing. It's making me cross. I might end up hating Cilla for ever. I don't want to hear Elisabeth humming sweetly; I want to know the dreadful news that she's about to tell me.

She moves the two cups over to the counter, places them down carefully and then bends to the floor. She's messing about in her handbag, but then stands up straight and puts a piece of paper on to the counter.

'I'm sorry,' Elisabeth says, pushing the paper across the counter to me.

I look at her; tears are streaming down from her eyes.

'What have you done?' I ask, and Elisabeth breaks her eye contact with me. Instead, she looks to the paper in front of me.

I look down. I see it.

Certificate of Birth
Name and Surname: Martha Elisabeth Graham
Date of Birth: Fifth February 1960

Elisabeth slides another piece of paper over the counter – my last poster. I let it rest next to the birth certificate. Next to my birth certificate. I have a name. I have a birthdate. My surname is no longer Lost.

I place my fingers on the square of paper. I close my eyes. My mind's full of images of Elisabeth holding a tiny baby. Elisabeth is young, too young. She's snuggling that tiny baby close to her. She's talking to her baby, and she's full of love. The baby's name is Martha.

I have a mother. My eyes open; my tears are beyond control.

'I'm sorry,' Elisabeth says. 'I'm sorry. I'm sorry.'

'You're my mother?' I ask. Elisabeth nods.

'Your name's not Martha,' I say. 'I thought it was a family name?'

'It's my middle name,' Elisabeth says, and then, 'We're the same, just a different way around.'

'But the words in the books . . . they didn't sound like you,' I say.

'I didn't want you to know it was me,' Elisabeth says. 'Not at first. I needed to know you could deal with the truth, doll.'

'You abandoned me?' I ask. Elisabeth nods.

'You left me here with HER?' I ask. I point my index finger up to the heavens. Elisabeth nods.

'I'm so sorry, doll,' Elisabeth says. 'I wanted to tell you. I wanted to get you away from that monster, but I left it too late. I was scared I'd lose you for ever if you found out who I

292

really was. You weren't like you are now; you're stronger now. She doesn't influence you now. She'd have locked you up; she'd have kept you away from me.' She pauses, tears streaming from her eyes. 'It killed me every single day, not being able to pull you close or protect you from her, but what could I do? I'd lost all rights to being your mum the day I gave you up.'

'Did you ever love me?' I ask. Elisabeth weeps in response.

I move to Elisabeth, and I touch her face. Her tears roll over my fingers. I can see how ashamed she was when she became pregnant. I can see her lying in bed. She's sobbing, and she's curled up into a ball.

'How old were you?' I ask.

'Fifteen,' she says. 'Your father was a piano teacher, a family friend. I'd never even kissed another man before him. He was so handsome and so clever. I loved him.' She pauses. 'He was married. Two kids.'

I can see him – my father. I'm watching him through Elisabeth's eyes. He's a lot older than she is. He's got children, and they're not that much younger than Elisabeth. I can see her watching him playing with his children at a picnic; it looks like it's next to a church.

'My parents were Irish, strict, religious . . .'

I see her mother, my grandmother, holding a leather belt with a metal buckle. My whole body shudders as the buckle smashes on to Elisabeth. I know about mothers with belts. Elisabeth's curling up, protecting her belly. She's protecting me.

'They wanted to send me away to a mother-and-baby home. I wouldn't tell them who the father was. They assumed I didn't know . . .'

I see Elisabeth in Lime Street Station. She's clutching a piece of paper, and she looks at it. An address.

'I came to Liverpool to have an abortion . . . I couldn't.'

293

I can see Elisabeth. She's looking at her fingernails – they're covered in grime, so dirty. She's crouched in an alley, and there are rats. She's putting her hand on her swollen belly.

'Eventually, I found work serving on tables in a café, and a good Samaritan gave me a bed. I hid that I was in the . . . that I was pregnant, but then my waters went when I was serving a big fat bloke . . . I had you and I registered you . . .'

My fingers are still touching her face. I see her leaving hospital, carrying me in a blanket. I see her going back to her room, being told there was no place for people like her. She lost her job. She lost her home. I see her being back on the streets. She's stealing, she's trying to keep us safe. I can feel that everything she's doing is for me. It's to try to keep me safe. She's desperate, she's so very alone, and her sadness is deep within her.

'I had to give you up.'

I look into Elisabeth's eyes. She fixes her stare on to mine. She's sobbing. I know that the day she gave me up she broke. I can feel her despair. I can feel that she thought she was doing the right thing for me, that she thought it would keep me safe. I was three months old. She'd tried everything she could think of to feed, to clothe, to protect me. She was at the end of her journey. She had no option. She had no one to offer her support.

'Walking away from here with nothing in my arms . . .' She stops talking. I can feel her sorrow.

'When you've had your everything taken from you, you have two choices. You fight to get it back or you crumble and die,' Elisabeth says.

'I was your everything?' I ask.

'You are my everything.'

'You came back for me,' I say.

'I was always going to come back for you,' Elisabeth says, and then, 'You're the most amazing person I've ever met.'

I'm sobbing snot and tears. All those years of not knowing who I am, all those years of thinking that I was unlovable, and all the time she was next door. She was watching and waiting and protecting. And now that I'm touching her cheek, I can see her sitting on the bench opposite the lost property office. It's during the years that she wasn't next door; it's every single day from the day after she left me outside of the lost property office. I can see her watching. She blends in, she's desperate, she's searching for me.

'I get it now,' I say, and then, 'I was the person who broke your heart.'

'No, doll, you mend my heart. Every single day,' Elisabeth says.

'You watched,' I say. 'Every day in those years that you didn't own the coffee bar.'

'Every day,' Elisabeth says. 'I wanted to claim you, but I knew what she'd do. I'd heard rumours in the station about her being religious. I thought at first that was a good thing; it was only after I left you that I saw what she was really like. I was only just sixteen, unmarried, no income and I'd abandoned you. I had no means. I couldn't support and care for you. I had to find another way to be near to you. I couldn't risk Mother finding out who I was and making you disappear or reporting me to the police. If she'd known I was your mum, she'd have kept you away from me. So, I worked my way out of the gutter, worked hard, saved hard.'

'Established a coffee bar right next door to where I worked and lived,' I say.

'What better way to be close to you? I would never have told you who I was . . . I was made up just to be your friend, just to be in your life . . . You're the best friend I've ever had.'

'But you sent the book . . .'

'I was testing the water. Knew you'd believe the facts in a book. I was terrified you'd stop responding to my words, or that you'd discover my identity before you were strong enough for my truth.'

'You never had any other children?' I ask.

'Never even had another boyfriend,' Elisabeth says. 'I should never have abandoned you. I swear I thought I was doing the right thing for you. I thought you'd be safe here . . . Then it was too late, and I couldn't risk Mother sending you away or making you hate me.'

'I could never hate you,' I say.

'Even if you can't forgive me, I'll still love you for ever,' Elisabeth says.

I reach up to the top shelf and pull down my battered brown suitcase. I lift the suitcase on to the counter and slide the catches until the release flicks open. I remove the contents and lay them on the counter. Elisabeth looks down at the posters.

'You kept them?' Elisabeth asks.

'For you,' I say. 'The words in the book said you wished you could keep them.'

And that's when we hold each other tight, and that's when I learn what it is to be held by a mother, by my mother. My tears and snot soak into her tweed jacket.

'About Town' column in *Liverpool Daily Post*

FLEEING FROM THE FAKE SUITCASE

Word about town is that Aussie rat Max Cole, 42, has run from our fair city with his tail between his legs.

Wanted in connection with the theft of ten thousand pounds from our city's very own Rocky Hooper, the police are keen to speak with Cole. The rumour mill is stirring and the word is that Rocky Hooper stepped in and stopped Cole from defiling one of our city's children. It seems that we were all fooled by the Aussie, whose wife and children are currently being detained somewhere in the city for questioning.

When contacted, Rocky Hopper said, 'I don't regret stepping in and stopping him from raping that little girl, but it's cost me ten grand.'

The city salutes our hero, as our men try to sniff out the rat that is Max Cole.

Keep your nose to the ground and let's pull together as a city and catch the Aussie, before he finds himself another of our little girls.

I've seen her before, of course, but now she seems different. Her eyes speak of such sorrow. She's standing in the doorway to the lost property office, and beyond her, sitting on the bench opposite, are her children, a girl and a boy. The girl's a little version of the woman in the doorway, blonde and beautiful. The boy's a teen – he's sitting with a protective arm around his sister. They're both watching. I'm sitting on my stool. I wave, but they don't wave back.

'Martha?' the woman asks.

'Angela?' I ask.

We both nod. She steps forward, close to the counter.

'I'm here to apologize for the behaviour of my husband,' she says.

'I didn't know he was married,' I say, and then, 'I'd never have. If I'd known. Not that I . . .' I say

'It's OK. Your mum's told me everything,' she says.

'My mum,' I say. I can't help but smile.

'I wanted to see you for myself, to make sure you were all right,' Angela says.

'You're brave,' I say. 'You could have written.'

'I'm sorry,' Angela says.

'I know,' I say.

'Did you know about that receptionist from the Adelphi?' Angela asks.

'Not really,' I say, and then, 'I've not really had much experience with men.'

'You thought he was one of the good ones?' Angela

298

asks, and I nod. 'Me too. He wrote me fancy letters . . .'

'Do you know where he is?' I ask, and Angela shakes her head. 'I'm so sorry. Look after them,' I say, nodding my head towards her children.

'He wasn't always a bad guy, you know. I think he lost his way. Maybe Liverpool brought out the worst in him,' Angela says.

I nod. I don't know if I believe her.

'Did he hurt you?' Her eyes look down to the bruises on my wrists. I rub the marks, wishing them away.

'I'll be OK,' I say. The words carry weight.

'I want you to have these,' Angela says. She fumbles in her huge handbag and pulls out a wad of paper, tied with paper-clips and elastic bands. She places it all on the counter in front of me. I can see photos, typed sheets and newspaper cuttings sticking out from the pile.

'I don't under—' I start.

'Max's research on Mal Evans. I want you to have it all. I think it should stay here, in Mal's Liverpool,' Angela says, and then, 'It's brought us nothing but misery. Might help you to understand . . .'

'What will you do next?' I ask.

'We're flying home, to our friends and family,' Angela says.

'They'll keep you safe,' I say, but Angela's not listening. She's already turned and walked out on to the concourse. Her two children stand. They walk to her as Angela pulls them close. Her arms seem longer. They stretch around both of her babies; they let the children know that she will protect them.

I don't know why I'm crying.

Dear Kevin Keegan,

You don't know me, but I'm writing to formally invite you to try one of my mum's French Fancies. She's been saying for ages that she'd absolutely love to give you one.

I only found out that she was my mum today (long story!), but she's been talking about your thighs for many months. We waited for you, after the UEFA Cup win. We'd heard a rumour that the players were arriving in Lime Street Station. Alas, you didn't. Mum had been all excited and then was truly disappointed. Unfortunately, that's the night Mother died (it's complicated!), and then I forgot about you until today. Many apologies for that, I know you're famous and should never be forgotten.

Anyway, my mum's name's Elisabeth Martha Graham, and she's thirty-two years old. I hope that isn't too old for you. She's only ever had one boyfriend (he was a married man!), but she's truly beautiful. She'd possibly be beautiful enough to be a Hollywood star. Mum's coffee bar's in Lime Street Station, right next to where I work in the lost property office.

Please do come and visit. Dress code is shorts.

Yours hoping,

Martha Elisabeth Graham

Xxx

PS: How do you say Brugge?

We're all sitting around a table in the coffee bar. Elisabeth's closed up for the day and prepared a little 'once-upon-a-time' party tea for me. It's not my birthday, not in any official way, but it's the day I heard Part One of my fairy tale.

Elisabeth must have told George Harris and William, as they've both wrapped a gift for me. There are three gifts sitting in the centre of the table. My eyes keep fixing on them. I can't quite believe that they're for me. We've all had cake; I even blew out one candle and made a wish. Now we're sipping Italian coffee and, mainly, smiling.

I've spent all afternoon with Elisabeth. We've been talking and crying and listening. We've still got a lot of talking to do. Small steps are being taken, but I hope we'll be all right. We searched through Mother's room. I'd not been in there since she'd died. I found a wooden box. The key, the one I'd found when searching for William's front door key, was a perfect fit. When I first touched the box, I felt Mother's fear, but I pushed past it. Inside the box were letters and cards, loads of them, all addressed to me. Mother had never opened them, but she'd not thrown them away. There were letters from solicitors, copies of official documents, everything in a wooden box full of my life. I opened a couple of the birthday cards, but then I had to stop. I felt that I was drowning. Elisabeth had thought about me every single birthday. She'd been next door. She'd always given me a special slice of cake on that day, but I'd not known the significance. Seeing all the cards and letters, it was enough knowing that my mum had been thinking about me and wanting to be part of my life. When I'm feeling stronger, I'll read them all, in order.

Elisabeth asked if I'd like to move into her house with her, but I said no, not yet. I'm still the liver bird of Lime Street Station. I'm not ready to sleep outside the station just yet. William's thinking about moving in with her, just as friends, and I'm already excited about going around to Elisabeth's home for Sunday lunch.

'I was here the night Elisabeth left you,' William says, and we all look at him. 'Her pain and mine, it's the same.' Elisabeth closes her hand over William's hand and gives it a squeeze.

'Thank you for not hating me,' Elisabeth says, to all of us.

I smile. There's no hatred in this room, but there has been a promise not to play any tracks by The Beatles for a little while.

'Have you called Management?' George Harris asks, and I nod.

'All sorted, job's mine, no heavies will be visiting. I am official. I even had a day to spare,' I say. I look around the table and everyone's smiling, real smiles. Elisabeth rolls her eyes then laughs.

'I read Max's research about Mal Evans,' I say, mainly to Elisabeth. 'I wrote him a letter.'

'I thought we'd been over this, doll. You need to stay away from—'

'Not Max. I wrote Mal Evans a letter – it's in with the research,' I say, and Elisabeth nods. 'And I wrote to Kevin Keegan too,' I say. 'Told him you wanted him to try one of your French Fancies.'

Elisabeth lets out a squeal. Her cheeks are flushed red and straight away she's shaking her head at William.

'I don't,' she says, and William laughs, but then George Harris coughs. It's a weak cough, yet we all turn to look at him.

'Erm . . .' George Harris says, 'I found this.' He slides a book across the table, knocking it into two saucers.

'Found it?' I ask. I run my fingers over the cover, but no images jump into my head. It's a purple book, an old one – I have one space left on that shelf. I open the cover. Words are written inside. I read the words, and I smile again.

'What does this one say?' Elisabeth asks. I don't answer; instead, I fix my eyes on George Harris.

'You wrote these words, didn't you?' I ask, pointing to the inscription inside. George Harris nods. 'And those other words too, in all those other books that you said you'd found?' I ask. George Harris nods again. His cheeks are the brightest of red. I smile.

'Presents,' Elisabeth squeals, clapping her hands together. She uses both her palms to shuffle the presents around the cups and saucers, across the surface of the table, towards me. I'm clutching my new book and looking at the presents, not quite sure which to open first.

'Here, open mine,' George Harris says. The gift's a small box, and there's a pink bow tied around it. It's almost too pretty to unwrap. I look at George Harris's fingers and realize that he's crossing them. I smile again.

'What is it?' I ask, and everyone laughs.

'Open it and find out,' George Harris says.

'Is it OK if I don't?' I ask, and then, 'I just want to look at them a little bit longer.' George Harris winks at me. I feel the heat rushing across my cheeks. 'You make my insides feel like I'm going to throw up,' I say.

George Harris looks unsure; Elisabeth giggles.

And so my fairy tale cotinues.

Dear Malcolm Evans,

You don't know me and now you're dead. It's too late for us to meet. William found you in the basement, below my lost property office. Your urn was our Holy Grail. We'd been following leads for weeks. I must admit that my motivation was to make a man love me for ever, which is utterly ridiculous, and I could have made a huge mistake and handed you over to him. But I didn't. Instead, Elisabeth held you in an urn and ran through tunnels with you. I would have carried you, but I had my arms full with the heart of Lime Street Station. We had our own adventure, you, Elisabeth and me. But now you're back with your family and you can rest in peace, Malcolm Evans.

But, and forgive me, I've only really known about you for a few weeks and now I've been given research notes all about you, with photos and anecdotes and newspaper cuttings. I'm not quite sure what I'll do with them all, but I know that I'll have to do something. I hope that your story will be heard.

From underwear to holidays, Malcolm Evans, you were the man who could find what The Beatles wanted. You were a big finder. I'm a little finder, and I feel that we could have been friends. And from all I've read, opinion is universal. People speak of your gentle nature and just how very nice you were. You were happy with The Beatles, weren't you? You loved the music and you loved that band that put our city on the map.

Protecting The Beatles was never about a search for personal fame, was it? For you, The Beatles were family. You respected them and you loved them. I can only hope that they loved you back. I'd hate to think about you ever feeling lonely, and I'd hate to think about you feeling undervalued and nothing. I wish that I'd been able to hear your story, Malcolm Evans, in your own words. Instead, I've been faced with a jigsaw puzzle, attempting to understand how you went from a GPO worker in Liverpool to being shot to your death in LA.

Because, Malcolm Evans, you were so much more than nothing. You were a friend to The Beatles when they couldn't have friends. You were a slice of normal, a link between the real world and their stardom. Not a manager, not a serious guy – I think you were a constant for them. When the world was screaming out for pieces of those young men, I think you kept The Beatles safe. You fetched, you carried, and I think you might have been the person that kept The Beatles grounded.

I wish that I'd known you, Malcolm Evans. I wish that we could have had a cup of tea and a slice of lemon drizzle cake together. I'd have wanted you to protect me. I'd have wanted you to pick me up and carry me around in your pocket. George Harris is a giant like you. I think he'd protect me, if I allowed him to. I think I'd feel safe in his arms. I think you'd have liked George Harris. I think you and him would have liked dressing up as Roman soldiers and stomping around the streets together.

I guess I'll keep searching for your missing archive. I guess I'll hope that one day your story will be told. Your name is important, Malcolm Evans. You're a legend, a giant part of Beatle history. Your story won't be forgotten, kind sir.

*Rest in peace, Malcolm Evans. I think you might have
been one of the good guys.*
Martha Elisabeth Graham
xxx

Martha Graham's Scouse Glossary

Balls to you, I'm fireproof: being indifferent and not caring what a person thinks.

Bevvied: drunk. I discovered that Max was a good example of this.

A blue: an Everton fan.

Blundellsands accent: talking in a posh accent. Not French though. Blundellsands is an affluent area of Merseyside.

A bobby dazzler: someone who is special, through looks or attire.

Brass: management. They've mostly gone away now, back to London.

Butties: sandwiches. Ham is George Harris's favourite kind.

Doll: a woman, often a term of endearment.

Down the fab of the nab: the DHSS. I'm still not exactly sure what that is, as I kept my job after all and didn't have to go there.

Gaffer: a boss. My mum, Elisabeth, says that I'm the gaffer of the lost property office in Lime Street Station now.

Give over: stop it!

A gob like the Mersey tunnel: someone who is loud-mouthed, or possibly cannot keep a secret. Jenny Jones is a good example, according to my mum, Elisabeth.

A jerker: someone who is deliberately annoying.

Jesus fluid: holy water, kept in a pan by Mother.

John: a term of address for any male in Liverpool.

Knife-and-fork tea: a cooked and ample meal, usually involves meat. We're going to have lots of these now that William lives in a real house and doesn't need picnics.

Lady/Lord Muck of Muck Hall: a female/male who is pompous.

Live over the brush: living together before being married. Which is inviting the Devil into your bed, according to Mother.

Liver bird: the symbol of Liverpool. Two bronze statues sit on the top of the Royal Liver Building. Local legend claims that if the birds fly away, then the city will cease to exist.

A nutjob: someone who is insane. Mother is a good example, according to my mum, Elisabeth.

Paddy's wigwam: Liverpool's Metropolitan Cathedral, shaped like a wigwam.

Plastic Scousers: people from the outskirts of Liverpool (includes the Wirral).

Queen: a term of address for any female in Liverpool, according to my mum, Elisabeth.

A quilt: an idiot. Max is a good example, according to my mum, Elisabeth.

Scouse: an accent from Liverpool.

Scran: food.

She'd pinch the pennies off a dead woman's eyes: someone who has no scruples or someone who is tight with money.

Short-arse: a person who is not tall.

Soft Mick: someone who is ridiculous or extravagant. I am a good example, according to my mum, Elisabeth.

Stop nebbing: stop being nosey!

Stuff your face: eat up!

Take a walk till your hat floats: go away! Maybe to the Wirral, I think, but not on the ferry.

Tilly mint: a female from Liverpool.
You're talking wet: you're being pathetic.

A Note to the Reader

The Finding of Martha Lost is fiction, but some features are close to fact.

The story of Mal Evans is true and I owe a debt of inspiration to him. He was a very close friend of The Beatles, becoming their roadie and later an executive of Apple. Mal Evans was shot dead by police in January 1976; his belongings went missing, and later his ashes did too. A suitcase was found and the contents were determined to be fake. He did write a manuscript (which is still lost) and he wrote a diary (which was also lost, though some extracts were later found). The mystery surrounding Mal Evans remains a continual point of discussion for Beatles enthusiasts. I include myself in this category, and it was when I was researching Mal that the seed for this novel began to grow. Despite the passage of time, my passion for everything to do with The Beatles remains fervent. I hope this never changes.

The Williamson Tunnels under Liverpool are real (but are not located under Lime Street Station) and they do contain a ballroom. They are an intriguing underground world created beneath the streets of the Edge Hill district of Liverpool by Joseph Williamson, a wealthy tobacco merchant – the reason for their existence is still unknown. My thanks are offered to Claire Moorhead at the Friends of Williamson's Tunnels for assisting with my initial research.

Acknowledgements

So many have aided in the writing of this story, but none more than my agent, Donald Winchester, who is shrewd, splendid, and possibly the most patient person in the publishing industry. His numerous readings and perceptive comments have been invaluable. Indeed all at Watson, Little have been infectious with their cheer and enthusiasm.

I am indebted to my wonderful editor, Suzanne Bridson, for her insightful editorial suggestions and her generous belief in my writing. I also owe a huge thank-you to the spectacular Ann-Katrin Ziser and the foreign rights team at Transworld. Thanks also to Kate Samano, Sophie Christopher and to the rest of the fabulously enthusiastic team at Transworld, who have all been so very supportive.

Special thanks to Joanne and Andy Harris, for trusting me to use their son's name in this story and for allowing me to create a Roman soldier called George Harris.

Admiration and a colossal bunch of gratefulness to Sophie Wright, Luke Cutforth and Josh Winslade.

An ongoing debt of gratitude is owed to Dr Ann Judge. The hours spent guiding and listening will never be forgotten.

Thank you to Bernie Pardue, Francesca Riccardi, Anne Cater, Dave Roberts, Lynne Machray, Birgitte Calvert, Katie Cutler, Clare Christian, Natalie Flynn, Matt Hill, Tracy Whitwell, Sophia Taylor, Alex Brown, Helen Walters, Jean

Ward, Cathy Cassidy, Paula Groves, Richard Wells and Margaret Coombs, for your encouragement, reassurance and friendship.

And, of course, my love and affection are given to the valiant LG. I like that our long fine journey began with an inscription in a novel. More thanks (and perhaps apologies this time, too) are offered to my children, who have had to brave my tantrums and my fears. Their support and love are gifts that I'll never take for granted. But particular thanks must be given to my beautiful daughter Poppy, for helping me to see just how magical the world can be, and for the countless times we've stood in Lime Street Station making wishes and looking for Martha Lost.

Finally, I am truly grateful to Arts Council England, who supported the writing of this novel by providing 'time to write' funding.

Caroline Wallace worked as a lecturer for several years before turning her hand to fiction. She lives in Liverpool with her husband and their many children.

Follow her on Twitter @Caroline_S